SOUVENIRS OF MURDER

Previous Titles in this series by Margaret Duffy

A HANGING MATTER
DEAD TROUBLE
SO HORRIBLE A PLACE
TAINTED GROUND *
COBWEB *
BLOOD SUBSTITUTE *

* available from Severn House

SOUVENIRS
OF MURDER

Margaret Duffy

This first world edition published 2009
in Great Britain and in the USA by
SEVERN HOUSE PUBLISHERS LTD of
9–15 High Street, Sutton, Surrey, England, SM1 1DF.
Trade paperback edition published
in Great Britain and the USA 2010 by
SEVERN HOUSE PUBLISHERS LTD

British Library Cataloguing in Publication Data

Duffy, Margaret.
  Souvenirs of Murder – (A Patrick Gillard and Ingrid
  Langley mystery)
  1. Gillard, Patrick (Fictitious character)–Fiction.
  2. Langley, Ingrid (Fictitious character)–Fiction.
  3. Great Britain. Serious Organised Crime Agency–Fiction.
  4. Murder–Investigation–Fiction. 5. Detective and mystery
  stories.
  I. Title II. Series
  823.9'14-dc22

ISBN-13: 978-0-7278-6810-7   (cased)
ISBN-13: 978-1-84751-174-4   (trade paper)

All Severn House titles are printed on acid-free paper.

Typeset by Palimpsest Book Production Ltd.,
Grangemouth, Stirlingshire, Scotland.
Printed and bound in Great Britain by
MPG Books Ltd., Bodmin, Cornwall.

ONE

In hindsight, it is difficult to decide which of the two was the most momentous; The Case of the Man who Tried to Take Over a Village and Ended up Dead or the fact that my husband, Patrick, had been given the job of catching a woman regarded as one of the world's most dangerous criminals and was accused of her murder. At the time, of course, the latter was the priority, the former not affecting me so personally, although it did others to whom I am close, very much so. My first, and at the time I hoped my only, contribution was that of finding the corpse.

Patrick had been an 'adviser' for SOCA, the Serious Organized Crime Agency – the inverted commas necessary as this particular operative goes to work armed to the teeth – for several months when he was given the assignment. It was felt by those in charge, namely Richard Daws, his one-time boss in MI5 who never seemed to be allowed to retire, and Commander Michael Greenway, a lesser mortal to whom Patrick now answers, that he was exactly the right man for the job. My unease started at this point. I knew full well – the novelist wife is on the payroll as 'consultant' to the 'adviser' – that he did not exactly have bucketfuls of experience in dealing with glamorous females who regularly execute those members of their establishment who fall short of expectations by personally garrotting them with a length of fine wire. I had pointed this out to Commander Greenway, adding that the harpy no doubt kept it neatly rolled up in her knickers' drawer and wouldn't an equally off-the-wall member of staff of SOCA, if there was such a person, be more suitable for the job?

Greenway had given me a wary smile. I know he values my contributions but has also learned that this female novelist comes at the price of asking the questions that Patrick, for several reasons, does not. His wariness was also due, I felt, to the fact that I was hugely eight and three-quarter months pregnant at the time and he thought of me along the lines of an unexploded bomb. I had every sympathy for him as, although a married man with a family, he did not want to have to play midwife on his office carpet.

'Patrick *can* do off-the-wall though, can't he?' he had remarked gently, the man in question a little late for the meeting, stuck in a traffic jam.

'Yes, he can, but with the kind of skill that impresses men,' I had replied. 'As you know, he's an ex-undercover soldier, used to dealing with terrorists and the like. He's only ever really operated in a man's world.'

And can reduce strong men to tears with his voice alone and at Christmas often cracks walnuts just with his fingers.

'With the help of criminal profilers we're going to turn him into the kind of person to impress this woman,' Greenway had said after a thoughtful pause. 'And look, although the assignment's not going to be achieved in five minutes the groundwork is being done by others – he's not going in alone.'

So I had had to resign myself to the inevitable.

This conversation was nothing to do with the fact that Mark was born the following day, at around four in the afternoon, not that I was actually bothered by what hour it was at the time. He was in as much of a hurry as Justin, our first, who had arrived in the ambulance, and Patrick made it to the delivery room with five minutes to spare. I was glad about this, he is not the kind of man to have the emotional stamina to be able to bear his partner yelling her head off in the throes of childbirth for any length of time.

We were living in a rented furnished house, having sold our home in Devon, while extensions were added to the old rectory at Hinton Littlemoor in Somerset that we had bought from the diocese. Patrick's parents – his father is still rector there – had been due to be rehoused in a gerbil hutch of a new bungalow, one of several being built on land that is, since the railway closed and all the culverts became blocked up, in effect, the village's flood plain, and the rectory put on the market. The prospect of this was simply too awful for words and Patrick's anger had honed his haggling skills to drive down the price: it was no secret that the building needed a new roof.

'No more babies,' Patrick had muttered just after the birth, rescuing his wrung hands that I had been holding so that he could mop my hot brow.

'I'll make an appointment for you at the vet's as soon as I get home,' I had promised, looking down into the little red crumpled face and praying that this one wouldn't be as stroppy as his brother.

That we have two children already – Victoria was the second – is something of a miracle, Patrick having been seriously injured in his Special Forces days before he joined MI5. Then Patrick's brother, Larry, was killed and we adopted his two, Matthew and Katie, and suddenly the Dartmoor cottage seemed rather small. I was desperately hoping that our nannie, Carrie, would be able to carry on. She had moved with us to Somerset but her overriding concern was her mother, who lived in Plymouth and did not enjoy the best of health. The matter was soon, and amazingly, solved to everyone's satisfaction when a recently widowed friend whom she had known at school – both ladies are natives of Bath – asked her if she would like to go and live with her on the outskirts of the city.

Just over a month later, my domestic arrangements more or less intact, I found myself, in a dismal February in the rented house, a barn conversion a mile from Hinton Littlemoor, with a new baby, a figure more redolent of a champion Jersey than that of any kind of consultant to a crime-fighting agency and a bad case of post-natal blues. At least, that was what other people who happened to be around when I suddenly burst into tears were calling it. I thought it had far more to do with the fact that I was not only site managing the building work on the rectory and had been right from the beginning, but now was lugging Mark around, by this time a healthy nine pounds in weight, for what seemed like hourly breastfeeds, never mind the aftermath. Patrick's parents were having an extended holiday while the worst of the mess at the rectory was going on – for a few weeks the house was uninhabitable – their son heaven only knew where undergoing 'training'. In view of the proposed assignment I was agog to know what this entailed.

And, of course, the business of writing books had gone right out of the window.

The builders, who were working to a very tight schedule, had at first tended to dismiss the pregnant and then somewhat dour nursing mother who turned up every day – I did not take the baby into the house while work was going on – as a dimbo to be smiled upon and ignored. After a few skirmishes along the lines of their being content to use the wrong roofing slates, not the ones we had ordered, they were now brewing me tea while bringing me up to date, exactly, with the work in progress and would I like to inspect what had been done since my previous visit?

Church services were being taken by a retired bishop, a lay reader and any other clergy who were deemed to be free. While John had been in need of a complete break from what is, in effect, a seven day a week job Elspeth had been particularly reluctant to go away with a new grandchild on the scene and while I might need help.

Late in the morning of the day when they were due back, a Saturday, I was on a mission to harry the decorators who were putting the finishing touches to John and Elspeth's new two-bedroomed annex. All on the level, it had been created from the old garage and stable with a new floor above that gave the house another two bedrooms, one with an en suite bathroom that would be for Patrick and me, the other for any visitors. A boxroom with a big cupboard was now the nursery with a connecting door to our room – Carrie's was just across the landing. My priority on this particular morning was to get John and Elspeth's new home fit to live in but if furniture could not be brought in or curtains fitted today because paint was not dry then it was not a disaster if they had to stay in bed and breakfast accommodation in the village for one night. This eventuality had been pencilled in at Rose Cottage, a short distance away just off the high street.

The main part of the rectory was still full of the racket of sawing, nail guns and drills but at least the doors of the rooms that were not being touched, most of those downstairs, had been sealed with special tape to prevent the entry of dust. This had meant that the furniture in them could remain in situ. Another single-storey extension was being built on to the kitchen to make it bigger, swallowing up an old integral coal store and outside toilet, plus providing a small room where the children could have their computer and do homework. Later, a large conservatory would be built over the courtyard outside with a door into it from the kitchen, another from the living room and yet another that was the entry to Elspeth and John's quarters so they would not have to go out into the open in order to join us. On the opposite side double doors would lead on to the garden. John would still have his book-lined study in the main house: that was sacrosanct.

My mind full of colour schemes – it had been difficult to organize these over the phone and in the end Elspeth had said it was safer to leave it all up to me – I first went round to where the painters were emulsioning the walls of the annex pale cream, the plaster too new to cover with wallpaper. I was told that they hoped to put the final coat of gloss on the wood-work in the afternoon and it was obvious it would not be dry in time for the rector and his wife to move in that day, the smell of paint notwithstanding. Therefore I would have to put off the curtain people and the carpet fitters.

This area was no longer a building site so I had Mark in a sling around my neck. He was sound asleep making very tiny snoring noises. I am not a cooing kind of mother but had to admit that he was extremely cute: Patrick was missing a lot. He had rung me the night before, sounding tired, but would not go into details about his activities, merely saying that he was fine and on a 'refresher course'. Ye gods. Doing what?

Quick footsteps crunched on the gravel outside and a woman peered through the open doorway.

'Oh! Aren't they back yet?'

'This evening,' I told a bad case of growing out black-dyed hair and a frown. This was Mrs Crosspatch, Elspeth's alternative name for the wife of the chairman of the PCC, Frank Crosby, who had been pointed out to me and in my presence spoken of as 'nosy, unpleasant and interfering'. 'Hello,' I said. 'I don't think we've met. I'm John and Elspeth's daughter-in-law, Ingrid.'

She ignored the introduction, marching agitatedly right up to me to say, 'It's after eleven and the church is still locked. It's most important that I check the flowers.'

'Isn't locking and unlocking the church the responsibility of the sexton while the rector's away?'

'Yes, but he often oversleeps and you're nearer. You've got a key, haven't you?'

Her voice had risen to tones of withering scorn.

I was not too sure about this and was about to point out

that we did, actually, have the builders in when I remembered seeing a large key of ancient and noble appearance hanging on a hook in John's study, one of the rooms that had not been closed off in case any of the parish records kept in the safe in there were needed. Asking La Crosspatch to meet me around the front of the house – I had already invented another nickname for her – I went across the courtyard and into the rectory, picking my way over toolboxes and around a platoon of men in dusty jeans and sweatshirts, hanged if I was going to ask my visitor to hold my son in case he caught something nasty from her bad breath. The key was where I remembered seeing it.

'The WI had to have their committee meeting in the parish hall, you know,' the woman said as we went through the small gate from the rectory garden into the churchyard. 'It really was most inconvenient not being able to have it here.'

'Where do you have your ordinary meetings?' I asked, knowing full well.

'In the parish hall, of course.'

'Well, I'm afraid you'll have to carry on having them there or somewhere else,' I said with regrettable satisfaction. 'The rectory is now a private house.' I was aware that what had been missing was Elspeth's home-baked cakes and a very comfortable setting. Elspeth had said to me that she thought it about time someone else did all the hard work and now was a good time to make the break.

Mrs Crosby's mouth snapped shut into a thin straight line and she stomped on ahead of me.

Keeping hold of the key – I was damned if I was going to give her that either – we went into the church porch. It was piled with autumn leaves blown in from the previous night's gale which my companion tut-tutted over with a glare in my direction as if to say that I should have dealt with them. I unlocked the door.

The flowers, some on the altar, a few arrangements on tables and a window ledge, were definitely not fresh.

'But this is disgraceful!' the PCC chairman's wife gasped. 'Nothing's been done! All I should have to do is check that they're ready for the services tomorrow.'

'Who was due to do the flowers?' I asked.

She went back into the porch, found her glasses in a pocket and consulted a list pinned to the notice board.

'Pauline Harrison.' A snort. 'You wait until I get on the phone to her.'

'No,' I said.

'No? What do you mean, no?'

'I happen to know that her father's been taken to hospital after suffering a stroke.'

'That's no excuse.'

I closed in on her. 'No,' I repeated in level tones. 'You will not phone her, other than to ask how he is. You will also kindly deal with the problem here. The village store sells flowers that are good enough for an emergency and you can help yourself to whatever foliage you need from the rectory garden. Is that understood?' We stared at one another eye to eye. I very rarely lose this kind of confrontation.

At last the woman said, 'Very well. But the box with the flower fund money's in the vestry which I would like to have access to as I didn't bring my purse with me. I don't live nearby.'

She knew where that key was; tucked out of sight on a ledge by the organ.

A well-built man was spreadeagled face up on the floor of the vestry. He was very dead and all I noticed just then was that the body had some kind of plastic tube protruding from the mouth.

Not necessarily a natural death then.

Having made his way between the police vehicles and personnel Detective Chief Inspector James Carrick swithered between admiring the new member of the Gillard family – he and his wife Joanna are friends of ours – and his professional duties and then caved in and grinned at Mark, who was awake and beaming gummily up at him, before gently touching a chubby cheek with a forefinger.

'He looks like you.'

I did a double take of my son. 'Really?'

'And I'd put money on him being the quiet, introverted and artistic one.'

'But I'm not like that,' I protested.

'Compared with that husband of yours and Justin you are.'

I had to admit that he had a point. Hadn't the two of them

recently fought a water pistols at dawn duel? Even at six years old Justin had thought himself a better shot than his father. Not so.

We were standing on the gravelled path leading up to the church near the lych gate where I had met Carrick in order to tell him of the circumstances of the discovery. I had thought it best that as Mrs Crosby had understandably been shocked – I had escorted her to a nearby friend's house where she was having a recuperative cup of tea – that I take over the business of flowers. They could be put in a bucket of water until restrictions of entry to the building had been lifted. I was hoping this would be in time for the services the following day. If not, Elspeth could have them.

Carrick excused himself and headed off to join his scenes-of-crime team. Then he turned and said, 'Were you alone when you found the body?'

'No, I was with the wife of the chairman of the PCC. She's two cottages away getting over the shock.'

'I shall need a quick word with both of you. But you don't have to hang around, Ingrid. I can catch up with you at home. And if you have any insider information about the village . . .'

'You'll need to talk to Elspeth and John about that. They'll be back later today.'

'Do you know who he was?'

'No, but I think Mrs Crosby does. It didn't seem my place to question her.'

He walked a few more paces and then stopped again. 'First thoughts though?'

I had to smile. 'Is this the Somerset and Avon Police asking SOCA for a professional opinion?'

'If you like,' he answered soberly.

'I had another look at the body after I'd dialled 999. There's what looks like a vacuum cleaner nozzle rammed into his mouth. But you can only see a short length of it so it's quite a long way in. Hardly an accident or suicide. Somebody hated him.'

Carrick nodded briskly. 'Thank you.' Then, 'It's odd how corpses seem to follow you and Patrick around.'

'Yes, but this one's *your* baby.'

And that was how I intended it should remain. I would

go home and write. Did I have any ideas for the next novel?
Not one.

Six days went by. Despite inches of rain work progressed at
the rectory, John and Elspeth, coping well with the ghastly
shock of the murder, expressing themselves delighted with
their new living quarters, although I doubted somehow that
Elspeth would relinquish her kitchen so happily when work
was finished and the Gillard family could move in. No matter,
if she continued to want to cook for everyone when Patrick
and I were at home I would be the last one to be stupidly
possessive about it.

Carrie, detecting oncoming exhaustion as most of the reason
for my miseries, had prised Mark away from me and put him
on the bottle, the natural product now petering out. I suppose
I had clung on to him for too long to the detriment of my
health, guiltily feeling that she had more than enough to do
with the two younger children already. But as the feisty Carrie
herself had said, 'What the hell else are nannies for? Go and
have some time for yourself, woman.'

The murder victim had been named as Squadron Leader
Melvyn Blanche, retired. He and his wife, Barbara, were
comparative newcomers to the village but, according to Elspeth,
had wasted no time in getting themselves involved in local
activities. Human nature being what it is clubs and groups had
been delighted that their two new members welcomed working
on the various committees.

'But before you could say knife everyone was complaining
that they were running the village,' Elspeth had told me. 'Oh
dear, was that the wrong thing to say? The poor man wasn't
stabbed to death, was he?'

'No,' I had said. 'He had been hit over the head with some
kind of blunt instrument that hasn't yet been found.' I had not
wanted to mention, right then, that the narrow vacuum cleaner
nozzle had then been forced down the victim's throat and
some kind of bleach-based cleaning fluid poured down it. This
had gone into the lungs and the latest update from James
Carrick was that the post-mortem findings were inconclusive
as to which event had actually been the cause of death. The
results of more tests were awaited.

'And whoever did it knew where the key to the vestry

was kept,' Patrick's mother had gone on in hushed tones. 'And they must have had access to one of the keys to the church too, otherwise how would they have locked up afterwards?'

I preferred to leave all this conjecture to the DCI, who with his sergeant Lynn Outhwaite, had, no doubt, closely questioned everyone involved with the day-to-day running of the building.

Another week went by. Mike Greenway rang to tell me that Patrick had started the job and that for his own safety would not now be able to contact me. All I had to reassure me, or otherwise, were his final words to me before he had set off to return to the aforementioned training three days after Mark had been born, this presumably the extent of SOCA's paternal leave.

'This won't be a protracted business, despite what Greenway might have said to you.'

And:

'Have a good rest. If I desperately need your help I'll contact you, somehow or other.'

It seemed to me that nothing had changed since the day Patrick had left MI5 because of personal danger and that to his family. And now where were we, I asked myself, with the main breadwinner still likely to come home for the weekend in a body bag? Not a protracted business? What, with possible changes of appearance and identity involved? Not all that long ago Patrick had spoken of giving up his job with SOCA to do something that would allow him more time with his family. He had actually been quite upset about the fact that the four children – this was before I knew I was pregnant with Mark – were growing up without his presence for quite long periods, something that was beginning to manifest itself in Justin's bad behaviour at school.

Resolving absolutely, definitely and utterly not to get involved with the just-under-my-nose murder as some kind of replacement therapy I busied myself – I simply could not concentrate on my new novel – finding out as much as I could about the mad-as-a-box-of-spanners hoodess Patrick was out to catch. There was not much information to be had, either on SOCA's internal website, to which I had the passwords, or that of the Met, courtesy of James Carrick. One of the names she used when in the UK was Andrea Pangborne, this utilized when she was passing herself off as what used to be called a socialite. She had others, a whole suite of identities and nationalities, some stolen, others invented, all using forged passports. She was a shadowy figure, very little was known about her and, like those who worked for her, she changed her appearance all the time. The only hard evidence – other than a string of serious crimes – that she was still in business was the occasional garrotted henchman left in her wake, usually literally in a gutter somewhere, the body having been pushed from a stolen car.

Yes, her business: it probably ought to be written her Business. This again was mostly about murder, internationally, for money, of course, and could involve anyone from a top politician to a drugs pusher if the price was right. Thrown in for good measure, and if required, was the wholesale slaughter of the target's nearest and dearest, including children, full-scale destruction of their houses, cars and any other assets that looked as though they could be satisfactorily firebombed, although anything particularly valuable along the lines of jewellery, artworks and so forth, was removed as contractor's perks. It was rumoured that she did the more 'interesting' jobs herself.

I do not bite my nails but they would have been down to my knuckles by now. OK, Patrick could, as Greenway had put it, 'do off-the-wall' but how, exactly, was SOCA going to play this?

TWO

Yet another ten days went by. The rectory roof was finished and, as the first floor extension had also been completed, the scaffolding was removed. The builders were now concentrating on the kitchen extension. Although settling in I knew that Patrick's parents were finding the annex a trifle small because the main rooms in the house were still sealed off, access to which they would have when all the work was finished. To give them a change of scenery and to help alleviate my own worry about Patrick I decided to ask them, and the Carricks, over for dinner. No, not the latter because I was agog to know how the murder inquiry was progressing, absolutely, absolutely not.

It was Elspeth who asked the question over pre-dinner drinks, she and John I knew were constantly badgered by their parishioners for news about the investigation, the more timid needing assurance, the victim's widow still apparently unable to live on her own.

The DCI knew that this was the time for straight-talking, not platitudes.

'I'm afraid we haven't got very far with this. We've eliminated quite a few people from the inquiry but anyone who has access to the key to the church and knows where the one to the vestry is kept is still a suspect as there appears to be no motive. Except those present in this room, of course. It's turning into one of those Agatha Christie stories where the more you delve beneath the surface of village life the more cans of worms you find.' He looked a little contrite. 'I hope I haven't ruined your impression of the rural idyll.'

'Good grief!' John exclaimed. 'There's no such thing and never has been. The so-called rural idyll was something invented by well-fed intellectuals who never went into the countryside to see the starving. These days, a good proportion of the people round here are pagans, worshipping their cars, money or pop stars and don't give a tinker's cuss for anyone. Newcomers complain about cattle mooing, the lack of street lighting and the church bells. There's even a suspicion that we've got a black magic outfit that's just been set up.' He added, darkly, 'I'm going to close *that* down if it's true. I'm not prepared to tolerate such filthy rubbish in the parish.'

'Good for you, sir,' Carrick said. Then he continued, 'It appears the murder victim was not a popular man, neither locally nor within his own family. His wife, Barbara, seems to be the only one to have anything good to say about him – and speaking in complete confidentiality I have to say I find *her* somewhat strange.'

'She thinks she can foretell who's going to be next to die,' Elspeth said. 'She's known as Morticia in the village.'

A smile twitched at the corners of Carrick's mouth. 'It looks as though she might have failed as far as her husband goes then. What I can't understand is that although unpopular, or at least it seems he was, they appear to be members of just about every local organization; the Garden Society, the Hinton Players, a drama group, the Bridge Club and he was on the PCC. Mrs Blanche has joined the WI and a keep fit class.'

'We'd only just returned from holiday when we spoke last,' Elspeth said. 'I've been doing a little investigating myself, mostly, I feel you ought to know, because of the general anxiety of a few members of the congregation. They tell me that they had words with him about something or the other just before he was killed – there were three, I think, who said that – and then I remembered that another two people had asked me prior to this man's death if they ought to mention to John something that he was steamrollering ahead with in a semi-official capacity that was not in the best interests of the village. They're worried that they're suspects.'

'What kind of semi-official capacity?' Carrick asked.

'Well, he'd just got himself on the village fête committee and proceeded to try to take over the entire running of it. And, while the usual person was away he somehow bullied the Hinton Players into letting him stage-manage the summer play. The village has a little festival in June – it's only been going for two years – and no end of people were upset about his interference. I have to say that only came to light yesterday as far as I'm concerned. There's been such a lot to do here,' she finished somewhat apologetically.

John said, 'I understand the poor man was hit on the head with some kind of blunt instrument.'

'Then a narrow vacuum cleaner nozzle was pushed down his throat and a bleach-based cleaning fluid poured down it,' Carrick told him. 'He actually drowned.'

Elspeth said, 'Those things are available to people on the cleaning rota, and they know where the key to the vestry is hidden.'

'Were he and his wife on the cleaning rota?'

'No, they're far too grand to do things like that. They were hymn snobs too.'

'*Hymn* snobs?'

'Yes, they'd only sing hymns that are in *Ancient and Modern*. None of what they called the "happy-clappy" stuff.'

'Are you? On the cleaning rota, I mean.'

'Yes, I do it with Molly Gardner. John always polishes the brass.'

'You'll have a copy of the current list then.'

'Of course. I'll let you have it. And there's one pinned up in the church porch.'

'How many keys are there to the church?'

'Three,' John answered. 'I have two, and the sexton another. One of those I hold is given to a church official if I'm away, one of the wardens usually, but I have to say we're not strict about it. The building is normally unlocked at around nine thirty in the morning by the sexton and locked up again at dusk – I usually do that – but a bit earlier than that in the summer with the long light evenings.'

'Had he unlocked it on the morning of the murder?' I asked.

'Yes.'

'So the murderer locked it up again.'

'Looks like it. This is going to turn into a jigsaw puzzle with several thousand pieces.' Carrick held out his glass for another tot of whisky as I proffered the bottle: Patrick's favourite, I had noted with a pang as I had picked it up.

Carrick noticed too. 'Have you heard from Patrick?' he said to me as I was about to ask who, exactly, had been in possession of John's spare key.

I shook my head. 'No, not since he started this job. He's not allowed to.'

Thankfully, he sensed that I preferred not to talk about it

right now and the conversation moved on to other things. I had not told John and Elspeth the nature of Patrick's latest assignment.

The next morning I took one look at the front page of the *Daily Telegraph* that had just been pushed through the letter box and snatched up the phone to call Michael Greenway, not caring that it was only six forty-five. The number being that of his mobile there was every chance of catching him. There were the usual strange clicks and clonks as the call went through whatever electronic wizardry SOCA uses to protect its operatives' communications and then he answered, with a mouthful of breakfast by the sound of it.

'Body found in Soho gutter,' I quoted tersely, forgetting to tell him who was calling. 'A man who had been garrotted. Can you put my mind at rest?'

'Even I don't know who he was yet,' Greenway admitted after swallowing his cornflakes, or whatever. 'I'll get right back to you as soon as I know anything. But don't worry, I'm sure he's fine.'

Later, the morning domestic scene going on all around me; children squabbling as they rushed to get ready for school, Vicky in her high chair serenely, and stickily, eating honey on toast, Mark asleep after his early morning feed, I really began to feel that I would go off my head with worry.

Patrick and I make a very good team, a partnership that enforced maternity leave was hazarding. I am not conceited but all I could think of was that he was out there somewhere without an important cog in the machine. Unless he was that body in the gutter.

The phone rang and I leapt at it.

'I'm going to Bath for a dentist appointment,' said Elspeth's voice. 'Do you want anything?'

'Er – no, thank you,' I mumbled.

'Only you mentioned a few days ago that you'd have to get some tinted moisturizer or other from Boots.'

'Oh, yes . . . sorry . . . yes please.' I gave her the name of it.

'Are you all right, Ingrid? You sound a bit under the weather.'

'Yes, fine. I didn't sleep very well, that's all.' Which was perfectly true.

'Patrick should have been allowed to spend more time with you. Having babies is an utterly exhausting business. Never mind, it's his birthday in three days' time. He always rings me if he's away somewhere so I'm sure you'll hear from him too.'

When I had put down the phone I shed the usual tears. In my present state of mind I had forgotten all about it.

Five minutes later the phone rang again.

'Negative,' Michael Greenway said. 'I know nothing more right now but you can rest assured it's not Patrick.'

'How *can* everyone be so sure?' I asked stubbornly, haunted by the images in my mind's eye of hideously bloated facial features.

'I asked them to check the right foot. It's a real one. OK?'

Humbly, I thanked him. Truly, having a baby had scrambled my brains.

Weak with relief, I went off into a welcome daydream, thinking how amazing it was that Patrick, through sheer hard work, the clichéd blood, sweat and even a few tears, had succeeded in getting fit after the Special Forces injuries that had meant having the lower part of his right leg amputated. It has been replaced by something that is just about the best in the world and cost a small fortune. Now, he might limp a little when he is very tired but can dance, run for short distances and no longer has nightmares of standing naked in the centre of some vast sports stadium with thousands of people shouting 'cripple!' at him.

Another week went by, each day seemingly an action replay of the previous one. I still could not work on the new novel I had started: I simply could not concentrate. I was aware that the police were continuing to make enquiries in the village, visiting those houses where people had not been at home when the first house-to-house questioning had taken place. James Carrick had not been in touch and I knew that this was not only because he was frantically busy but, sensitive soul that he is, would refrain from badgering me, knowing that I would call when I had anything to tell him.

Realizing that I was sitting in exactly the same place, worrying about exactly the same things as I had been seven days previously I wearily got to my feet, automatically picked up the toys and garments that the children had left in their wake and, berating myself that I was still in my dressing gown, made my way upstairs. I heard Carrie coming back from taking Justin to school.

The phone rang but before I could get to the nearest one it stopped after four rings. Calling whoever had changed their mind a few names under my breath I carried on up the stairs. Then, up in the bedroom, my mobile, which was in my bag, rang four times. Not for me silly tunes.

Four rings.

Back in the mists of time – a few months, no weeks, previously – that was the code Patrick and I had used when we urgently wanted the other to get in touch.

'But why not just ring me?' I asked out loud.

Because he wanted me to ring him, that was why, stupid.

I stuck to the rules and left it for a short time, six minutes to be exact, and then rang his mobile number from the land-line, heart thumping and suddenly feeling a thousand per cent alert.

There was a click and then a rough voice said, 'Who's that?'

'Doctor Astrid von Bremen,' I answered. 'Is someone trying to contact me?'

'Oh!' There was a short pause. 'Your number was called a while back on this mobile belonging to a bloke wot's been hurt in an accident. I'm trying to identify him so I can call his family. He says his name is Patrick Gillard.'

I went ice cold.

'I don't think he's a patient of mine,' I said.

'Can you check, like?'

'I'm right in the middle of my morning surgery,' I told him. 'Have you called an ambulance?'

There was another little silence. Then, ''Corse.'

He was lying.

'Surely if he's able to tell you his name he should be able to say who his next of kin are.'

'No, he's . . . sort of . . . like . . . rambling on.'

'What kind of accident has he been involved in? Has he been knocked down by a car?'

More silence, but for faint music.

'Can I speak to him?' I risked asking.

There was a click and then the line went dead.

My first instinct was to arrange immediately for my mobile number to be changed. No, it might be the only life-line Patrick had. But I would have to use another phone until I was sure that no one was now tracking my own. Then I remembered that Patrick had called the house landline first. Which meant they probably had that too. And, for heaven's sake, unless he had erased the other numbers in his phone's memory persons unknown were now party to all the numbers of family, friends, Uncle Tom Ballsup and all.

'What the *hell* were you doing having your own phone with you?' I raged to the four walls of the room.

'Are you all right, Ingrid?' Carrie enquired up the stairs.

'May I borrow your mobile?' I asked, throwing on clothes. 'No, on second thoughts . . .' I went down. 'Carrie, I think the wrong people may have got hold of Patrick's phone with all our numbers in and I don't know if they have the wherewithal to listen in. Does Patrick have your number?'

'Yes, he has. In case there's something wrong with the ordinary one.'

'So they'll have his parents' number too,' I said in despair.

'There's a phone box in the village,' she reminded me.

I was halfway out of the door when she called, 'You could use Matthew's. You bought it for him after Patrick went away and they're not allowed to take them to school.'

I tore back up the stairs.

'Someone's got Patrick and it sounds as though he's under some kind of duress, even truth drug,' I told Michael Greenway without preamble. 'They know his real name.' I related what had happened.

He swore under his breath.

'I can't understand why he has his own phone,' I said.

'He probably hasn't. He was issued with one that has a completely false set-up and for emergency use only. Your number could have been one of those in it.'

'He still might have told them the codes for it.'

'It wouldn't have done them a lot of use as someone calling themselves Auntie Mamie answers and yatters on for fully half a minute about life in Frinton before anyone can get a word in edgeways.'

'He's a very poor subject for truth drug actually,' I recalled, forcing myself to be pragmatic. 'Keeps singing and going to sleep. I could hear someone singing in the background.'

'I'll do everything in my power to pull him out,' the Commander promised before ringing off.

I sat on Matthew's bed staring at the shiny new phone, my mind in a whirl. It seemed inconceivable that Patrick, so professional in everything he did, had had his own phone with him and I hoped Greenway was right. Unless he was living in some kind of rented accommodation that had been raided by whoever had rung me – and I wondered if it was the Thug in Charge working for the Executioner – and his personal possessions, which I knew would have been well hidden, had been found.

But under truth drug he might have told them where they were. It was possible he had told them everything about himself, about me, the children, where we lived, everything.

But on the other hand . . .

I reasoned that it must have been Patrick himself who had rung me originally as he had allowed it to ring only four times: the emergency call using our own prearranged code that Greenway did not know about. Even if the person who then acquired his phone had been given the information for what reason would they want me to phone back? The man had presumably used the last number redial facility in order to see who he had been trying to contact. Was his cover, in fact, blown? What had he told them other than his name? Was he even alive?

I stared at the phone and then slowly, fearfully, having to know something, *anything,* dialled his number.

It rang and rang.

Then, just before I knew the messaging service would cut in, there was a sudden silence. Then, laboured breathing.

'Patrick?' I shouted. 'Patrick! It's Ingrid. Where are you?'

There came the ghastly sound of someone vomiting, on to the floor, probably.

'Oh, God, where are you?' I cried.

'I – I don't know,' Patrick's voice said faintly.

'In your room?' I asked. 'Is it your room?'

'Yes . . . it's my room,' came the answer after several very long seconds had elapsed. He then sang the first verse of a rather rude Rugby song.

'Are you hurt?' I managed to get in before he could start on the second.

'I don't know.'

'Have those people gone?'

'What people?'

'The people who were with you. I rang after you tried to contact me and a man answered.'

'I can't remember anyone else being here.'

'Think!'

Another long silence followed during which I could picture a man trying to gather his drug-addled wits while he fought nausea. He lost on the latter count.

'Patrick, please talk to me when you can,' I pleaded, not knowing if he could even hear me.

'Yeah, that's right,' he gasped, finally. 'They broke in. They've gone to get her.'

'Then get out!' I shrieked. 'You know what happened to the others!'

'I don't think I can walk. They gave me a jab and I passed out.'

'Does Greenway know where you are?'

'Who?'

'Greenway. Michael Greenway. Your *boss*.'

'I don't know.'

'He said he'd get you out. He *must* know where you are.'

There were scuffling and grunting noises that went on for far too long for my peace of mind. Then, panting for breath, Patrick said, 'Yeah, I can stand. And walk – sort of. I'm going to get her.'

'No, that's what *they're* doing,' I frantically told him. 'Save yourself! Find a taxi, or a bus. Just *go*!'

'I'm going to get her,' he repeated. 'It was part of my brief.'

I opened my mouth to again implore him to escape but he had gone.

The news broke at around four thirty that afternoon. There had been a shoot-out at a house in Muswell Hill in London with several fatalities. The police were saying very little, only that, at present, the incident was being treated as a battle between two rival gangs. Three people had been taken to hospital, one of whom was a girl around eight years of age who had died shortly afterwards from her injuries. A man found collapsed and in a confused state nearby, armed and with his clothing bloodstained, had been arrested.

THREE

'Patrick hasn't been arrested,' Michael Greenway said. 'That was for the benefit of the media. We actually carted him off to the private clinic SOCA uses when we want a little anonymity.'

By this time I was fuming because of being, in effect, on the far end of a very long piece of wire. 'Am I permitted to resume duties?' I enquired stonily.

'You can talk to him over the phone if you want to. No restrictions there.'

'Where are the restrictions to be found then?' I countered.

He had a habit of chewing his bottom lip when he was thinking and I could imagine him giving it hell now.

'What I meant to have said was that you can talk to him about everything but the job over an open line.'

'Please answer my question. Can I get back to work so I can help Patrick deal with this?'

'Are you sure you're fit? I mean, I wouldn't want you to—'

'I'm fit,' I interrupted.

'Well . . . yes. Of course.'

'I'm coming to London – now. Where do I find him?'

'Ingrid, before I give you the address I feel I must tell you that he does appear to have killed or injured several people. The woman who sometimes called herself Andrea Pangborne was among the dead. It was the drugs he'd been pumped full of, of course, and no one's talking about arresting him until he's recovered and can make a statement.'

'Is he supposed to have shot the little girl?' I asked him, shivering now.

'We won't know until his clothing has been DNA tested but I'm afraid it would appear so.'

'I spoke to him,' I revealed. 'When he'd just regained consciousness.'

'Come to HQ and we'll talk about that. I'll take you to the clinic afterwards.'

*   *   *

'It might not be as bad as we think,' was Greenway's opening remark when I entered his office later that day. Not for the first time, I wondered if his wife and family ever saw him. 'Would you like some refreshment?' he went on to ask.

'No, thank you,' I replied, my insides still churning with the sheer horror of the situation. 'What might not be so bad?'

'Well, for a start, one of the people taken to hospital, a woman who said she was a cleaner, was locked in a cupboard by a man who fits Patrick's description. She broke her wrist trying to batter her way out. The other person receiving treatment turns out to be a passer-by who said he was about to investigate a wide open front door and the sound of smashing bottles but before he could enter the house was grabbed by a man, who again fits Patrick's description, and found himself chucked into a bush. His hand is gashed as there was some broken glass beneath it. So it sounds as though our man was at least lucid enough to try to save the innocent from injury, not someone who was crazed and off his head.'

I wondered if that actually made things worse and said, 'I must ask you something before we go any further. Patrick's last words to me before he hung up were that he was going to get her. The people who had been with him had told him that they were going to get her and I understood that to mean that they were going to fetch Pangborne so that she could deliver the coup de grâce after whatever it was he'd said broke his cover. I thought he was confused – he *was* confused for God's sake! – and shouted at him to get out while he could. But he repeated that he was going to get her, adding that it was part of his brief. Was it?'

Slowly, Greenway shook his head. 'No, he had no orders to do away with the woman, or even arrest her, if that is what he meant when he said it, only provide intelligence that would lead to her arrest. I don't have to tell you that SOCA isn't in the business of killing criminals. We might never know, Ingrid, what he meant. The first results of blood tests indicate that he was up to the eyeballs with a cocktail of stuff, including, as you correctly surmised, truth drug, Sodium Pentothal.'

'He always reacts very badly to those kind of substances. He was throwing up everywhere.'

'Tell me about it,' Greenway said with a grimace. 'I've just come back from his digs. I've got scenes-of-crime people there to see if we can find out who his visitors were – if indeed they were all in that room when you spoke to them.'

'Patrick remembered them breaking in,' I said. 'They must have given him the jab, or jabs, and he told them his name.'

'Rest assured he had none of his own things at that address so they won't have got hold of his private mobile with all the family numbers in. When I first briefed him for the job he told me he would leave everything in his locker here at HQ. Can you remember both conversations well enough to be able to write them down?'

I opened my bag to extract my notebook. Tearing out a few pages I handed them to him. 'I wrote out what was said on the train,' I told him. 'But I can't guarantee it's word for word.'

I had included background noises, even Patrick throwing up, how voices had sounded, everything that might provide clues as to what had happened.

'You have a very good memory,' Greenway murmured, reading.

'It comes in handy if there's a power cut and I haven't been saving my work properly,' I told him. 'How is Patrick now?'

His quick glance in my direction was full of sympathy. 'He's being treated for continuing nausea and dehydration, and also closely watched as his memory's returning and he's understandably suffering from shock.'

'He actually remembers shooting those people?' I gasped. I could never recollect Patrick ever suffering from shock, not after any of the ordeals we had been through together.

'No, not in the stark way you mean. He can remember hearing shots being fired but there's a dreamlike quality to his memories. That's caused by the after-effects of the drugs. I don't want him questioned yet, not by cops anyway.'

For dreamlike read nightmarish, I thought.

'Not by cops?' I repeated. 'But by his wife?'

'That's absolutely at your discretion. The questions, that is. You're perfectly free to talk to him about anything else you want to now if you think that's the best thing to do.'

'I think that before I do anything I'd prefer some background information.'

'You can visit the crime scene if you want to.'

*   *   *

'It's what we're calling her London HQ,' Greenway explained as we got out of the car and he had asked the driver to wait. 'The woman had been under surveillance for just over six months in several countries and it's only recently that a clearer picture's emerged, partly, I have to say, because she's appeared to have become overconfident. As soon as crooks get cocky and careless it makes it easier for the law to catch up with them. And as you can see, although this isn't exactly the West End she believed in living comfortably.'

The house in Park Road was a large Victorian semi overlooking a recreation ground cum park and I could glimpse open water, probably a reservoir, in the distance. The road had been closed, except for access to residents, but was virtually blocked by police and associated vehicles anyway.

During the drive over Greenway had told me that Pangborne, real name either Horovic or Larovic – nothing about the woman was certain – had been born in the north of Serbia in the late sixties. Seemingly either abandoned by her parents or an orphan she had been raised by nuns, eventually leaving the convent to work as a waitress at an hotel. She and a junior chef had almost immediately run off together and started a life of crime, earning the nickname The Mad Wolves as they had tended to carry out raids, holding up filling stations and other retail outlets that were open during the night. Others joined them, all who tried to stand in their path were ruthlessly gunned down.

Life had gone on like that for some years but when the country was in turmoil and at war the gang had split up and gone their separate ways. Pangborne had by then rid herself of her partner in crime, by shooting him dead, having met more wealthy and organized criminals, one of whom, Jethro Hulton, she lived with. She never lost her taste for killing. Hulton was thought to be the eight-year-old girl's father.

The Commander lifted up a section of incident tape so I could duck beneath it and said, 'Obviously the bodies have been taken away now but you can get the gist of what happened.'

I said, 'May I first see where Patrick was found?'

'Of course.'

Greenway then had to show his ID and explain who I was: clearly, the Met was running this side of things. We went down a path between the buildings that ran down the side of the house, walking carefully as there had been overnight frost and there were icy patches, emerging in a wider lane at right angles to it that gave access to garages sited at the ends of the gardens. A small area at one side had been cordoned off with more tape, the ground covered in dumped and mostly rotten grass cuttings and other garden refuse. There was a hollow of sorts in the heap.

'There,' Greenway said. 'He probably passed out.'

There was nothing for us to see here and we started to walk back. I said, 'Have you ever had any experience of truth drug?'

'I've never come across anyone wandering around with it in their veins but from what I can remember of training I was told it makes you feel hellishly sick and a complete zombie. Have you?'

'We had to experience all kinds of horrible things during training for MI5. You tend to lose inhibitions and that makes some people friendly and chatty although most retain self-control. You become more suggestible but less wilful. High doses can render people unconscious which is obviously what happened to Patrick, but mostly, you just want to go to sleep. And you're saying he killed and injured several people despite having had a skinful of the stuff?'

'I did tell you that he wasn't under arrest. How did Patrick behave during training?'

'Although tending to yarn endlessly about his army days and sing his self-control remained in charge. As I've already said, he was a bad subject. He's a good liar – you have to be for undercover work.'

'Doesn't that make you feel a bit uncomfortable?'

'We're talking about work,' I retorted. 'He doesn't lie in his private life.'

Greenway spread his large hands in a gesture of peace. 'Sorry. What about when he's had a drop too much of his favourite single malt?'

'Maudlin, soppy and in love with the whole world,' I replied.

'Um,' was Greenway's only response to this. 'But he still must have told them he was an undercover cop or whoever it was wouldn't have said he was going to fetch Pangborne.'

'It's perfectly possible.'

A constable on duty at the front door stood aside for us

to enter. I knew without being told that I must not touch anything and there would be rooms which we would only be permitted to look into from the doorway. This was the case with the first that we came to on the right in the wide hallway, a large, bright living room within which white-suited figures moved carefully, collecting microscopic samples, examining fingerprints or taking photographs.

'The souvenirs of murder,' Greenway said quietly, wrinkling his nose at the smell of stale blood. 'There's not much to see in the rest of the house. The child seems to have been shot on the upstairs landing judging by the bloodstains and somehow made it into the bathroom where she collapsed. At least, that was where she was found. It's all guesswork at the moment, as you're aware and until test results confirm otherwise or Patrick remembers what went on here that's how it'll have to stay.'

We gazed into the room. Bottles and drink cans were all over the floor, and on a side table was the remains of a buffet meal of sorts: crisps, shop-bought sausage rolls and other party food, an untouched sickly looking, lipstick-pink 'strawberry' gateau. I suddenly noticed that someone had vomited all over a nearby armchair. Otherwise the room looked as though several people had been executed by firing squad, the walls on one side splattered and smeared with blood and brains.

'How many were killed?' I asked.

'Seven, including Pangborne and the child. As I said earlier, those who survived can be described as innocent parties slightly injured in other ways.'

'Who were the other five?'

'We know that three were part of Pangborne's empire and wanted for crimes in other countries, namely, France, Germany and Italy. They were a trio who had worked together sometimes over the years. The other two are, as yet, unknown to us but photos have gone off to various agencies. My guess is that they were illegal immigrants and that we'll find forged passports when we discover where they lived.'

'I take it Hulton wasn't among the dead.'

'No.' Greenway took a deep breath. 'Shall we go and see Patrick?'

*   *   *

Housed in a large, bland but beautiful house in a terrace very similar to SOCA's HQ the clinic was situated in a quiet square in Richmond. A discreet sign on one of the gateposts gave the information that the establishment was run by the Nightingale Memorial Trust.

'Florence is still helping injured soldiers then,' I remarked to Greenway with a flippancy brought on by sheer nerves.

'Oh, I understand it was one Nathaniel Nightingale, a Victorian mill owner, whose original quest was to rescue fallen women from the streets of London.'

'I'll tell Patrick that.'

'I already have. He wondered if they still had any stashed away somewhere.' Greenway shot me a look. 'Don't worry, he was right off the planet.'

'I wasn't aware that you saw him earlier,' I said reproachfully.

He held open a door for me. 'It was never my intention to keep the fact from you. He went straight back to sleep after he'd said that.'

In a silent lift we travelled up to the second floor and walked down a corridor through a hushed and opulent world of marble panelling, works of art and the scents of aromatherapy.

'I'll wait here,' the Commander told me when we had stopped outside Room 46, gesturing to a waiting area. 'And have a very quick word with him afterwards. Stay as long as you like. I could do with an excuse not to do much for a little while.'

I went in, not of the opinion that wives should knock. The room had an adjoining private bathroom in which the occupant was having a shower so I had to sit down and wait a few minutes, more like hours, actually.

Wearing what can only be described as a voluptuous cream towelling robe the man in my life finally appeared. There was a small graze on the side of his cheek, a bruise on his jaw and he was as white as the immaculate bedding, only with a greenish-grey tinge. I surveyed him closely as he registered surprise when he saw me.

'Hi! I'm off the drip,' he said, somewhat unnecessarily. 'No more honking.'

I got to my feet and went over to him. Close up, the fine grey eyes looked a little strange, which was to be expected.

'It all went horribly wrong, didn't it?' I said, putting my arms around him.

'Yes,' he replied.

'You've had a hell of a time.'

He hugged me tightly and then, his head on my shoulder, wept.

Good, it would help.

The room was quite large with armchairs in it, over to one of which I steered him after a couple of minutes when the worst was over. There was a jug of orange juice on a bedside cabinet and I poured some into a glass for him.

'Flushes through the system,' I said matter-of-factly, handing it over, together with a tissue.

'How's the new boy?' he asked when he had mostly recovered, making an heroic effort to behave normally.

'Bouncing,' I told him. 'James Carrick thinks he's just like me.'

An eyebrow quirked and I suddenly realized that a joke about the likelihood of fallen women being stored away for possible further use did not *have* to mean that a man was stoned out of his noddle on drugs. There was such a thing as putting a brave face on things too so I became even more confused as to his real state of mind.

'You saw James then?'

'Yes, there was a murder in the church.'

'What, at Hinton Littlemoor? At *home*?'

I nodded. 'It happened a few hours before your parents came back from holiday.'

'Who died?'

'You probably don't know him. A Squadron Leader Melvyn Blanche.'

'I do know him. The man was insufferably rude to me. He came round while you were in hospital after having Mark and told me we had no business to buy the rectory.'

'On what grounds?'

'He didn't say but I rather got the impression that he'd have gone after it himself if the place had not been sold by private treaty before it went to auction.'

'Don't tell James – you might find yourself on his list of suspects.'

Patrick actually smiled. 'So he hasn't got anyone for it yet then?'

'No.'

'How have Mum and Dad taken it?'

'As they usually cope with what life throws at them; splendidly. Your father's asked the bishop to hold some kind of reconsecration service.'

There did not seem to be much wrong with his recall of family matters.

'Before the funeral presumably.'

'No, that's going to be held somewhere else. Your mother told me that the woman's making it no secret that she'll never worship in St Michael's again.' There was a short silence before I added, 'Can you remember what happened this morning?'

'Some of it,' Patrick answered shortly.

'Do you want to talk about it?'

'No, I'm trying not to think about it at all,' he retorted harshly.

I waited.

'She's dead, isn't she?' he then said so quietly I could hardly hear him.

'Who? – Andrea Pangborne, or whatever she was calling herself at the time? Yes, she is.'

Patrick shook his head. 'No, Leanne, her daughter.'

'The eight-year-old?'

'Yes.'

'I'm afraid she is too.'

This was all so utterly ghastly that I was feeling faint.

'As I said to you when you rang, I went to get her. I failed.'

My ears roared. 'You mean you went to get her *out*?'

He gave me a very straight look, his eyes still swimming with tears. 'Of course. What else did you think I meant?'

'You were still a little wuzzy and I didn't know what to think you meant.'

Patrick looked appalled. 'Someone filled me up with drugs thereby finding out that I was an undercover cop, took my gun and then had themselves a massacre. I couldn't stop it. And didn't save Leanne.'

'You didn't fire a shot?' I exclaimed.

'I'm not too sure but probably not.'

'Patrick, you were carrying a gun when you were found, your gun.'

'I'm pretty sure I didn't fire it.'

'What can you remember, clearly?'

'Really clearly only carrying Leanne as she didn't want to leave the house. The bastard shot her in my arms. He was probably out to get me.'

Patrick's voice broke as he uttered the last words and he put his head in his hands.

'Do you know this bastard's name?' I asked gently.

'No, I didn't really get a look at him. I'm not sure why.' A few seconds elapsed before he added, 'D'you mind if I go back to sleep?'

I got up immediately. 'Of course I don't mind. I shouldn't be asking you all these questions.' Quickly, I went over to him and kissed his cheek. 'I'll come back when you're feeling better and take you home.'

'Ingrid . . .'

I turned from going over to the door.

'I've been going out with the woman.'

'That was part of your brief?' I enquired, more shocked by the tortured look on his face than what he had just said.

'Yes. I should have refused, shouldn't I?'

I made myself remain pragmatic. 'You've done some iffy things in the past in order to take dangerous criminals out of circulation.'

'There was a party at the house. I could have been dosed with something then, in a drink, as I can't really remember it at all. I might have slept with her.'

When men say 'might' in this kind of context they usually mean 'probably did'.

'At least, I can remember wanting to,' he muttered to the floor. 'She was naked at some point during the evening. I feel a real shit.'

'You're not and we'll talk about it when you come home,' I told him. 'But if that's all SOCA wants you for then you'd be better off in neck-end Bath selling second-hand cars for a living.'

I shut the door very gently behind me.

'So then,' I said to Greenway, rounding a corner and making him start slightly. 'He's screwing she-crooks to get their plans, ambitions and secrets. Is that what the training was for? All the latest techniques, positions, advice on the best aftershaves and talcs to drive women wild?'

He opened his mouth to speak but I ploughed on.

'Did you have a vote among your female staff as to who would be the best-looking guy for the job? Oh, yes, Gillard's got quite the prettiest eyelashes and is actually quite a stunner when you think about it. Never mind that he's a clean-living bloke, even when he was in the army, and can't actually make much of a stand against filth who drug his drinks, strip off their clothes and then get their minions to drug him again. I told you he wasn't the right man for the job and he wasn't. My husband is crying in there, Commander, because a little girl he was trying to rescue – God knows how, the state he was in but I got the impression that it was part of his orders that she should come to no harm – was shot in his arms. We've had a murder in our church at home and the bishop is going to reconsecrate the building. Shall I ask him to do Patrick while he's at it?'

I walked off, aware that I had yelled the last couple of sentences.

'Ingrid, listen – please!' Greenway desperately called after me.

I swung round. 'If he's not been brought home by ten tomorrow morning I'm releasing everything I know about this wretched business to the media.'

FOUR

The media beat me to it, the front page of a tabloid newspaper braying SOCA MAN IN GUN RAMPAGE on the counter of the village post office when I went in there to buy stamps shortly after it opened the following morning. The story went on to report that the name Patrick Gillard had been mentioned by an 'unofficial source' but nothing had been confirmed. I earned the thorough disapproval of the proprietors by establishing, there and then, that the story was carried, to a greater or lesser degree, by several other papers, all of which referred to the previous day's news of a gun battle in London. They went on to report that the police were continuing their enquires and were not denying that police personnel might have been involved.

I immediately rang Michael Greenway to tell him that I had not been guilty of leaking the story, and would hardly have mentioned Patrick's name if I had, but had to leave a message as his phone was, unusually, switched off. I could imagine him in a top-level meeting, perhaps with Richard Daws. He returned the call shortly afterwards.

'We know you didn't,' was his first remark. 'There was an anonymous call to a news agency from a man who described himself as an insider.'

'I do know insiders,' I said.

'Yes, but – well – Ingrid, we knew you wouldn't really do it. He's on his way home for at least a week's leave, by the way.'

'I'm sorry I bawled you out.'

'It looked very bad from where you were standing yesterday. It *is* very bad with the death of the child. And please believe me when I tell you that Patrick's training was no more than a refresher course with weapons and so forth and a regime to get him as fit as possible.'

I knew that if I was to carry on working with Greenway I had to believe him. A short while later the phone started ringing; friends, acquaintances and finally, when he could get through, Patrick's father, all wanting to know what was going on. All I could say to everyone was that he had been working undercover, adding that he was not under arrest and had had nothing to do with the killings. John I invited over later, with Elspeth if she wished, so they could talk to him themselves. It was all I could do.

Carrie put her head around the living room door. 'I take it the news about Patrick is a smoke and mirrors thing and there's nothing to worry about.'

'There's a little concern,' I told her. 'But no, basically, you're right. Patrick'll be home later and if Matthew and Katie ask questions we'll deal with it.'

'Oh, good. That baby of yours has been nominated for a sainthood, by the way.'

It was actually a little after eleven when a car pulled into the large gravelled parking area in front of the rented house – not a blade of grass, tub of plants nor tree in sight, a situation that had led us to call it 'the helicopter landing pad' and making me desperate to move to my new home, which was at least another three weeks away. Patrick got out, went round to retrieve a bag from the back, waved his thanks to the driver and the car left immediately.

I went out to meet him.

Standing face to face after a kiss and a hug Patrick said, 'I'm OK. Are you?'

He was not at all OK and I rather felt from his guarded expression that he was asking me if I was going to divorce him. 'Absolutely fine,' I told him, meaning it.

'Is the sprog asleep or am I allowed to have a quick gloat?'

Mark woke up, blinked twice and then drifted off again in his father's arms. Patrick sat down with him in the first floor living room, facing the picture window that gave a fine view over the Somerset countryside, while I brewed coffee.

'He seems very placid,' Patrick commented when I went in.

'Heaven after Justin,' I said. I had brought a shawl. 'Lay him on the sofa in this while you have your coffee in case you spill it on him.'

'Can I let it get cold so he won't be scalded if I do?'

I had to smile. 'If you want to.'

'He's all right though? Not quiet because . . .'

This time I laughed. 'Of course he's all right! You can bath him tonight if you like and hear him yelling for his feed.' I sipped my coffee. 'So you're on a week's leave.' I had hoped that he would look better than he had in the clinic. He did not: still like something poisoned.

'In a way.'

'There had to be a catch.'

'Greenway's working on the theory that the so-called insider who leaked the story is either the killer or someone with a big grudge against me. The call was made from a mobile phone.'

'Sorry to be so negative but how can everyone be really sure that you didn't go right off your head with the mixture of drugs you'd been given and fire shots in all directions?'

'Overnight testing has proved that the shots *were* fired from the gun I was holding when I was found nearby. It *was* my Glock 18. But my prints are the only ones on it, just the one set, not lots of others of mine that would be the normal state of affairs. Which would suggest it had been wiped and then put in my hand.' At this point Patrick changed his mind and rose to place Mark in the shawl on the sofa, watched for a few moments to make sure that all remained peaceful and then sat down again and picked up his coffee mug. 'As you might know already they were all killed with a single shot to the head, except for Leanne who had been hit in the chest.'

I respected the silence that followed, Patrick turning away from me, in the direction of the window.

'Apparently it was a mass execution,' he continued, after clearing his throat. 'In the living room, where they were found.'

'Greenway took me there.'

'Someone said that it would have been a medical impossibility for me to have fired such accurate shots in the condition I was in.'

'So what did the killer do, line them all up against the wall and shoot them?' I said, aware of occasions when this man of mine had achieved things not reckoned at the time to be medically possible, like laughing when he was in intensive care, for example. 'He would only have been able to kill one at a time. Did the others just line up waiting to die like sheep?'

'A scenes-of-crime team is still working there. No one knows – yet.'

'You went back to the house to try to get Leanne out. That means you must have been mobile, after a fashion.'

'Look, Ingrid, I didn't kill those people!'

'I know, sorry, but I'm playing your hard-hearted consultant and trying to get to the bottom of this. Frankly though, I can't understand why you're not under some kind of arrest or suspension. After the party you went back to your digs, presumably in the early hours of the morning, and were still under the influence of whatever you thought had been slipped into your drink. *Then* someone broke in and doped you with truth drug. It was after that, after I'd spoken to you, that you went back to the house to rescue the girl and that's when the shooting started. How did you get there?'

'I can't remember,' Patrick answered after another silence.

'*Why* did you feel she needed rescuing?'

'I'm not sure now. It might have been because she was around during the party – or rather binge.'

'Around?'

'Saying she was hungry and why wasn't there anything to eat. I got her out of the room, made her some supper, and told her to go to bed.'

'While her mother was high on God knows what and having it away with any number of men.'

'Drink and drugs yes, but as far as sex went only with Hulton.'

'Not you?' I enquired ruthlessly, not knowing how much he could recall of what he had told me the previous day.

'No.'

'No?'

'No. The situation's clearer to me now. She was too scared of him to go with anyone else.'

I left that subject, thankfully, and said, 'Why didn't you get Leanne out of the place while the party was going on if you were worried about her safety?'

'I didn't think she was in the kind of danger you're thinking about. A bad situation for any child, I know, but she was used to such happenings and had only come downstairs because she was hungry. And at that stage I didn't know anyone suspected me.'

'It might follow then that when those people broke into your digs they said something to you that made you think *everyone* at the house was in danger, not just Leanne.'

Patrick shook his head. 'If they did I can't remember what it was.'

'Why didn't you phone Greenway? They must have left your mobile behind because I rang you.'

'It was my work mobile I had with me – which is fixed up so that your calls are automatically forwarded. I still have it with me. Mine's in my locker at HQ.'

'In that case, with that literally at your fingertips, why didn't you call out the cavalry instead of going back to the house on your own?'

Patrick had a mouthful of coffee and then said, 'You're getting as good at interrogation as me. So if I ask you for something to eat before I answer any more questions you refuse, eh?'

We eyeballed one another. He hadn't exactly been joking.

'I don't know why I didn't call Greenway,' Patrick then said. 'But if it wasn't because I was sozzled and had forgotten the codes I might have been hoping I could salvage the job even at that late stage.'

'Please tell me what your rôle was as far as this woman was concerned, your undercover rôle, I mean.'

'I was brought in by someone who penetrated the gang years ago and who worked as a kind of Bloke Friday; driving their cars, fixing things and so forth. He then had a faked road accident and was pulled off the job. I'd been introduced as an ex-serviceman with a grudge against this country after being injured and invalided out who had plenty of specialized knowledge about MoD installations and weapon stores and wanted a job. The idea was that she'd find me – well – attractive and confide in me.'

I stood up. 'I'll fix you something to eat.'

The kitchen was on the ground floor, reached through a wide archway from the dining area, this part of the house being mostly open plan. This was a pity as I could have done with a door to shut right now. Mind a blank I found myself looking into the fridge. Yes, that's right, lunch. Bread rolls, tomatoes, ham, butter . . . I took a double handful of stuff to the nearest work top and dumped it all down, tears dripping on to the pack of rolls.

I became aware of Patrick standing in the archway.

'It's called baby blues,' I told him, or rather gulped. 'Quite common and I had it after Vicky was born. Take no notice of me.'

'She didn't,' Patrick said.

'What, confide in you? That's a shame,' I said brightly after a big sniff.

'No, find me attractive.'

'Oh.'

'She preferred hairy men.'

I stared at him. '*Hairy* men!'

'Yes, Hulton's like a yak. It was rumoured that he carries a gun hidden under all the fur.'

I really thought for a moment that he was having me on but he came over and solemnly dried my tears on his handkerchief.

'I think I'll put smoked salmon and cream cheese in the rolls,' I said with a silly laugh. 'And we'll have a glass of wine with it.' Then I said, 'Did you try to make yourself attractive to her?'

Patrick kissed the end of my nose. 'No, but don't tell himself.'

'I forgot to wish you a belated happy birthday. Your presents are upstairs.'

Which were a bottle of his favourite single-malt whisky and a large framed photograph of George, his horse.

'Greenway told me that Hulton wasn't among the dead,' I said later after we had eaten and Patrick had slept for an hour and a half.

'I can't remember seeing him when I went back but that doesn't mean he wasn't in the house. Or he might have either left the previous night or did a runner when the trouble started.'

'Would he have killed Pangborne if she'd had sex with another man?'

'Hulton'll kill anything.'

I was just going to ask Patrick if he thought the man guilty of the murders when a car drew in.

'It'll be your parents,' I said. 'Do you want to talk to them alone?'

'No, by no means,' Patrick replied emphatically.

Dreading any awkwardness I went down to let them in.

Elspeth delightedly commandeered the latest addition to the family who had just been given a feed and was wide awake. John said nothing, other than to greet me, and led the way upstairs.

There was a little general conversation; the ongoing police investigation into Blanche's murder, the building progress, the weather, and I stuck it out, unwilling to leave the room to make tea and thereby abandon Patrick with them. I could understand their concern but although they love him dearly they are not the sort of people to be pleased by anything they regard as a drop in standards so, from their point of view, were facing family disaster.

Then John said, 'This job of yours seems to be getting totally out of hand.'

'No assignment goes strictly to plan,' Patrick told him.

'Are you under suspicion for these murders?'

'Unofficially, yes.'

I heard Elspeth gasp.

'But as you can see I'm not under arrest,' Patrick went on. 'I can't water this down for you but feel you ought to know that I was sent in to try to bring to justice a woman and her gang who were international criminals; killers and thieves. Someone, somehow, must have suspected me. I was drugged and dumped in a lane behind the house and a person unknown must have put the gun in my hand that had been used to commit the murders so I would get the blame. It was my gun. I hadn't fired it. I know when I've fired a gun because my right wrist aches slightly for a few hours afterwards, a legacy of old injuries. My memory is returning but I still don't have the full mental picture because of the drugs. That's all I can tell you. It's the truth and, frankly, Dad, I don't need you coming here wearing your dog collar and with a face as long as a fiddle. I *do* need your support, a prayer perhaps or a blessing so that I don't feel so bloody wretched about trying to get a child away from danger only to have her shot in my arms.'

I left the room to put the kettle on. He did not need my presence. Not only that, he had remembered being dumped out the back, something that I had not mentioned along with other details at Greenway's suggestion. When I returned with the tea things I rather got the impression that a prayer had been said and a blessing administered – verified by Patrick later – because the atmosphere was much more relaxed and Elspeth was smiling broadly as she talked to Mark in her lap.

'We should have helped you with that,' she said to me. 'Oh, you wouldn't like to come to dinner tonight, would you? Only we've asked James and Joanna as he's managing to have a couple of days off and it's a bit fogeyish for them with just us two.'

'Fogeyish?' John queried. 'Is that a word?'

'Of course it is,' his wife declared. 'Besides, someone's given us a huge chicken. Folk are so generous, you know. And as we were saying just now, the builders have finished making a mess indoors and have cleaned up as best they can so if we all turn to for an hour or so now to do a bit of hoovering and dusting I think we can unseal the dining and living rooms and use them this evening. That's if it's all right with you two. I mustn't forget that it's your house now.'

'It'll always be home to you,' I said, as ever in total admiration of her tactics.

FIVE

Nothing further was said about the shootings – the Carricks remaining tactfully silent on the subject – until later that day after dinner when Patrick's parents had retired for the night. We were seated in front of a blazing log fire – which was needed as it was snowing outside – in the living room of the rectory and by candlelight, Elspeth having completely forgotten that there was no power, water, or central heating reconnected yet in the old part of the house.

Patrick gave James Carrick a rueful smile. 'I'm innocent until proven guilty,' he observed. 'But Greenway told me to surrender my passport and stay in Hinton Littlemoor.'

'You've been debriefed, I take it,' Carrick said.

'Not in so many words. I'm not being told too much as he wants to see how much I recollect on my own. He's coming here the day after tomorrow accompanied by what he described as 'colleagues', by which time I'm supposed to have rid my system of all the dope. Rightly or wrongly he was handling me with kid gloves at the time and what he really meant was that I'll be grilled by people from Complaints. I'm forbidden to investigate this myself, on pain of dismissal.'

'You're actually suspended then.'

'Oddly enough, no. I think Richard Daws might have had something to do with that.'

'Is there anything I can do to help?'

'Thanks, but I don't know what. You might let me know if a guy by the name of Jethro Hulton turns up on your patch – that's one of the names he goes by, anyway.'

'He's the one with drugs baron friends in Colombia, isn't he?'

'That's him.'

'Hardly likely to be found opening a church fête in Farrington Gurney then.'

'Now you mention it, no.'

'He's not been out of jail that long, if I remember correctly. Served five years for his part in a bullion robbery. The prosecution couldn't make it stick that he'd masterminded that and other crimes of a similar nature.'

'The difficult bit's getting people to testify against them,' Joanna commented. At one time she had been Carrick's sergeant. 'What else do we know about this character?'

Patrick said, 'Born 1970, five feet nine inches tall, thickset, brown eyes, swarthy complexion, usually heavily bearded and also grows his hair long. He walks in a strange hunched-over manner, possibly as a result of a back injury, which makes him look shorter. In his youth he served three years of a life sentence for murder in Mexico but was busted out of a prison van taking him to another jail by cronies and fled to Europe. He's connected to all kinds of rackets but as Joanna said, it's getting the charges to stick or even grab the bastard in the first place. Part of my brief was to manoeuvre him into a situation where he could be arrested, along with the woman.'

'A sting operation then.'

'If necessary.'

'Could he have recognized you from something that you worked on in the past and busted your cover?' Carrick said.

'No, I've never come within a mile of the bloke before. He's a common crook, not someone to interest MI5.'

'Might Hulton have murdered these people?'

'He could well have decided to turn over to a new page of his life and tidy up the clutter. That's exactly how his mind works. We'll have to see what forensics turns up.'

The DCI smothered a yawn and said, 'In the meantime you could always have a go at the murder in the vestry case to keep your hand in. We don't appear to be getting anywhere with it.'

'OK,' Patrick said.

'I was only joking!'

'I'll make your tea for you,' Patrick wheedled.

'Earl Grey for preference,' Carrick said after a few moments. 'There's a little shop in Green Street that sells estate teas.'

It seemed staggering to me that any kind of official permission would be forthcoming on this proposal but the following morning, a full twenty-four hours before Commander Greenway was due to arrive for the debriefing, he rang to inform Patrick that he was extending his permitted area of freedom of movement to a twenty-mile radius of the village. There was then a call from a superintendent at the Avon and Somerset force's HQ at Portishead, near Bristol, acknowledging Patrick's temporary secondment to Bath CID and informing him that an official letter was on its way. He made it clear that he, Patrick, would take orders from Detective Chief Inspector Carrick and have no authority over anyone. He emphasized that the arrangement was purely temporary.

In receipt of the news of this development I said, 'Patrick, I don't think you've really thought this through.'

'In what way?'

'It's already a bit difficult for your parents and now you're going to be crawling all over the parish breathing down the necks of the locals, some of them their close friends – while you yourself are under some kind of investigation for murder.'

'I don't think Greenway's too bothered about offending people round here.'

'No, I appreciate that, but *you* should be!'

'I am. And there's also a lot of folk here who would like me to follow in Dad's footsteps and even take over from him one day. This'll be a good test of sentiments. It might even scare them into not telling me any porkies.'

Are men's brains weirdly, drastically and differently wired to women's? Oh, yes.

'So where do I fit into all this?' I enquired grumpily, having realized, with a sinking feeling, that I ought to be involved.

He considered and then said, 'There might be room in my briefcase for a nursing mother.'

'I'm not now, thank you.'

'OK . . . What shall we call it then?'

'Tea-buyer and squeeze-of-the-moment?'

'I'll go for that.'

Before further consulting with James Carrick we visited the scene of the crime with a view to calling on John and Elspeth afterwards to give them the news. The church was unlocked, as it was normally during the day and there were no longer any restrictions of movement. (The entire building had been closed for just under a week while scenes-of-crime personnel had gone over every inch of it.) I knew that the bishop of Bath and Wells had paid a private visit and prayers had been said, the feeling being that too much of a 'song and dance', as Elspeth had put it, would only heighten the sense of tragedy and get the story in all the papers again, thus attracting yet another dose of gawpers.

John was in the church, up by the altar laying a clean white cloth on it. I heard Patrick sigh as he went forward. Despite present and past difficulties there is a close bond between them but I knew he was not looking forward to this encounter. Hearing movement, his father looked round as Patrick approached.

'Any good news?' he asked bluntly, his voice carrying effortlessly to where I was standing near the door.

Patrick came straight to the point. 'I'm to assist James with the murder here until ordered otherwise. I thought you ought to be the first to know.'

John said nothing and went back to what he was doing. Then without turning he said. 'Your mother and I have a very good relationship with everyone in this parish.'

Except for the black magic practitioners, one imagined.

'I'm fully aware of that,' Patrick replied. 'And I sincerely hope nothing I do changes that.'

His father spun round and barked, 'It had better not, Patrick!'

He turned his back on the pair of us.

'It's no good, I can't concentrate on the job while he's here,' Patrick whispered when he rejoined me. 'We'll have to come back later.'

'Coffee with your mother then?' I suggested.

'Oh – all right.'

'You don't have to knock!' Elspeth exclaimed, answering the door of the annex.

'Well, I've just taken a full broadside from Dad and holed below the waterline,' Patrick said with a wry grin as we followed her into the kitchen. 'If the rigging goes as well . . .'

'Oh, he's like a bear with a sore head this morning. It's this thing about women bishops. He seems to think that if we eventually get one here everyone'll have to start calling God Madam.' She paused in carrying the kettle across to the sink. 'But John doesn't usually take things out on you.'

'No, I'd just told him that I'm going to be helping James with our murder inquiry.'

'*Really?*'

'I admit he was half joking when he asked me but, as you know, the man's always overworked and hasn't really got anywhere with the case at all. He seems to think that because I'm an insider of the village I might be able to solve the case.'

Elspeth filled the kettle, switched it on and then said, 'I can foresee a *bit* of a problem. Some of the elderly people are already very nervous and, rightly so, are worried that someone living near them is a murderer. If you roll up and interrogate everyone like the Gestapo . . .'

Patrick looked exasperated. 'But—'

'Like that!' his mother declared, pointing an accusing finger. 'Like that! When you look like that! Cross! You'll frighten all my old ladies silly!'

Her son got to his feet. 'A little rôle-play then.' He winked at me and jerked his head in the direction of the kitchen door.

We both left the room and closed the door behind us with Elspeth saying, 'Where are you going? Patrick? Patrick! I'm sorry if I—'

He knocked.

'Oh, come in,' said Elspeth crossly.

'Mrs Gillard?' Patrick said, breezing in.

'You jolly-well know it is.'

'My name is Patrick Gillard and I'm with the Serious Organized Crime Agency.' Here he showed her his opened wallet in lieu of the warrant card which was still in a safe place at SOCA HQ. 'This is my assistant Miss Langley. I was wondering if you could give us your assistance in connection with the recent murder in the village by answering a few questions.' All this with a smile that would have made Cybermen coo.

'All right,' Elspeth said, playing along. 'I was just making some coffee. Would you like some?'

'Lovely,' I said. 'Thank you. Neither of us takes sugar.'

Patrick seated himself at the small kitchen table and appro-priated a shopping list pad and pen, which he handed to me. 'With your permission Miss Langley will take notes.'

Elspeth smiled at me.

'How long have you lived in the village, Mrs Gillard?'

'Getting on for twenty years.'

'And your husband is rector here?'

'That's right.'

'Did you know the deceased?'

'Yes, but not as a friend. He was on the PCC and other local organizations.'

'What kind of person was he?'

'From what I knew of him not a very pleasant one. He would buttonhole one for information on this and that matter without even a good morning or a thank you. No manners at all.'

'You mentioned to us before that several people – five, I think you said altogether – had spoken to you, worried that because they'd had words with him they might be suspects. May I have their names?'

Elspeth frowned. 'I'll have to think about that for a moment. It was before we went on holiday. We were away when it happened, you see.'

I hid a smile. She had forgotten for a moment the real identity of the man to whom she was speaking. I have never been able to fathom whether it is the easy manner inviting confidence, or hypnosis, that results in witnesses and others telling him everything they know. With those who could be described as real criminals there is an entirely different approach.

'Shall I write them down?' Elspeth offered. 'I'll find it easier to remember if I do.'

I gave her the pad and pen and she wrote busily. 'That's the five but I have an idea there was someone else,' she mused a couple of minutes later, giving us our coffee. 'An unlikely person.'

'Unlikely?' Patrick queried.

'Um.'

'Where were you when this person spoke to you?'

'I'm not sure. Oh, I know! It was in Sainsbury's in Bath. That's right, I saw Miss Trelawney and she told me that Melvyn Blanche had threatened to take her to court over her trees. She's their neighbour and has what amounts to a small arboretum at the end of her garden. She's a very knowledgeable lady about plants and trees and the ones she has are rare and lovely varieties. He told her he wanted most of them cut down as they took all his light.'

'Do they?'

'Not at all! They're to the north east of his property so actually shelter his place from cold winds. She was very upset, as you can well imagine.'

'Is she on the cleaning rota?' I asked.

'Yes, she is. Oh dear!'

'But an unlikely person to commit murder?' Patrick queried.

'She's gentle,' Elspeth said. 'A real lady from an old landed Cornish family. Vulnerable and the kind of person to be easily bullied.'

'Would she have had the trees felled just because of what he'd said?'

'Oh, no. They're her children. I have an idea she talks to them.'

'*Not* easily bullied then.'

'All right, in every other respect,' Elspeth corrected.

'Were you ever invited to the Blanches' place for dinner, or drinks?'

'Oh, no. I don't think they ever entertained.'

'Do you know if there are any children?'

'I can't remember them mentioning any. They're not the kind of people you ask personal questions of.'

'Do you know anything about this black magic sect?'

'No, you'll have to ask John when he comes back as he'll have gone into Bristol by now. He deals with that. I don't want to know about things like that.'

'But you must hear rumours,' Patrick remarked gently. 'The WI, the Mothers' Union . . .'

'All I know is that it involves incomers. And we're not talking about batty females who roll naked in the dew and concoct potions to cure warts but real Satanists.'

'Shame about no naked females,' Patrick murmured, grinning at her and thus breaking the spell. 'How terrorized by me were you on a scale of one to ten?'

She thought about it. 'Oh . . . nine.' And then laughed.

John's car had gone from outside the church so we went back into the building.

'Tell me exactly what you did, before and after, when you and Mrs Crosby found the body,' Patrick said, gazing around as though he was seeing the place for the first time.

'There was nothing of real interest to the investigation about it,' I told him. 'As I've previously said she came to the rectory asking for the church to be unlocked as it wasn't and ought to have been. She wanted to check the flowers. I told her that the sexton should unlock when your father's away but she retorted that he often oversleeps and—'

'Do we know if he had overslept?' Patrick interrupted.

'No, he hadn't. He'd unlocked the church, presumably at the usual time, around nine thirty.'

'What time was Blanche killed?'

'I don't know.'

'Didn't Carrick mention that?'

'I don't think he knew when I last spoke to him. And I haven't been too interested in this up until now as my husband is in trouble and I didn't make a point of asking him.'

He had scooped up the shopping pad and pen after I had given them back to Elspeth having torn off the written-on sheets and now noted this down, glancing up to give me a raised eyebrow look. 'Always in trouble, is he, Madam?'

'A complete tosser,' I answered in a bored voice.

We both giggled.

'Ingrid, why am I doing this?' Patrick said, flopping down in a pew.

'To try to take your mind off the trouble.'

He gazed at me and I saw the depthless misery in his eyes.

'You didn't kill those people,' I said quietly. 'And even if you had because you were off your head with the drugs I would still love you to bits.'

He gave me a wan smile and then turned his attention to his notes. 'Right, you and Mrs Crosby came in, unlocking the door with the key that hangs in Dad's study. Then what?'

'The flowers hadn't been touched, still last week's. She got on her high horse, consulted the flower rota in the porch and said she would phone the woman who should have done them and give her a piece of her mind.'

'Who was it?'

'Pauline Harrison. I told her not to as I knew that Pauline's father had been taken ill with a stroke.'

'How did you know that?'

'By a fluke. I'd overheard a conversation in the village

stores. I have discovered since, from Elspeth, that Pauline had had to drive up to Cambridge. Her dad died.'

'I must remember that if we have to talk to her. Then you unlocked the vestry door.' Patrick got to his feet and went in that direction. 'Why did you need to go in there?'

Following him, I said, 'I'd asked Mrs Crosby to take care of the flowers in the circumstances and she said that as she didn't live nearby and hadn't brought her purse with her she would need to take money from the flower fund box – which is kept in the vestry.'

'Did you believe that? Don't women usually take their hand-bags, or purse, with them everywhere?'

'No, I didn't believe her. I think she didn't want to have to pay for the flowers herself.'

'Mean old bat. Then what?'

'I didn't open the door, she did. The key's kept on a ledge by the organ. I didn't know where that one was.'

'I wonder how many other people do.'

'Loads. James can probably tell you who they are.'

Not surprisingly, Patrick knew where the vestry key was kept and unlocked the door. The room was some twelve feet square and all seemed as I had seen it last time except for the carpet which had been removed by the forensic team and was presumably still being examined in a lab somewhere. He stood still for a moment, staring at the floor and then opened the one large cupboard the room possessed revealing a vacuum cleaner, dusters, a long broom, a dustpan and brush and brass cleaning materials. There were also flower arranging items on an upper shelf.

'It must have been one of the tools from that cleaner that was forced down his throat,' I said.

Patrick rummaged. 'There isn't a narrow nozzle tube here so that must have been it. But why did Blanche come here that morning? We know he wasn't on the cleaning rota, nor were he and his wife on the flower rota – I looked in the porch on the way in. There are no parish papers kept in this room: they're all in the safe at the rectory. You don't have to come in here to gain access to the tower in order to wind the clock either. Anyway, a retired farmer by the name of Bill does that.'

'He might have been dragged in here having been hit on

the head somewhere else,' I suggested. 'Does James know what he was struck with yet?'

'He hadn't when we last spoke but there might have been developments. We'll have to go to the nick.'

I wandered back into the nave. 'Where are the heavy brass candlesticks kept when they're not in use?'

'At home, in the safe with the communion silver. They're all valuable antiques.'

'And your father cleans those too?'

'Yes.'

'But someone else must have had the keys to the safe while your parents were away.'

'Good thinking.'

'Would that be the sexton as well?'

'No, *probably* someone like the Chairman of the PCC.'

'Mrs Crosby's husband then.'

'It's a priority we go to the nick so that we can read up the notes on the answers to questions that have already been asked. No point in asking them all over again unless people gave evasive answers.'

Outside, a couple of minutes later, I surveyed the acre or so of graveyard and said, 'Have the police really searched every inch of this for whatever it was that Blanche was attacked with?'

'They must have.'

'Only it's quite overgrown in places. What about the rectory garden?'

Part of this is literally over the wall towards one end. The drive to the house, with more garden bordering it, runs along the church boundary on the southern side.

Patrick rang Carrick.

'They did, but, as yet, only as far as what was regarded the distance someone could throw something like a heavy hammer,' he told me, Carrick still on the line.

'What about the builders?' I said. 'Were they interviewed? Had they had any tools stolen? Had any of them known the murder victim? Or have previous convictions?'

Patrick gravely passed over his mobile.

'Hello, Ingrid,' said the DCI. 'I heard nearly all of that. Come to the nick and I expect you'll be able to find most of the answers.'

We agreed that the pair of us would do so at around two that afternoon.

'There's time to search,' I told Patrick, setting off in the direction of the little gate that is in the boundary wall. 'The killer might have gone right into the rectory garden to dispose of the weapon.'

'What, look for a hammer or something similar?' he said, staying where he was. 'I was thinking of an early lunch.'

I turned and held up one hand, fingers outstretched, palm towards him. '*Five* children,' I said. 'Like you, I've signed a contract so this will be *my* job with SOCA for a while if there's no happy ending to your spot of bother.'

He caught up with me and we went through the gate.

'I'd clean windows, wash floors, mow lawns, anything.' Patrick said.

I saw that I had really offended him and he was also tired. 'Sorry, that was very unkind of me. I know you would. Perhaps I'm just trying to say that I don't want you to lose your edge.'

'Have I?'

'From your MI5 days? Yes, you have a bit.'

'Am I relying on my consultant too much?'

'Perhaps. At one time you would probably have towed me through all these hedges, looking, and be damned with lunch.'

For answer he grabbed me, gave me a big munching kiss, took my hand and soldiered off into the rectory garden.

After half an hour of soggy searching through the remaining rapidly melting thin layer of snow we found it.

SIX

The heavy hammer had been in the shrubbery long enough to have started to rust a little but had arrived sufficiently recently for the leaves of an evergreen plant, a branch of which it had borne to the ground, not to have yellowed beneath it. Only an Olympian would have been able to throw it to this spot from inside the churchyard so whoever had done so had either come into the garden or tossed it from a window of the house, the latter not an easy option either.

'There's paint on the handle,' I said as we gazed down at it. 'I'd put money on it belonging to one of the builders.'

'It doesn't mean they had anything to do with the killing,' Patrick pointed out. 'There have been vans parked out here for weeks with the rear doors open and any number of tools in full view. They only take the valuable stuff indoors with them. And this might not be the murder weapon.'

He drove to our present home to fetch a sample bag and gloves from his briefcase – which for some reason was not in the car – rang Carrick to tell him what we had found and we then went straight to Bath, only pausing to buy some sandwiches at a corner shop. We found that the DCI was on his way back from somewhere but would be with us shortly, this information given to us by Derek Woods, the duty sergeant.

'Glad to have you back, sir,' said Woods, referring to a stint that Patrick had done with Bath CID the previous year. 'And you, Miss Langley.'

'Thank you, Derek,' Patrick responded. 'Tell me, is it more likely to be a man or a woman who would murder a bloke by hitting him on the head with a hammer and then shoving a vacuum cleaner nozzle down his throat and pouring cleaning fluid down it?'

The sergeant grimaced, sucked in his breath through clenched teeth, thought for a few seconds and then, in his soft West Country voice, said, 'It might depend if the body was moved at all and on how heavy the murder victim was.'

'We're assuming until it's proved otherwise that both actions occurred at the same place, in this case a church vestry.'

'Then first of all I'd start looking for a woman with a horrible grievance. She might have been aided by a male accomplice, of course. He may have wielded the hammer.'

'Thank you. My thoughts entirely.'

'Is this the investigation at Hinton Littlemoor?'

'It is.'

'There have been complaints coming from that quarter of what people have called "dodgy goings on". Not the usual antics of youngsters coming back from the pub and making nuisances of themselves but adults drinking and making a lot of noise around a bonfire. It might have nothing to do with the case you're working on though, sir.'

'Is this activity centred on any particular area?'

'I understand it mostly involves the new development down where the railway station used to be.'

'When does this happen?'

'Seemingly during the night.'

'That's where the new drainage scheme's being put in,' Patrick mused. 'Thank you.'

'And where the diocese was going to rehome your parents,' I said as we strolled in the direction of Carrick's office.

'Noble reward for half a lifetime's service,' Patrick said sarcastically. 'A bunch of shitty little bungalows that tended to flood in winter soon to be joined by phase two, another bunch of shitty little bungalows with gardens consisting of subsoil and rocks from the holes dug to put in drainage pipes. I gather that all the topsoil they could scrape together was sold off to provide beer tokens for the hard-working lads.' And, on an afterthought, he added 'I must ask Dad about that black magic lot.'

'But as Derek said . . .'

'Yes, it probably has nothing whatsoever to do with our murder case.'

'Do you know what time Greenway's due to arrive tomorrow?'

'At around ten thirty.' Patrick gave me a big crazy grin. 'How many Micky Mouse degrees do you have to have these days to be a street sweeper?'

James Carrick swept around a corner to the rear of us,

Lynn Outhwaite behind him. I instantly got the impression that there had been a difference of opinion.

'Ah,' Carrick said when he saw us. 'One moment and I'll get you all the info.'

Patrick held out the bag with the hammer in it. Carrick scooped it from him on the way by, imploded into his office and emerged seconds later with a file that he thrust into Patrick's hands.

'There. Sorry, can't give you any more time – there's something very pressing on right now.'

His sergeant brushed past us with a brief smile – or at least, bared teeth – and the door of the room was practically slammed in our faces.

'Yes, the English *were* particularly nasty to William Wallace,' Patrick said to the grubby paintwork. He turned to me. 'So it'll have to be the canteen and sticky buns.'

'We've just bought sandwiches,' I reminded him.

'They won't chuck us out for eating those in there as well, will they?'

The information contained in the file was a neat and thorough record of all evidence gathered during house-to-house enquiries, interviews with witnesses – that is, Mrs Crosby and me – the murder victim's wife, neighbours and a couple who were described as 'friends'. There were scenes-of-crime findings – predictably the fingerprints of what was probably half of north Somerset had been found in the church, the results of DNA tests – again representative of possibly hundreds of people with no pattern. No useful evidence of any kind was on the vacuum cleaner nozzle other than that pertaining to the victim, blood and saliva, which suggested that the killer had worn gloves.

Patrick exhaled noisily. 'All of this adds up to sweet FA,' he muttered.

'James did tell you he'd run into the wall with it,' I said.

'Which means that we'll have to start from the beginning again. What d'you reckon was going on just now?'

'Between James and Lynn? Heaven only knows. Nothing probably. Just tempers getting frayed under the pressure of work.'

'We'd better go and solve this one for him then – starting with the wife.'

'May I make a suggestion?'

'As always I treasure every contribution of yours,' the man in my life said, looking up from stowing papers back in the file to flutter his eyelashes at me.

'Fool. Someone nicknamed Morticia probably deserves it. I suggest you let her stew for a while.'

'Yes, I suppose we ought to regard her as a suspect.'

'Or perhaps I'm merely being horrible.'

'Um.'

Miss Ann Trelawney was a surprise. Expecting for some reason to find a somewhat frail lady of a certain age with the saintly aura of one who communes with nature and has a cellarful of seething home-made ginger beer, wine and yoghurt we came upon a lanky person under the bonnet of an elderly Land Rover.

'You know what?' she said, having obviously heard our vehicle's arrival and turning to look at us with a splodge of oil on her chin. 'This thing is an utter, utter bastard.'

'But when they do go, they're with you to the death,' Patrick observed.

She fixed him with a dark-eyed stare. 'I agree. But what the hell is one supposed to do the rest of the time?'

'What's wrong with it?'

'It won't start. It's almost impossible to find people to fix things like this these days. They say there's no money in it.'

Patrick peered into the engine compartment. 'There's a guy called Pete in the village who lives and breathes Land Rovers. He'd look at it for you. Meanwhile though –' here he performed a little tweaking – 'one of the leads on your battery was loose. Now try.'

The engine roared into life.

'Thanks, but it's terribly corny,' said Miss Trelawney when she had stepped down from the driver's seat and we had introduced ourselves. 'Like a detective story on the box. The sleuth comes along and fixes the heroine's car and they murmur sweet nothings over the cylinder head gasket. I take it you want to talk about Melvyn – only one had to call him Squadron Leader, of course.'

She was around forty-five, with hair as dark as her eyes, and had a round face with a snub nose. I deduced the clothes she wore were the ones she was hoping to go out in when we had left and not those she had put on to try to fix her car. Whatever their purpose they were pricey; immaculate white slacks and a deep orange sweater, brown leather moccasins, a bag to match on the passenger seat.

So why run an old car like this?

Because she loved it, that's why.

'The man wasn't friendly, you understand,' Miss Trelawney said, unprompted by a question. 'I don't think anyone really got to know him.'

Patrick said, 'Even though he and his wife joined so many clubs and groups?'

'I reckon they joined so he could run them. It was a substitute for the RAF. Never happy unless he was bossing people about – getting them to fly in formation. He came over here one day and told me he wanted my trees felled. Just like that, no discussion, no nothing. I told him they couldn't possibly be causing him any loss of light as they were roughly to the north of his place. He wouldn't listen. Cut them down, or else.'

'Did he actually threaten you?'

'With solicitors. Oh, and he was going to write to the council about them. You know, this business of over-tall boundary hedges being deemed a nuisance. I sent him on his way, I can tell you! Boundary hedge! As though my beautiful trees were wretched Leylandii.'

'May we have a look?' I asked, ever ready to be nosy.

She smiled delightedly. 'Of course.'

The house was the middle one of a group of three that formed a tiny hamlet just off the road from the village to the junction with the main Bath to Shepton Mallet road. Patrick had told me on the way there that they had been built on the site of a market garden some time in the late eighties. The business of planning permission for the development had always been a matter of controversy, the general feeling in Hinton Littlemoor being that certain favours had been involved but it was best not to ask. The properties themselves were ordinary but pleasing, three or four bedrooms, I guessed, and all seemed to have large gardens.

'So that's the Blanches' house?' Patrick enquired, indicating the roof of the house next door that could be glimpsed to the left above a neat beech hedge.

'That's right,' said Miss Trelawney. 'The Taylors live on the other side. You can't see their place from here as the house is slightly skewed and behind that evergreen oak.'

She led the way down the garden, which, even in winter, was like an illustration from an upmarket homes magazine. At the end, through a little wicket gate, was her 'collection' as she called it. She rattled off a lot of Latin names for the trees within the copse we found ourselves in but they were lost on me: I just stood there entranced: despite most of the branches being bare, it was indescribably charming. There was nothing pretty-pretty here, just somewhere where you could sit all day and dream the stuff of lost legends. If it were mine I would defend it to my last breath.

'Miss Trelawney, I understand you're on the church cleaning rota,' Patrick said, bringing me down to earth with a thump.

'Yes, I am,' said the lady, looking him right in the eye. 'But I didn't kill the horrible man. I can't kill anything. Not even bluebottles, and they're about the filthiest things that have ever flown that aren't planes.'

'So where were you on that particular Saturday, the first of last month?'

'Here. I don't go out much. I was knocked down by a car in London, and nearly died, before coming to live here and it put me off venturing very far. It's one of the reasons I have the old Land Rover, I feel safe in it.'

'Were you alone?'

'Yes.'

'And on the Friday evening?'

'I went to a recital in the village hall. Everyone saw me.'

'Were the Blanches there?'

'No – at least, I didn't see them. But they might have come and then gone away again without me noticing. It wasn't a very good recital – they hadn't practised enough.'

'I take it you weren't on the cleaning rota that week.'

'No, but someone asked me if I'd swap. Pauline and I did it on the Thursday so we can't help you really.'

'Pauline Harrison?' I queried.

'That's right.'

'Wasn't she down to do the flowers?'

'Yes, but most people do them on Friday or Saturday so they're at their best for the Sunday services. You pick up your flowers when you're in Tesco's or wherever doing the weekly shop. But as you probably know, Pauline had to drop everything and drive up to Cambridge when her father was taken seriously ill.'

'Have you any idea why Melvyn Blanche should have gone to the church and into the vestry that Saturday morning?' Patrick asked.

'No, he was on the PCC but with no actual portfolio, as it were. I imagine he would have resigned soon – there's no controlling that. The rector's too strong a personality.'

Oddly, she appeared to have made no connection between him and the man to whom she was speaking.

'I understand Blanche somehow jockeyed himself into the job of stage-managing the summer play. Are you involved with that?'

'We call ourselves the Hinton Littlemoor Players. I write the plays. I should imagine his behaviour over that caused more bad feeling than all the rest of the things he did put together.'

'Who's normally stage manager?'

'Stewart Macdonald. He was in Scotland when it happened. To be fair though – and I have to say I don't want to be – he had seemed a bit reluctant to do it again this year.'

I said, 'I would have thought one needed a bit of experience in that line.'

'Blanche didn't have any. He actually said that it was something any bloody fool could do.'

'Is Macdonald back from Scotland now?'

'God, yes, he was only away for a week.'

'Where does he live?'

'In the old smithy, with his partner, Cindy Crane. He's actually a woodcarver by trade.'

'Have you any theories about this, Miss Trelawney?' Patrick enquired after a short silence.

'I'm sure the answers will be found in Blanche's past. And your murderer's a man. No woman would think of using a vacuum cleaner nozzle as a funnel in order to try to kill someone.'

'Is that right?' Patrick asked me when we were heading back towards the car. 'Would you?'

I pondered. 'I'm not sure. Did the cleaning fluid come out of a bottle stored in the vestry?'

'That's a good point.' He hurried ahead, opened the vehicle and found the file. 'Yes,' he reported, reading. 'Jeyes. Which was removed and now presumably Exhibit B.'

'A spur of the moment thing, then. Having hit Blanche on the head with the hammer, whoever it was realized he wasn't dead, and decided to be nastily creative in finishing him off. I think we're looking for a man and a woman.'

Patrick wilted against the car. 'As James said, this is turning out to be a can of worms. We have the list that Mum gave us of people who had had words with him, plus another of the folk on the cleaning list who know where the vestry key is hidden and had some of the tools to hand, just about everyone in the local clubs and groups, the whole village come to think of it. No, we'll have to go and talk to the widow. Miss Trelawney may be right and it's someone from his past who caught up with him.'

A female minder opened the front door and, without introducing herself, haughtily informed us that Barbara Blanche had been interviewed already, twice, and in the circumstances could not be further disturbed.

Patrick assumed his MI5 persona. 'Mrs Blanche is perfectly within her rights to refuse to see us. I should just like to hear it from her personally.' He refrained from adding, 'And not from some bossy cow on the doorstep,' but, really, his expression has a way of saying everything.

She went away leaving the door open, defeated but resentful, and we waited. Patrick's mobile rang and he walked away for a short distance to answer it, returning very quickly.

'He was killed in the vestry,' he whispered. 'Tiny spots of his blood on a wide area of the carpet. The pathologist reckons he died some time between ten and eleven.'

'After the sexton had unlocked the church door then.'

'Yes.'

We carried on waiting. We could hear them whispering. Then, finally, when I knew Patrick was on the verge of barging in anyway, the woman put her head around the doorway in the entrance hall through which she had disappeared.

'You may come in.'

'This is an intrusion,' said the woman who must be the murder victim's widow. 'I resent it.'

'May we sit down?' Patrick asked.

There was a pause.

'Yes, I suppose you'd better,' she said grudgingly. 'This is my sister, Felicity, in case you were going to ask. She's staying right here.'

'And this is my assistant, Miss Langley, who will take notes,' Patrick batted back at her, glancing up from extracting the case file from his briefcase. 'I have been seconded to Bath CID to help Detective Chief Inspector James Carrick who is seriously overloaded with work. You must have met him. Your sister didn't listen too closely when I showed her my ID so I'll tell you that I actually work for the Serious Organized Crime Agency and I am normally based in London. Your husband's murder is a serious crime and I expect your full cooperation. Do I have it?'

'I suppose so,' Barbara Blanche said. 'But if I'm going to be asked exactly the same questions all over again . . .' She shrugged.

She was not to be reassured on that subject but I was a little disappointed that Patrick had not given her our condolences before launching into the questioning. Even under pressure he usually retains common politeness and I could only think that he was far more stressed about the prospect of the following day than I had imagined.

He said, 'You've already intimated that you had no idea why your husband had gone to the church that morning – and it has just been established from forensic evidence that he must have died in the vestry between ten and eleven. His body was discovered shortly before midday. Did he say anything to you before he went out?'

'I didn't know he'd gone out. But Melvyn could be a bit like that, not always saying what he was going to do. I had stayed in bed, I didn't feel very well.'

'Are you aware of anything particular that was on his mind?'

'No.'

She was far younger than I had expected, at least fifteen, or even twenty years younger than her late husband, who had been sixty-one. Grief, strain, and anger made her appear pale and drawn – she wore no make-up – but discounting that she was still unattractive and frumpily dressed. Her sister was a slightly older version, with the frumpiness times two.

'Did you go to the recital at the village hall the night before he died?' Patrick enquired.

'Yes, we had tickets. But we didn't stay long. It was terrible – they hadn't a clue how to play Brahms so we didn't risk the rest of the programme.'

'Did you come straight back here?'

'No, we went for a walk. We were rather disappointed and didn't want to come home just then.'

'Was it a mutual decision to leave?'

'Of course.'

'I ask because it would appear that your husband was a controlling type of person. There seems to have been a certain amount of resentment caused by his—'

'People always resent a clever man!' Barbara Blanche butted in with. 'Melvyn was clever. He believed in showing how things should be done. He couldn't bear the second-rate. If people resent that it shows how small-minded they are.'

'That's only a matter of opinion,' I was stung to say. 'I'm married to a clever man but people don't resent him, they admire him. He wouldn't dream of imposing himself on people. Bath CID have statements from a large proportion of the local residents, a good percentage of whom, I have to tell you, are professional people, and at least twenty of them stated that your husband was insufferable. *That,* Mrs Blanche, can be the basis for murder.'

She opened her mouth to take issue with me but I swept on. 'Whether you accept it or not he must have made at least one real enemy, either now, or in the past. Was there anyone in Hinton Littlemoor with whom he'd had a serious argument?'

She glowered at me, then said, 'I thought you were here just to take notes.'

'Please answer the question.'

Stiffly, she said, 'There had been a few tiffs with people who didn't like what he was doing. It was inevitable.'

Patrick said, 'So he didn't take the hint and back off a little?'

'No, why should he? Melvyn was brave as well as clever. He used to fly bombers.'

Well, that would figure, I thought.

'Was there anyone in his past who might have borne a severe grudge?' Patrick said.

'No one that I can think of.'

'Please pause to think for a few moments. It's very important.'

'No, no one,' came the immediate reply.

'How long had you been married?'

'Fifteen years. Really, I don't see how—'

'But why was he in the church?' Patrick persevered. 'Neither of you was on the cleaning or flower rotas, and no parish documents are kept in the vestry.'

'I have no idea why he should have been there.'

'Did he know where the key to it was kept?'

'I don't know.'

'Do you?'

'No.'

'What did your husband do before he went in the RAF?'

'He gained entry when he left school. In those days you didn't have to be a graduate. It was something he'd always wanted to do.'

A truly crazy idea hit me. I quickly wrote on my pad and passed it across to Patrick who read what I had written and gave me a brief, quizzical stare.

'Tell me,' he said slowly to Barbara Blanche, 'Do you know anyone who lives down on the small estate where the railway station used to be?'

'I – er – think a couple, no – er – two couples we've met at quiz nights, or something like that, live in that direction,' the woman stammered. 'But I really wouldn't describe them as friends.'

'Have you been to their homes?'

'No, hardly, as they're not friends of ours.'

'Not for meetings?'

'Meetings!' she shrilled. 'No!'

'Committee meetings, I mean.'

'Oh! No.'

Patrick got to his feet. 'Thank you. That'll be all for now.'

She had flushed. 'When can I have Melvyn's body and arrange the funeral?'

'Not yet. You'll need to ask Detective Chief Inspector Carrick about that. He's in overall charge.'

We left.

'Thanks for the compliment,' Patrick said when we were outside.

'Any time. I have an idea she's as horrible as he was,' I muttered,

'The question about friends down the hill seemed to press a panic button.'

'So where *are* the wine and communion wafers kept before they're consecrated during services?' I asked.

'In a small cupboard in Dad's study.' He whistled softly. 'I wonder if that's what he was after? Or anything else with sacred connections for black magic ceremonies.'

SEVEN

To interview everybody on the various lists again would be an enormous task and, personally, I felt would be mainly a waste of time. James Carrick was thorough and the fact that nothing he had turned up so far had lit any fuses probably meant that the answers lay elsewhere; with a new line of enquiry. First though, it seemed a good idea to discover the reason for Barbara Blanche's apparent awkwardness when asked a simple question.

'Do we really have to talk about this now?' John Gillard asked when we called round on our way home, partly to assess the builders' progress.

Patrick said, 'Let's just say that someone we were talking to this afternoon got their tongue in any number of knots when asked if they had friends on the new estate.'

The rector shook his head. 'Black magic's a load of obscene nonsense.'

Elspeth lost patience. 'John, this is Lieutenant Colonel Patrick Gillard, only he doesn't use his rank, of the Serious Organized Crime Agency and his assistant Miss Langley. Please answer the question.'

This reproof had the effect of making John chuckle. 'And if I offer him a dram to forget all about it for now he'll accuse me of trying to bribe a police officer.'

'Of course,' Patrick said. 'But I wouldn't mind one anyway.'

His father paused in fixing them both a tot and said to Patrick, 'Look, I'm sorry I've been a bit over the top about everything.'

'Nothing to apologize for,' Patrick said. 'This is terribly stressful for you.'

'Oh good,' Elspeth said. 'Some sherry for me, please John, one of those lovely schooner glasses. And whatever Ingrid wants.'

'Most people would say that it's none of my business what people do in their own homes, or in their own time,' John began, Elspeth having left the room, with her sherry, to attend to the cooking of their evening meal. 'But when my parish-ioners are frightened by something that's going on in their midst I feel it is my duty to do a little investigating with a view to persuading people otherwise. Last Sunday I made it the subject of my sermon again. I've mentioned it before but didn't pull any punches this time.'

'Please be careful,' Patrick said. 'Those who mess around with what they're pleased to call the black arts are often very unpleasant.'

'I agonize about the young ones being drawn into such things in such godless times,' said John.

'What exactly have people been saying to you?'

'There's a piece of spare ground behind the housing development higher up the hill and in the opposite direction to where the drainage system's being put in. One day, no doubt, it'll be Phase Three of the estate. There's a footpath running through it that eventually leads up to the boundary of Hagtop Farm.'

'I know it,' Patrick said.

'Several parishioners have seen lights at night, and fires with masked people dancing around them. Screams, drunken singing. Animal and poultry remains have been found in that area together with extensive bloodstains on the grass. Whatever it is, Patrick, it's not good for children to find headless chickens and what's left of someone's poor cat. Of course it might be nothing more serious than wild bonfire parties and the activities of foxes.'

'Dad, I agree it's suspicious but honestly can't see how thundering from the pulpit is going to help. You're literally preaching to the converted.'

'Am I?' asked John with an ironic twist to his mouth.

'Are you saying that you think some of the members of your congregation might be involved?'

'It's happened elsewhere and it would be stupid of me not to think Hinton Littlemoor's full of angels because I know all too well it isn't. It's not unknown for followers of that kind of thing to try to get hold of communion wafers to use in their wretched ceremonies. I understand people become ensnared and then blackmailed into stealing church items after being photographed naked, or something along those lines, when they'd gone to what they thought was a perfectly ordinary party, only to be drugged or have their drinks spiked. I need to prove if anything's going on. So a bit of thundering might draw someone's fire.'

'Any ideas why Melvyn Blanche was in the vestry that morning?'

The rector stared at his son. 'I don't think you're changing the subject, are you?'

'No.'

'He wasn't the sort to be easily intimidated.'

'Oh, no, he'd have had to have gone in for something like that quite willingly. Does that fit in with the man you knew?'

'But I didn't know him very well. I don't think anyone did. I have to say I found him overbearing and high-handed. It was the reason I always resisted him having any real responsibilities on the PCC, and he didn't like it. He may well have eventually resigned. The man didn't really want to do any work, you understand, just be in a position to tell other people what to do.'

This time it was Patrick who chuckled. 'And a one-time Royal Naval Reserve officer isn't going to take any nonsense from a retired member of Crab Air.'

'No, quite,' John said with feeling. 'But you know, to be fair, I can't see Blanche getting involved with people cavorting around Devil worshipping.'

'He might have known those who did. Someone who had a hold over him.'

To John I said, 'We found a hammer in the garden here this morning. But it might not be the murder weapon.'

'That's a thought!' Patrick exclaimed. 'Have you lost any tools lately, perhaps just before you went away on holiday – dropped a hammer in the bushes?'

'What, me?' said his father. 'You ought to know by now that I never open my tool box if I can possibly help it.'

'Perhaps you'd check if there's anything missing.'

'They're probably all rusted together.'

Later that night I wrote up and printed the notes we had made of the day's work and put them in the case file. Tomorrow would be another matter.

Michael Greenway arrived dead on time with the two expected members of the Complaints Department who were introduced

as Commander David Greenshaft and Detective Chief
Inspector Helen Hurst. Carrie had been forewarned of their
impending arrival and the house had been cleared of the two
noisy little people by the simple expedient of her taking them
to stay with Elspeth for most of the day, John busy with his
parish duties.

Whether Greenway had made some kind of stand with
regard to my presence at this interview was open to conjecture but the pair did not quibble when, after having shown
them all into the first floor living room and served coffee
and biscuits I sat down in a chair that I had previously carefully positioned, slightly away from the centre of the room
but nearest to where I had suggested to Patrick he should
sit. OK, I had set the stage; the three visiting policemen
placed so they were not ranged in front of the 'suspect' like
a firing squad.

'Nice house,' was Greenshaft's opening remark after he had
set the recording machine going. He was a tall, thin individual
and, if in the acting profession instead, would have made a
first-class Stasi officer. Nobody had asked Patrick if he had
fully recovered. He had not.

'It's rented,' Patrick told him. 'We've sold our place and
bought the rectory that my parents were going to be chucked
out of. Quite a bit of work had to be done to it to make room
for the family.'

'Expensive, no doubt,' the man murmured, glancing up from
extracting a fat file from his briefcase and opening it.

'Mum and Dad helped with the cost as it'll be their future
retirement home.'

Up until now Patrick had been tense and monosyllabic after
a practically sleepless night but now appeared to be as relaxed
as our cat, Pirate, who was curled up on the hearth rug in front
of the log fire. Unlike Pirate though Patrick is ferociously good
at hiding his feelings when necessary.

'Sorry to be nosy but why were they being evicted? Hadn't
they paid the rent?'

So he was a bastard: he must have been in receipt of all
Patrick's personal details – which may or may not be in the
folder on his lap – and in SOCA's case these I knew were not
so much in-depth as bottomless.

Patrick gave him a patient smile that said I think you're

in this job because you're a bastard. 'No, my father's the rector here and the house belonged to the church. It was going to be sold.'

'Oh, I see. Right then, I'll read out the statement that you made to Commander Greenway before you were sent home. If you've remembered anything else please tell me.'

This he did, and Patrick hadn't.

'So what drew you to working for the Serious Organized Crime Agency?' Greenshaft then asked.

'Mostly Colonel Richard Daws.'

'He was a big wheel in MI5, wasn't he?'

'Yes, I worked for him when he headed up D12.'

'So what went wrong there?'

'Nothing, the department was disbanded, or rather absorbed into another, he retired and I resigned because my family had been under threat from a criminal gang and the protection wasn't up to scratch. When SOCA was set up they raked him out of his castle as they needed people with his kind of experience. He thought he could use me.'

'Castle?' queried Helen Hurst; short of stature and frankly, nondescript, speaking for the first time, her initial greeting having been an unsmiling and tiny nod.

'He's the fourteenth Earl of Hartwood in his spare time,' Patrick explained.

'You've *dabbled* in various careers, haven't you,' Greenshaft commented distastefully, thumbing through the file. 'You entered the police on leaving school and then resigned at the end of your probationary period to join the Devon and Dorset Regiment. Why?'

Yes, he was the one who would try to make Patrick lose his temper, a serious failing that has had repercussions in the past and something they might now try to accuse him of having done, whether or not under the influence of drugs, and killed several people.

'It wasn't exciting enough.' Realizing that something more was expected Patrick then added, 'The West Country was extremely law-abiding in those days.'

'Lots of sailors getting drunk and going on the rampage in Plymouth surely.'

Patrick shook his head. 'No, it's drunken civilians who go on the rampage. Besides which, the Navy do their own policing

– that's what Masters at Arms are for. Besides, I wasn't after punch-ups.'

After giving Patrick a cold stare Greenshaft continued, 'And then you entered Special Services, a unit that I understand is similar to the SAS. Tell me, how many people have you killed in your time?'

'I don't keep a tally,' he was told.

'Can you remember the last person you killed?'

'Yes, I was indirectly responsible for the deaths of a couple of hoodlums when I caused an explosion in a gas-filled basement last year. Ingrid and I were running for our lives at the time and she'd just rescued me from being tortured with a red-hot fork. It would all have gone bang anyway, I just hastened things along a little.'

'I was in on that one,' Greenway said. 'Ghastly burns on his stomach.'

'Do you tend to lose the plot when you're under pressure?' Hurst said, ignoring the SOCA man. 'You know, get a bit desperate?'

'No,' Patrick said, giving his boss a shut-up-for-God's-sake look.

'Never?'

'I've been known to lose my temper when in immediate danger of losing my life.'

'You could well have lost your temper that morning in Muswell Hill.'

'No, I was intent on rescuing the child.'

'Have you remembered exactly what happened?'

'No. Only of being at the house, carrying Leanne and having her shot in my arms.'

'Her blood was found on the clothes you were wearing.'

'That has an obvious explanation.'

'Where were you when that shot was fired?'

'I'm not sure – it's all still very hazy. Possibly upstairs. She didn't want to leave.'

'Why?'

'Her mother was still there.'

'You know that? Were they still alive then?'

'I don't know but must have assumed everything was still relatively normal. Although I know I entered the house quietly.'

'But surely you'd have known if there was a pile of murdered bodies in the living room.'

'Not necessarily. I was in a bit of a state. I might have entered the house through the back. Yes, I've just remembered. I got in through a rear first floor window.'

'How, for pity's sake? It says here that you have an artificial right leg.'

'The artificial bit is below my right knee and I'm still quite good at climbing trees as most of my strength is in my hands and arms. That's right, I climbed the tree outside a bedroom window. It's actually an old vine of some kind or a wisteria.'

'How did you know this child was in particular danger?'

'That's still a grey area. But it might have been because of something the men said when they broke into my digs and had me under truth drug.'

'Who were they?'

'They had masks of some kind or stockings over their faces. But they must have worked for Pangborne – they said they were going to fetch her. She preferred to question and then finish off interlopers herself.'

'But you'd penetrated this gang. Surely you must have a rough idea who they were, even with their faces covered.'

'Have you ever been injected with Sodium Pentothal?'

'No, I haven't.'

'If you had you wouldn't ask questions like that.'

For some reason Greenshaft rounded on Greenway. 'Have you asked yourself about this?' he demanded to know. 'Questioned his account? Also mentioned in these records is that this man is an accomplished actor, a seasoned liar and has been known to kill with his bare hands. You felt quite happy with that, employing such a person, did you?'

I suddenly realized that Greenway might be being officially called to account here too.

'I was there when Patrick killed someone,' I said. 'A top policeman in the Anti Terrorist Branch had been permitted to set up a school for terrorists in the Brecon Beacons with a view to finding out their plans and eventually arresting them. It's all in the file. We went in to find out what was going on. We were captured to improve this madman's standing and cover – he employed real criminals for the same reason. He ordered Adjit, an Egyptian, one of the instructors, to slice

Patrick around a little with a knife. This man had overseen
the severe maltreatment, the previous day, of Patrick's wife,
me. Patrick, who was unarmed at the start of this confrontation, killed him. As I said, it's all in the file.'

Greenshaft cleared his throat but before he could speak
Greenway said, 'I have every confidence in Lieutenant Colonel
Gilllard's credentials and I do have to point out that you simply
cannot equate national security operational criteria with those
that are the norm in the police.'

'But nevertheless he is now working for the police,'
Greenshaft remarked. 'And has to abide by the rules. I wasn't
one of those in favour of bringing ex-service personnel in to
either SOCA or for more general duties when it was trialled
a short while ago. I see he was involved with that too.'

With a crooked smile Patrick said, 'There's no history of
MI5 killing a roomful of criminals with a view to tidying up
an investigation. You need to look to the likes of Jethro Hulton
for that.'

'The police forces of several countries have warrants out
for his arrest,' Greenshaft muttered absent-mindedly, still
reading the file. 'Do you think you'll ever remember what
happened?'

'I can't be expected to answer that. Possibly not. You might
have to ask the medical profession about it.'

'It's all rather convenient, isn't it? Yet you were found with
the gun that killed these people in your hand.'

'We already know that the weapon had been wiped and
only one clear set of fingerprints were on it, mine. I would
hardly have done that myself.'

'Did you have the gun on you when you returned to your
bedsit?'

'I must have done. I wear it in a shoulder holster during
the day and it went under the pillow when I slept.'

'Could someone have taken it off you?'

'No.'

'Not even when you were doped?'

Patrick stared into space for a moment and then said, 'Yes,
they did. But I seem to remember him throwing it back at me.'

'What about when you returned to the Pangborne place the
next morning?'

'I had it with me. I could feel the lump on my side. But I didn't fire it. I know when I've fired a gun, my wrist aches for a while.'

'Even though you say you were groggy and confused.'

'He was,' Greenway said grimly. 'Medical fact.'

'My point is that would he have noticed a mere ache?'

'Yes,' Patrick said. 'I would.'

'A consummate actor?' Hurst said in an offhand manner with a thin smile. 'A practised liar? We don't seem to have a timescale for any of this, do we? You say that something must have been slipped in your drink the night before the murders – what were you drinking, by the way?'

'Orange juice,' Patrick replied doggedly. 'I needed to keep a clear head.'

'Didn't anyone find that suspicious?'

'There were no comments. I'd said I wasn't feeling well.'

'So it's perfectly possible that someone doctored your drink as some kind of joke.'

'Perfectly possible.'

'Do you think anyone suspected you of being an undercover policeman at that stage?'

'No.'

'Any idea who might have done the doctoring?'

'Not a clue. I'd fixed it myself.'

'Do you know the names of those who were there?'

'Most of them, but there was no guarantee that the names they were using were genuine. And you must understand that people were wandering in and out. There was always open house on Friday evenings. Some of those present were neighbours who one must assume were perfectly innocent.'

'And the next thing you remember was being woken up in your room in your digs some distance away by men kicking the door in?'

'That's right.'

'How had you got there?'

'No idea.'

'I still think your story's too bloody neat by half.'

'Do you have a case against me that'll hold water?' Patrick asked him grittily.

The two men exchanged glances.

'Yes, we do,' said Greenshaft. 'The cleaner whom you locked in a cupboard and who subsequently broke her wrist

trying to get out has made a statement to the effect that she
freed herself in time to see you kill six people with shots fired
in rapid succession. You then turned to come towards the stairs
where she was observing this over the bannisters. She ran and
hid in a bedroom and subsequently heard another shot fired
and the child screaming. Then there was silence during which
she dared not move in case you found her.'

I thought the silence would never end so decided to break
it myself.

'And while this woman was trying to batter her way out of
a cupboard upstairs everyone else was just carrying on
normally as though it was an everyday occurrence,' I said
scornfully.

Greenshaft said, 'She said there was a hell of a row going
on downstairs. Shouting and banging about. They would not
have been able to hear her.'

'I shut her in the cupboard for her own safety,' Patrick said.
'She was scared stiff.'

'I'm not surprised if you were waving a gun in her face,'
Hurst remarked.

Patrick had his eyes closed, trying to remember. 'No,' he
said quietly. 'I didn't have anything in my hands. She was in
the room, cleaning, where I'd just climbed through the window
and was understandably alarmed by my appearance. I put my
finger to my lips to warn her to silence – I don't think her
English was too good – whereupon she pointed in the direction of the stairs, whispering "Hulton! Hulton!" That was
when I hid her in the cupboard, with her full permission, I
must add. I didn't hear her trying to break out. That must
have been afterwards when she thought she'd been forgotten.'

'After what?' Greenshaft snapped.

'After whatever happened next. That's all I can recollect at
this stage.'

'Why should she lie?'

'Because she's been threatened,' I said. 'I hope you've given
her police protection *now*.'

No one spoke for a few moments and then Greenshaft said,
'I've been digging around for people who knew you in your
MI5 days. In fact I spoke to Commander John Brinkley who
was, you might remember, your department's liaison officer
with the Met. He thinks you're mentally unbalanced and so

obsessed with getting the job done your way you're perfectly capable of going right over the top and committing murder, especially if under the influence of drink or drugs, if a job got too much for you. Did it, Gillard? Did this assignment have you floundering? Was it right over your head?'

'So why did he offer me a job?' Patrick said softly. 'I refused and he took it very badly.'

'Hardly surprising as it appears you swore and shouted obscenities at him.'

'No, I don't have to shout.'

'You don't deny it then.'

Patrick took a deep breath. 'My anger was not directed at him but at an Assistant Chief Constable by the name of Judd and a Superintendent Norman. They had messed around with a case I was working on to see how I would react and seriously jeopardized the rightful outcome. Brinkley was in the room but my remarks were not addressed to him. Since promotion to Commander he's become overweight, groomed like a dog ready for Crufts and horribly full of himself. I declined the job offer a little later but at the time to which you're referring told him he smelt like an Albanian knocking shop. It didn't appear to put him off making the job offer.'

'Has Brinkley ever seen you under the influence of drink or drugs?' Greenshaft asked.

'No, hardly.'

'Did you work closely with him so that he would be able to build up that kind of picture of you?'

'No, and any conversations I'd had with him were invariably over the phone. He was just a bloke I asked for information from, for God's sake!'

I cleared my throat and Patrick shot a sideways look in my direction. No, no, don't get angry, I mentally tried to beam at him.

'You haven't answered the question,' Hurst persevered. 'Was the job over your head?'

Patrick shook his head. 'It wasn't. But not one I would have chosen. You can't pick and choose.'

Greenshaft returned the folder to his briefcase and leaned back in his chair. 'Enough. I think, knowingly or not, purposely or not, consciously or not, you shot those people. I cannot, however, call you guilty of murder as my personal opinion is that you were unaware of your actions at the time. I don't see how it can ever be brought to court. It's not a case the Crown would win as there's no firm evidence either way and you'd be acquitted.'

'Then arrest me and take it to court,' Patrick said. 'I can't be expected to live the rest of my life with this vague accusation hanging over my head.'

'No, it would be a waste of public money and all for nothing. It's not the final decision, of course, as I shall have to present a report to my superiors. It's no disgrace, Gillard, you were obviously not in your right mind having been forcibly given dangerous chemicals. I'm afraid it'll be the end of your career with SOCA though.'

Patrick just sat there and calmly regarded him and did not have to voice that in his opinion the man was slipshod, incompetent, small-minded and, as before, a bastard.

EIGHT

They left, Greenway miming to us on his way out that he would get in touch later. A deep silence fell.

Patrick spoke first. 'I have a dreadful feeling the man's right.'

I said, 'And I have a dreadful feeling things are going to be left like this because funds are tight and, hey, those killed were only a bunch of crooks on any number of wanted lists so why spend a load of money on finding out what really happened?'

Patrick merely shrugged.

'Why *Brinkley* of all people? There are dozens of folk who would give you a good character reference. The grapevine must be fizzing with this affair. Did he come forward with revenge in mind?'

'I don't think I'll bother to ask him.'

'No, but it might be worth talking to Richard Daws.'

'I honestly can't see what good it would do.'

'You need some kind of official backing to investigate this yourself.'

'It's already come right from the top that that's not an option.'

'Lunch,' I decided. 'I can't think on an empty stomach and I don't know about you but I didn't have any breakfast.'

'We could go to the pub,' Patrick suggested, showing a bit more interest.

'And where will Greenway have taken the Inquisition for something to eat as there's nowhere else for miles around? To the Ring o' Bells.'

'I could thrash 'em at darts.' He responded glumly.

'Don't forget you still have a job to do.'

'That's right, it is only SOCA I'll be given the boot from. You know the very worst thing about this? Being blamed for the child's death.'

'It's completely unacceptable,' James Carrick said when he 'just happened by' that afternoon. 'And, frankly, I'm staggered.

What are the Met's findings? Did Greenshaft even consult
with them? Besides which, it's very early days to come to
any kind of conclusions. With your permission I'll get on to a
couple of contacts in London and ask them to find out what's
going on with regards to the investigation. I'm surprised you
haven't been interviewed by the Met, actually.'

'Up until today I've been regarded as goods still
contaminated by mostly illegal substances and Greenway's
been doing all the talking,' Patrick told him. 'And thanks for
the offer of help.'

'How are you getting on with the Blanche enquiry?'

'Are there any preliminary findings on the hammer?'

'No, not yet.'

'It isn't one of Dad's, I asked him to check and he rang me
just now to say that nothing's missing. I shall need to have it
back when the lab's finished with it – if it is thought to be the
murder weapon – to show to the blokes working on the rectory.
Some of them have completed their share of the work and
gone home so it'll involve a bit of chasing around.'

We spent the rest of the afternoon dodging yet more heavy
rain showers interviewing those on the church cleaning rota,
learned nothing of real interest apart from some hair-raising
gossip with not the remotest connection to the case and drank
endless cups of tea. We had just come in the front door when
Patrick's mobile rang and I got on with the usual domestic
matters while he answered it.

'That's it,' Patrick said, finding me in Katie's room. 'Carrick's
had a call from HQ. They've pulled the plug on me.'

'Greenshaft,' I said.

'He hates ex-military in the job, doesn't he?'

'I'm so sorry,' I said, putting my arms around him.

'James is livid. But he's helpless. He's still going to sound
out his contacts in the Met about the other business though.'

We both suddenly realized that Katie was standing in the
doorway, just back from playing hockey after school.

'A threesome cuddle is the latest trend,' Patrick said and
we made room for her. 'Good heavens, your head's almost
up to my chest now.'

'Someone at school said you'd killed some people,' Katie
whispered. 'Please tell me it's not true.'

Patrick sat down on the bed and patted the space beside him.

'Some people *were* killed,' he said when she had seated herself. 'And I was somewhere nearby. But I don't know what happened because someone else had given me an injection so I can't remember. But to answer your question properly, no, I'm as sure as I possibly can be that I didn't kill them.'

'And you still can't remember?' said Katie in a small voice. 'No.'

She put an arm consolingly around him in a natural fashion that I found utterly wonderful. 'They say that if you go back to where something happened that you can't remember about it helps you to remember again.' She regarded him with her hazel eyes. 'Uncle Patrick, please go and do that so I can tell everyone it's not true.'

'I will,' Patrick said.

'Promise?'

'I promise.'

'Tomorrow?'

'OK, tomorrow.'

She kissed his cheek and skipped from the room.

'Tomorrow,' Patrick said, gazing at me steadily. 'We tell the Greenshafts of this world to go boil their egos.'

'It'll have to be handled very carefully,' I said a little later when we were discussing what ought to be done. 'I'm sure I'm only echoing your own thoughts when I say that this is not a situation where you can pretend to be a meter reader in order to get into the house in Muswell Hill as you might have done in D12 days or break in at night. It'll still be a sealed crime scene. To do so would be to jeopardize your own case, in more ways than one, and would actually be very unprofessional. Besides which, you've been expressly forbidden to look into this yourself: I can see the wisdom of it. The Met has its own investigation and may have already turned up vital evidence that clears you completely. That needs to be established before we do anything else.'

Patrick, who had invited this consultant's opinion as a preliminary to making decisions, grimaced. 'I agree with everything you say but it sounds like several thousand very good reasons to do absolutely nothing. Ingrid, I must do *something*.'

'Yes, I suggest you get on to James, now, and reiterate that you value his offer of help and please would he get on with it.

While he's doing that, why don't you and I go and see Richard Daws? He has a lot of influence and talking to him can hardly be a waste of time.'

The phone rang and I answered it.

'Do you think you could both come over?' said Elspeth. 'That's if it's convenient.'

'Is something wrong?' I asked, knowing from her voice that there was.

'John's been roughed up. He – he's not badly hurt and I don't need to call an ambulance or anything but—'

'We'll be right there,' I told her.

As his father had undergone a heart bypass operation not all that long ago Patrick phoned their GP, Anne Walker, who is a family friend and lives nearby. All three of us arrived at the rectory together. Anne immediately, and carefully, checked over her charge, who was in the kitchen of the couple's annex drinking sweet tea, and declared him unscathed but for a couple of bumps and bruises plus a small graze on his hand, which Elspeth had already dealt with. She then, apologizing profusely, rushed off saying that she had promised to visit an elderly and frail friend but would call in later.

'You were right to urge me to be cautious,' John said to Patrick. 'I received a phone call to say that people were messing around on that spare ground on the estate. Whoever it was said they thought drink was involved and young children were there as well. I went down there but there was no sign of anyone. A couple of youths jumped on me from behind a bush.'

'Was it a man or woman who rang you?'

'A woman – I think. I'm fairly sure whoever it was was trying to disguise their voice.'

'Did you recognize these youths?'

'No, it was too dark.'

'No idea at all then, who they were?'

'There can't be many youngsters in the village who would do such a thing. I had taken my stick with me and got in a few whacks with it so perhaps that's the reason they ran off quite quickly.'

Predictably, Patrick then pointed out that he himself could have borrowed John's overcoat and gone instead – the two are practically identical in stature – and thus would have been able to nab them.

'You have enough to contend with at the moment,' the rector said.

'Yes, and I could have had a dead Dad to contend with as well!' Patrick countered. 'Oh, for God's sake! – sorry – let's have a dram and snivel into our beards together!'

He flung himself out of the room.

John and Elspeth looked at me.

'He's off both jobs now,' I said. 'Complaints seem to have it in for him.'

'Oh, *dear*,' Elspeth said.

Patrick came back with a tot of whisky for the patient and went away again with an expression on his face that I did not like at all.

Rather a long time elapsed before we moved into the living room and Elspeth started to cook their dinner. I thought about phoning James Carrick to report what had happened but decided to wait in case Patrick had already done so.

'Have you been in to see the latest progress?' Elspeth called through the open kitchen doorway to me. 'The new central heating boiler's been put in and tested and the electrician's finishing off all the rewiring tomorrow. Just a bit more plastering and then the decorating and the job's done!'

I had not. I had pushed it from my mind. So much for being site manager.

Had he taken the rest of the Macallan off into the sticks somewhere? I glanced around. No, it was still on the dresser. I looked at my watch. Everyone at the barn conversion would be expecting their dinner as well. I rang Carrie, who is used to an erratic life, and asked her to do something big casserole-wise with chicken joints that were in the fridge plus anything else she could lay her hands on.

Ten minutes later, when I was just about to leave, Patrick returned, dishevelled and a little out of breath. As soon as he had heard the outside door open John had risen from his seat, poured a tot of whisky into a clean glass and now, handed it to his son as he dropped into an armchair.

'No sign of anyone hanging around,' Patrick reported after a hefty swig. 'I spoke to a couple of people and they hadn't seen youths running away. But the bus had left shortly before so they may have got on that. I went in the pub and no one had seen anything suspicious. Everyone was horrified and word'll get round. I'll get them if it's the last thing I do.'

'It's my turn to urge caution,' John said quietly, waving an admonishing finger.

'This is nothing to do with any murder case as far as I'm concerned, although I did report it to James Carrick,' Patrick told him. 'This is me finding the little shits – sorry – who beat up my father.' He tossed down the rest of his drink and shot to his feet. 'Are you absolutely sure you're all right?'

'Perfectly,' John assured him.

'Please don't walk in unlit places in the village after dark until this is sorted out. And do let me or James Carrick know if you get any more phone calls or any threats.'

'Yes, of course. But I'm actually more concerned about you.'

Patrick gave him a wide smile. 'Justin seems to think I'm a Time Lord like Doctor Who at the moment because I always seem to turn up suddenly when he's doing something he shouldn't. So if things get a bit awkward I'll just regenerate.'

On this carefully engineered light-hearted note we left. Utter despair was only allowed to surface when we got home.

'Look, you can't blame yourself in any way for what happened,' I said, when Patrick had gone to stand over by the large window, his forehead on the glass, arms braced on the window ledge. 'You haven't been asking questions about witchcraft, it's your Dad who has a bee in his bonnet about that. We've only made very tentative connections, all guess-work, about Blanche and that kind of activity and it was in a private conversation with your father alone.'

'I should have gone down there, not a man in his seventies. He could easily have fallen, hit his head on a stone and died.'

'Of course, but he didn't tell you what was going on. And I think you're exaggerating a bit, John's a lot tougher than you think.'

Patrick said nothing.

Miserable introspection could not last for long as soon as we all, but for baby Mark and Carrie, who has her meals in her room as she likes watching television to relax, sat around the large table in the farmhouse-style kitchen – the dining room here was minuscule – for dinner. Tactful child that she is, Katie made no mention of the earlier conversation although I knew she would have shared what was said with Matthew. I wondered if anyone at school had made remarks to him and resolved to find out.

'Ingrid and I are going to London tomorrow,' Patrick suddenly announced after being in receipt of a piece of fresh pineapple that Vicky had thought he might like from the bowl of fruit salad in front of her and thrust under his nose. 'We might come back that same night or stay for a few days.'

I saw Katie's little private smile and Matthew's unhappy expression but had no worries about Justin who was in a world of his own indulging in his favourite hobby: eating. In Devon there had been behaviour problems, one of the reasons Patrick had initially thought of leaving SOCA so he could spend more time with his family. As soon as we had moved he had become a different boy and I had been forced to blame something wrong at his previous school. His grandmother had a lot to do with the improvement too for, after all, she had sorted his father out, hadn't she?

'D'you have any homework?' I asked Matthew when the two older children had finished helping me clear away.

'Yes, English,' he replied.

This was by no means his strongest subject.

'D'you need a few pointers?' I offered.

He grimaced. 'Yes, I do really.'

'Come and do it in the living room with us while we have our coffee.'

People have told us that we are too strict but the children are only allowed in the living room in the evenings – when we are there, that is – if they're going to read or engage in some other quiet activity. What we will not tolerate is their TV programmes or computer games dominating everything and even though Matthew has a computer in his room, where homework usually gets done, it is closely monitored. My children are not going to unwittingly communicate with weirdos on the Internet.

'It's an essay,' he groaned, arriving a couple of minutes later, 'And it mustn't be printed off.'

'Whoopee!' I said. 'How else is your handwriting going to improve? What's the subject?'

'We can choose between our pets and witches. I've already done one about Pirate so I thought I'd do witches.'

I had primed Patrick that we might need to talk over a

problem with Matthew and he had suggested I take the lead. He sat quietly, flipping though a magazine, in a corner, his coffee on a small table at his elbow. Behind him, a pale full moon was rising over the distant Mendips.

Matthew gazed at the wide expanse of glass. 'Do you ever close the curtains?' he asked.

'Yes, when it's really cold,' I answered. 'Do you want them closed?'

'It's a bit spooky,' he mumbled.

'I'll do it,' Patrick said, getting up.

'So it's witches,' I said brightly.

'The teacher asked us for ideas on what to write about. Greg suggested pets and Clem wanted witches. He seems to be in to them. His Dad's a wizard, or something like that. No, a war something.'

'Warlock?'

'Yeah, that's it. Auntie, are there such things?'

'People can call themselves whatever they like, I suppose.'

'But I mean, he brags about going to people's houses, meet-ings, or whatever where they do strange things. He's not allowed to go to all of them but says people dress up and drink a lot. He thinks it's great – really cool.'

'Does the teacher know all about this too?' I enquired, keeping my tone matter-of-fact.

'No. It's just between us and Clem. He asked me if I'd like to go to his house and see all the magic stuff when his Mum and Dad aren't there. I didn't really want to. I think it's scary. He called me a coward.'

'You're *not* a coward,' I told him firmly. 'But what you are is sensible in not wanting to get involved in anything so silly.'

'There's something else that even he thinks is scary,' Matthew went on. 'I didn't believe him really. It was too awful.'

'What?' I asked gently.

'Some of the people kill little animals and chickens and put the blood on each other.' His voice sank to a whisper. 'They try and call up the Devil. Grandad would say that was terribly wicked, wouldn't he?'

'Yes, he would. And you've been brought up to know it's not right either. Where does Clem live?'

'In Southdown St Peter. But he said the meetings are mostly here, down at the bottom of the village somewhere.'

Southdown St Peter: home of all local iniquity, past, present and presumably future. I said, 'Matthew, I wish you'd told us about this before. Is it what you were unhappy about earlier?'

His face cleared. 'Oh, no. I was just a bit miserable that you were both going away again.'

'We'll *all* go away,' I promised. 'Just us two and you and Katie, I mean. At half-term perhaps.'

'That would be great!'

'And now,' said Patrick, finishing his coffee. 'How about you and I going for a walk in the moonlight? Country folk used to call it the parish lantern. We'll look out for owls and badgers and if we go down to the river and stay very quiet we might even see an otter.' He got up. 'Coming? You could bring that big torch for the dark bits.'

'My essay though,' Matthew said sadly.

I said, 'Do it when you come back. I'll write a sentence as the idea for each paragraph you need to write. Look up the history of it on the Internet. And don't forget to finish by saying that it was a cruel persecution of innocent women. Oh, what's Clem's surname?'

'Huggins.'

He went off happily and I was confident that Patrick would ask him if anyone was bullying him at school about the shootings.

They had just gone out and I had filed the name Huggins under Unfinished Business when the phone rang.

'I don't know what to say about this morning – not politely anyway,' Michael Greenway said.

I told him that Patrick had just gone out but would be back in about half an hour and then went on to say that he had been taken off the murder case as well.

'I don't think Greenshaft has that kind of authority,' was Greenway's furious reaction.

'Oh, I'm sure it was a matter of a phone call here, a hint there and what's the country coming to with these ex-army bods playing at policemen and going round shooting everyone up?' I said, trying not to sound as bitter as I felt.

'I should imagine Carrick's bloody angry too with his help gone.'

'I think he's more angry for Patrick's sake. He said he'd

get in touch with people he knows in the Met to see how they're getting on with the Muswell Hill investigation. Commander—'

'Mike.'

'Mike, whatever Patrick's future is with your department and if permission is forthcoming from the Met would you have any objection to his having a look round the house to see if it helps him to remember what happened?'

'No, none.'

'It wouldn't be construed as investigating this himself?'

'I'll make sure it isn't. It's a good idea, in fact I'll say it was *my* idea, and in everyone's interest. Meanwhile I'm going to get on to Complaints and put in an official one about Greenshaft and Hurst. The last thing they're supposed to be is biased.'

Quite late that night when we were throwing things into suitcases just before getting into bed the phone rang and it was Carrick.

'I've fixed it,' he said. 'If you're at the crime scene at ten tomorrow morning someone called Harry Rundle will be there. He's heading the case and is enormously interested in talking to the unofficial suspect. Shall I confirm that with him?'

'I'm sure you can,' I said. 'But you'd better speak to Patrick.'

'An early start then,' Patrick said a couple of minutes later. He looked cheerful for the first time in days and gave me a foxy look. 'Will we sleep better if I ravish you several times on the carpet?'

'Natch,' I said. 'But in bed would be more comfortable.'

'Are you—?'

'On the pill? Too right.'

He swept me off my feet and on to the bed.

'You know what?' I whispered, a breathless half an hour later.

'What?' he mumbled, almost asleep.

'Whatever happened I'd stay with you for the sex alone.'

'I don't think that counts with the complaints mob.'

NINE

It had rained all night and the pavements were greasy, puddles reflecting the orange glare of the street lights, most of which, even though it was getting on for nine thirty in the morning, were still lit. The gloom was compounded by a large fire at an industrial estate nearby, black smoke rolling up and merging with the already leaden sky. Sirens wailed.

We parked near the murder scene and found somewhere to have coffee, both of us subdued, as we had been for the entire journey. Patrick, I knew, was aware that he was facing some kind of nemesis. I thought of asking if it would be a good idea to visit his digs but desisted: one thing at a time.

Harry Rundle turned out to be a tired-looking individual sitting smoking in a car parked right outside the house. As soon as he saw us he tossed the cigarette out through the open window where it was instantly extinguished on the wet pavement and got out.

'DCI Rundle,' he said tersely. 'I knew it was you: Jim Carrick said I would.' He eyed Patrick with professional interest. 'Got over the acid trip, or whatever it was, then?'

'I hope so,' Patrick said.

'So you're Lieutenant Colonel?'

'Not these days. It was one of the senior people in SOCA who suggested I use my army rank: as he put it "so some jack-in-office doesn't confuse you with one of the cleaners". But it's not practical, causes confusion and as you know SOCA personnel are nominally only constables to enable them to arrest people.'

'So what do *I* call you?'

'Patrick. This is Ingrid, my wife and working partner.'

Rundle nodded a greeting to me and then said, 'As far as our records are concerned you're remanded in custody on suspicion of murder. Those records won't be updated until we have some idea of what went on here. As far as *I'm* concerned this meeting is off the record.' Without waiting for any reaction to these remarks he then led the way up the front path to the house. Although I had been here before I doubted if I would have been able to identify it from the outside, all the long row of houses seemed to look the same and for some reason I had not noted the number. I did, however, shudder when we entered the hall and saw, again, the sickly yellow wallpaper, the row of grubby anoraks and jackets on hooks by a mirror, and smelt the odour of stale death and wanton living.

I placed a hand on Rundle's arm. 'I suggest you let him have a wander around first. The most important thing is that he remembers what happened here.'

The DCI shook his head. 'No, I need to be right there when any remembering's done. Sorry, but I've several murders to deal with here and I don't want to give people time to cook up fairy tales.'

I opened my mouth to protest but Patrick quickly said, 'It's all right,' and headed for the stairs, Rundle and I in his wake.

It was a bigger house than I had realized, a second, narrower, staircase going up to what must be loft rooms. But for now we remained on the first floor, Patrick walking slowly down a passageway. 'This is where I climbed in through the window,' he said when he arrived in the end bedroom.

'Did you shut it behind you?' Rundle asked.

'No, I left it as I'd found it, ajar.'

'Go on.'

'The cleaning woman was dusting. She was alarmed but as she recognized me . . .' He stopped speaking for a moment and then went on, 'Yes, that's right. She was going through the motions of dusting but was scared already. That was when she whispered "Hulton! Hulton!". Then I hid her in the cupboard.'

'Why though?' Rundle said.

'She was terrified. Thought she was going to be killed.'

'By you?'

'No, she had no grounds to be scared of me. She went in there of her own free will.'

'Yet now she's made a statement to the effect that she saw you fire the shots that killed these people.'

Patrick countered with, 'Then, for some reason, she's lying. She said she broke her wrist trying to get out of the cupboard. Would a woman who was that scared draw attention to herself in that way? Why would I have locked her in the cupboard if I intended to kill everyone?' He added, 'I'm supposed to be a one-time special services soldier. So would I have done something guaranteed to create a hell of a racket just before I turned up to take everyone by surprise?'

'Because you were off your head on drugs and didn't know *what* you were doing, that's why.'

Patrick just shook his head wordlessly and walked back down the corridor. We had passed the cupboard on the way, an old-fashioned linen store of some kind, not built-in but free-standing. He examined the door-catch and lock without touching anything. I could see no sign of damage.

'Has the key been removed by forensics?' Patrick said to the DCI. 'I left it in the lock.'

'Yes.'

'This thing doesn't look as though it's been subjected to any force, either from within or without. It's strongly, although roughly, built and I suggest to you that anyone inside wouldn't have been able to break out, even if they'd used their feet. And the woman involved is quite slight.'

'What nationality would you say she is?'

'Spanish. Her English isn't too good and although I'm half decent at French and have a little German there was no proper communication between us.'

'*Then* what did you do – after you'd secured her in the cupboard?' Rundle enquired. 'Incidentally, weren't you worried she might run out of air?'

Patrick pointed to gaps at the tops of the doors, which did not fit very well. 'No.'

'He noticed that when he was half off his head with drugs,' I commented. 'Thought about her welfare too.'

'I *am* exploring all angles,' Rundle said to me.

I apologized, having just realized that fact as soon as I had spoken.

Moving from there, Patrick went back to the bathroom, the floor covering in which had been removed. Standing in the doorway he gazed back along the corridor.

'That's Leanne's room,' he said, gesturing towards the first doorway on the left. 'I was coming back from where I'd hidden the cleaning woman in the cupboard when she came out, saw me but before she could say anything I put my fingers to

my lips. She must have just woken up because she was still
in her pyjamas and looked half asleep. I went to her and whispered that I must take her somewhere safe. Then I seem to
remember I took her back into her room and shut the door
so we could talk without being overheard.'

We went to stand by the doorway. Patrick was the only one
not to look inside, his expression taut. I glanced in quickly;
lots of pink, teddies, pictures of pop stars on the walls, just
like Katie's room.

Rundle said, 'Could you hear anyone else in the house?'

'No, it was very quiet.'

'All those downstairs could have already been dead by then.'

'And I would have had an hysterical child on my hands
instead of one who had just woken up. Would she have slept
through all that gunfire?'

'Kids do sleep deeply,' the DCI pointed out. 'And the weapon
might have been silenced.'

'But it wasn't. It was my Glock 18, which wasn't silenced.'

'Do you *know* you had it on you when you entered the
house that morning?'

'Yes.'

'You're quite sure you had it with you and hadn't left it
behind, or had it lifted off you the previous evening when you
say someone must have spiked your drink?'

'I'm sure I had it with me, in its shoulder harness.'

'Which you were wearing when you were found in the lane
out the back, the weapon in your hand.'

'I have no memory of being found.'

'OK. Then what happened?'

'I can recollect impressing on Leanne that we must leave.
She wanted to go and find her mother. But she'd . . .' His voice
trailed away, a frown creasing his forehead.

I held my breath and so, probably, did Rundle.

'Yes, she'd twisted her ankle in the garden the day before,'
Patrick said in an undertone. 'That's why I carried her. I told
her we'd find her mother but actually had every intention of
taking her out of the house as fast as I could. That meant
going down the stairs and out through the front or back doors,
of course. But we didn't make it.'

Neither the DCI nor I broke the silence that followed while
Patrick went away from us for a short distance. Then, turning to

us he said, 'I think I'd just left her room, carrying her when there was a shot. Leanne screamed. That's all I can remember.'

'Take your time,' Rundle said sympathetically.

'Everything else is a blank until I woke up in that clinic. No, I have a vague memory of lying somewhere out the back here, on a pile of stinking grass cuttings.'

'Yet the child was shot with the same weapon that killed all the others,' Rundle said. 'That doesn't tally with your account.'

I said, 'Patrick, you said you *think* you'd just left the room when there was the sound of a shot. When I spoke to you in the clinic you said you didn't get a look at whoever fired the shot but weren't sure why. Could any period of time have elapsed between you leaving Leanne's room with her and the gun being fired?'

'It was a bit hazy,' Patrick said after a pause. 'Yes, I suppose so. But—'

'Where could the shot have been fired from so that you would not see whoever it was?'

His eyes darted around with expert assessment. 'Nowhere. Even if he'd been standing up there on the next flight of stairs I'd have seen him. Any higher up the stairs and he wouldn't have been able to see his target.'

'But it was hazy,' Rundle reminded him.

Patrick grimaced. 'You can't be expected to understand or believe it but I've been as good as boiled in that kind of training. When you've done exercises using live ammo it's part of how you exist.'

'You didn't see this guy?'

'No.'

'He could have rushed out of one of the other rooms.'

'He didn't. I'm quite sure about that now.'

'Or behind you out of the room down the end you'd gained entry into.'

'Then he'd have shot me in the back.'

'And we still don't know what drove you to return here on that morning to rescue the girl – if that's really why you were here.'

'As I've said before, several times, it must have been something that one of the men who broke into my digs said.'

Rundle took a deep breath and let it go gustily. 'This is—'

'One possible explanation,' I interrupted. 'Is that someone

crept out of one of the rooms behind you, having been in there either before you arrived, perhaps asleep, or concealed them- selves in there when you closed Leanne's door in order to talk to her. When you came out of the room he clouted you with something from behind, rendering you semi-conscious. He then grabbed your gun and shot the child, who was then probably lying by your side on the floor. It's quite likely you would have heard that shot.'

Rundle said, 'That's possible but goes nowhere to solving the problem of people downstairs not hearing all that going on, or of Patrick not hearing them.'

'Perhaps they were doped,' I said. 'Everyone might have had their drinks spiked, not just Patrick. They were all shot neatly in the back of the head. Easy if they were unconscious, or nearly so.'

'But they were killed when they were standing up!' Rundle persevered. 'There's blood and brains all over the walls.'

'So someone was a little artistic with finger painting,' I said. 'Have the carpet and floor been examined for bullets that penetrated the victims' skulls and then emerged or for the kind of chemical traces left when shots are fired at close range?'

'Everything's *being* examined,' the DCI replied. 'It was like a slaughterhouse in there and tests will take a while longer.' He led the way downstairs and into the front room.

As with the bathroom, the carpet had been removed, as had sections from several floorboards.

'This is a Victorian house,' Rundle said. 'It was impossible to tell due to the seepage of blood and other fluids into the floor, plus dirt, whether holes in the wood were recent or history. You have a point though, they could have all been out for the count when Patrick arrived. It still doesn't prove that he didn't kill them. I suggest we start right from the begin- ning and visit these digs you had. You might remember what they said to you.'

But the digs, some five minutes' drive away, a bedsit on the top floor of another Victorian semi, were in the process of being deep-cleaned, the van of the company doing the job parked outside.

Rundle went ballistic.

Patrick and I left him to it, going back outside to stand on the pavement, where we could still hear the DCI shouting and the high-pitched protestations of the landlord, a skinny Welshman. I could appreciate the latter's point; that the place was uninhabitable and therefore he could not rent it out, but when police seal a room they expect it to remain so. I had every expectation that Rundle would arrest the man and charge him with interfering with evidence.

'But surely there's no real evidence there now,' I said. 'Forensics must have gone over everything.'

Patrick had appeared to be daydreaming but was not as he is not prone to such activity and did not respond. Then he said, 'I must have walked. We'll walk back in a minute.'

I was finding the whole thing very difficult because the pair of us had never been in this kind of situation before. We had helped James Carrick recover his memory after having been struck down in a hotel car park and I knew Patrick had experience of amnesia among those under his command in his army days. But drugs are different and I was becoming resigned to his never being able to reclaim that short period of his life. And of course if he had been rendered unconscious, again, on the first floor of the scene of the crimes then that was that, no amount of effort trying to remember would be of any use.

Two down-in-the-mouth workmen exited the house, gave us filthy looks, flung themselves into their van, wound down a window and lit cigarettes. Then Rundle appeared in the doorway.

'You can come up now,' he called to us.

All the furniture had been removed from the room, the lock on the door of which was still broken, the curtains and carpets also gone leaving us facing an empty box. It was full of steam from some kind of scrubbing machine with connecting hoses that we had had to squeeze by on the landing. Patrick went into the room for a few seconds alone, had a perfunctory glance around, shrugged, and then came out again.

Something strange was happening.

'Please stop right there,' I said, a hand on his chest.

For a moment I thought he would carry on walking and knock us aside.

'What?' he said harshly, seeming to look right through me.

'Because there's some kind of mental chemistry going on and you need to stop and quietly think about what it is.'

He did not want to think about it and I was worried that he was about to slam out of the house in a temper. We were in grave danger of showing Rundle exactly how several people might have been done to death.

I stared into Patrick's unseeing eyes, willing him to calm down.

After what seemed a long time his vision cleared. Then he turned abruptly and went over to the window, seemingly to look out. Again, time went by and I was grateful to Rundle for keeping quiet.

'The bastard said he was going to sell Leanne to a paedophile ring in Belgium,' Patrick muttered at last, addressing the dirty glass before him.

'Who, Hulton?' I said, or rather gasped, before Rundle could speak.

'Yes. At least – and I must be careful here – they were all wearing balaclavas. He said he was Hulton.'

'But his own child!'

'He thought it was really funny.' Patrick broke off, shaking his head. 'But, as I've just said, this was all dreamlike. Anyway, whoever he was he seemed to think I should find it amusing too. Then he got the other two to hold me down and gave me the jab. I didn't pass out then – truth drug doesn't tend to make me talk but I can remember giving him my real name. It appeared to mean nothing to him. Everything's a blank after that until my phone rang and it was you.'

'D'you reckon he'd brought you here in order to question you? I can't see how you could possibly have made it under your own steam.'

Patrick turned to face me. 'I must have done because I can distinctly remember them breaking into this room.'

'Who else might have done, brought you here, I mean?'

'I've simply no idea.'

'And you have no memories of leaving that house and returning here?'

'No, none.'

'I can only think that you were followed. How else would they have known where you lived?'

Rundle said, 'Well, a picture's emerging but I have to say

I don't necessarily believe it's the correct one. There's a watch on airports and railway stations for the man so all we can hope for is that he's soon nabbed. Meanwhile,' he went on dismissively, 'nothing much has been achieved.'

'Who was the man who Patrick was supposed to have tossed into a bush outside and who gashed his hand on some glass?' I asked him. 'Commander Greenway told me that he was a passer-by who had begun to investigate the sound of smashing bottles coming through the open front door.'

'He was actually the postman,' the DCI answered. 'D'you have any recollection of that?' he went on to ask Patrick.

Patrick thought about it. 'I have a vague recollection but I don't remember anyone in postman's uniform. He was quite an old guy – must have been getting on for retirement.'

'Was there any broken glass?' I enquired.

Rundle said, 'Yes, out the back. Someone must have been throwing empty bottles at a wall.' Addressing Patrick he said, 'If the front door was wide open why didn't you go in that way?'

'There's an old saying: "Never go down the path that your enemy has strewn with rose petals."'

'Did you hear bottles being smashed?'

'No. I don't remember the postman saying anything about it either. As far as I was concerned he was rather persistent, in my way and I didn't think he was anything to do with the snake pit indoors so I heaved him into the bush in case he carried on nosing around and got hurt.'

Rundle gave Patrick a hostile stare. 'So what standard of competence, mental and physical, do you reckon you possessed at that time?'

'By the time I returned to the house probably seventy-five to eighty per cent of norm all round. The fresh air –' Patrick nodded briskly – 'Yes, I did walk from here. The fresh air made me feel better.'

Which percentage brought him down to Mr Average-man-in-the-street, I supposed.

'OK,' Rundle said, glancing at his watch. 'I can't spare any more time right now. Are you sticking around?'

'We're staying with this until I've cleared my name,' Patrick said.

The DCI guffawed. 'You might have to stay a long time.'

'No, I shall go and find him myself.'

'Don't,' Rundle grated.

'I have an adopted daughter – she's actually my niece – who's been hearing from the kids at school that her uncle's a killer. I promised her I'd come to London and find out what really happened. Nobody, no cop, *no* one, is going to stop me from doing that.'

TEN

Perhaps wisely, Rundle made no further comment on the subject and went off after sourly telling the landlord that the cleaning team may as well continue as any damage had already been done. We also left the premises and, Patrick already having decided to walk to where we had left the car, set off, Rundle possibly having forgotten that he had given us a lift there.

'It doesn't look as though there's much choice of routes from here to Pangborne's place unless you deliberately went a roundabout way,' I said, tucking my arm through Patrick's. 'And you probably weren't in any state to find your way through back alleys.'

'I'm sorry I nearly lost it back there,' Patrick said, giving my arm a squeeze.

'I meant what I said when I spoke of chemistry,' I told him. 'It'll take a bit longer for you to fully get over this.' I glanced at him quickly. 'Are you really going after Hulton?'

'Yes, I am.'

'Your consultant here is really freaking out over it. I honestly don't think you're yet fit enough to go after someone like that – never mind what those in charge are saying.'

'He's only a stupid grown-up yob who's been sheltering in the organization of a clever woman.'

I didn't have an answer to that right then.

It had started to rain again and I put up the hood of my coat. In the distance could be seen the pall of black smoke from the fire as it rose above the rooftops. Traffic was light.

'None of this means anything to me,' Patrick said, looking around when we were probably halfway there. 'All I can remember is a breeze on my face and just roads and buildings.'

'Hardly surprising as it all looks very much the same,' I replied.

'There's something else you ought to know that I haven't mentioned before and didn't want to tell Rundle about.'

'What?'

'All through that morning I was hallucinating. It's very difficult for me to pick out what's real. I have to keep censoring
out all the impossible bits.'

'Like people with two heads and fire-breathing double-
decker buses, you mean?'

'Fantastic colours, feeling as though I was flying, everything
distorted like looking through a special effects camera lens,
seeing people who couldn't possibly have been there.'

'Like who, for example?'

'Mum and Dad riding bikes and, somewhere or the other,
the Queen taking some corgis for a walk.' He added, giving
me a grin, 'She stopped to tell me what a splendid job I was
doing.'

'She's always been a fan of yours.'

This was not entirely make-believe on my part. During his
service days there had been several commands to assist at
investitures, because, it was breathed, she found him amusing.
Her Majesty, one gathered, was another born mimic.

We walked on in silence and, a few minutes' later, reached
the car.

'At least we now know why you came back to this house,'
I said.

'But we still don't know if I'm a mass murderer or not,'
Patrick answered before grimly falling silent.

We had just booked into an hotel in central London – we
needed time to plan our next move – when Patrick's mobile
rang. I gathered from hearing half a conversation that it was
Michael Greenway and that he wanted to take us out to dinner
that night.

'He said he'd be in the Dover Street wine bar at seven
thirty,' Patrick reported.

'How did he know we were in London?'

'Apparently he rang home as we'd switched off our mobiles
while we were at the murder scene this morning because we
didn't want any interruptions and Carrie told him.'

'What's it all about?'

'Probably to soften me up before giving me the guilty
verdict.'

But he was wrong because Greenway's first words to us
were, 'Let's be quite clear on one thing; as far as I'm concerned

you're still working for me until I hear otherwise. My priority – and bugger the Met – is to get hold of Hulton. He's the key to this, whether he's guilty of murder or not. What would you like to drink before I fill you in on the latest?'

I wondered if the tone of this opening meant he was about to engage with us in a council of war but it appeared that the Commander was reckoning this to be mostly an evening off and had every intention of enjoying himself.

'So what is the latest?' Patrick prompted him, in receipt of his second whisky double.

'He hasn't left the country,' Greenway said. 'There's been a sighting of him here in London.'

'By a member of the team that you initially assured me did all the groundwork before Patrick went in to the Pangborne gang?' I enquired. 'Those who were the basis for your statement that he wasn't going in alone? The same ones who mysteriously disappeared while all the action was taking place so witnessed bugger all?'

For the first time I got the impression that Greenway was genuinely angry with me.

'It wasn't like that,' he said stiffly.

'What *was* it like then?' I persevered. 'Other than a monumental cock-up?'

After a somewhat overwrought silence the Commander said, 'There was round-the-clock surveillance – by the Met – from a house nearby but as you know the Pangborne place faces a park so observation from a house opposite was impossible. They were a little farther down the street on the other side. I was liaising with the officer in charge, a bloke called Rundle, and for some reason that has not been subsequently explained there was a mess up with the rota. Only one person was on duty that night and he had a bad attack of the trots. No one turned up at six that morning to take over from him, by which time he was obviously suffering from food poisoning and subsequently admitted to hospital. I don't *think* there were any suspicious circumstances in all this.'

'So who's seen Hulton?' I said.

'One of Rundle's team who's routinely working undercover in a nightclub in Acton much frequented by people who ought to be helping us with enquiries but aren't. You must appreciate that he couldn't simply order in a raid – he had his own

cover to think about. Hulton was tailed to Chiswick by
someone else but lost when he dived down into a tube station.'

Patrick said, 'We met Rundle today. Following your permission Ingrid and I went to the murder scene to see if it helped
me remember anything. There was not much of a result but
I did at least remember Hulton – or someone I thought was
him – telling me he was going to sell Leanne to a paedophile
ring. It must have been why I went back to the house.'

'He wouldn't have baulked at shooting the poor child then,'
he commented quietly.

'I told Rundle I was going after him myself.'

'Well, you aren't,' the SOCA man replied smoothly after a
sip of whisky.

'That's what Rundle said.'

'Leave Hulton to me. He may well have told you that to
ensure you went back to the house and had it all tidily planned
so that you would end up as number one suspect for the
killings. OK, suppose you do go after him. He might have
oppos whose orders are to start shooting when you arrive on
the scene. You end up in the frame for injuries to innocent
parties as well as all the others as he'll be prepared to swear
under oath that he saw you kill them. It's too risky.'

'He's too fond of his own skin to make plans that would
involve his being in any kind of shoot-out and I'm pretty sure
he doesn't have any sidekicks,' Patrick argued. 'Believe me, I've
spoken with him. The only plans he ever makes involve what
he's going to eat for his next meal and when he might get blind
drunk and enjoy killing someone.'

'So do I have to lock you up somewhere to stop you
disobeying orders?'

'He would,' I said to Patrick.

'I'm sorry, Patrick,' Greenway said after an awkward
silence. 'But you aren't working for MI5 now. Everything is
more *accountable*.'

There was another pause that was broken by Patrick's mobile
ringing. He apologized and left the bar to answer it.

'That man is still not well,' Greenway said in an undertone. 'I don't like his colour and I'm worried about his mental
state. I wonder if the tests the clinic carried out did pick up
everything he was dosed with. Mixtures of drugs have to be
horribly toxic.'

'I don't want him to go after Hulton either,' I said. 'Although – and I think you should take this on board – I think time will prove him correct with his summing up of this character.'

'Can you stop him?'

'No. He promised Katie he'd clear his name. That means everything to him, keeping the promise.'

'So what do I do, Ingrid?'

I looked Greenway right in the eye. 'You might have to lock him up.'

'It would have to be a safe house. But surely someone who's served in special services would find it quite easy to break out of a place like that, even if I put people armed with Tasers on the door.'

'Yes, you'd either have to chain him up or rely on his cooperation.'

'Are you saying, in effect, that there's no easy answer?'

'There never is with Patrick. I think though that if you closely involve him in your plan to get hold of Hulton, telling him it's *initially* in an advisory capacity, you'd get that cooperation.'

At this point Patrick returned and I could tell from his expression that all was not well.

'That was Elspeth,' he said. 'There's been a break-in at the church and people have held some kind of pagan or black magic ceremony. They did a lot of damage and Dad's suffering from shock and none too well.'

'What, last night?' I asked.

'Yes.'

'Why on earth didn't she ring you earlier?'

'She didn't like to bother us at work.' Patrick sat down suddenly. 'God, I'm staggered that people could do such a thing.'

'What did you say?'

'I told her that one or both of us, you probably, would drive down as soon as possible.'

'You both go,' Greenway said. 'And Patrick: I've decided on my next move. I'll get my team together and we'll provisionally map out how we're going to get hold of Hulton. I want you closely involved, initially in an advisory capacity. When you've sorted out the trouble at home get straight back here and we'll trot past you what we're thinking of doing.

This is on the strict understanding that nobody's going off to try to grab Hulton on their own. If anyone's going to get killed as a result of grabbing this bastard it's going to be him. Agreed?'

After hesitating fractionally, Patrick nodded and said, 'Agreed.'

I almost fainted with relief.

We arrived at Hinton Littlemoor at almost midnight having phoned Elspeth on the way. She was adamant that although it was late it would do John good if we could call in briefly before we went home.

I hardly noticed at the time, merely registering a certain spaciousness outside the rectory, and only realized later that all the skips, piles of building materials and rubbish outside my new home had gone. I parked the Range Rover – having done all the driving as Patrick was exhausted as well as having had a couple of whiskies – and we let ourselves in through the front door. That of the annex was ajar, Elspeth having obviously heard our arrival.

'I'm sure you're hungry,' was her opening, and characteristic remark, after returning our hugs.

'We're both absolutely famished,' Patrick assured her. Dinner with Greenway had had to be abandoned.

'Good, I'll find you something to eat.'

I held back. Sometimes even a wife can be an intruder in her husband's family but Patrick motioned to me to accompany him as he went to see his father.

John was in bed.

'You've been thundering from the pulpit again,' Patrick said to him after I'd kissed him and Patrick had grasped both his hands, which I noticed shook a little.

'Not really, I was asked to take a midweek morning service at Southdown St Peter and mentioned my worries. Your mother shouldn't have dragged you all this way,' said the priest. He looked pale.

'She didn't,' his son replied. 'We came as soon as we heard.'

'You did warn me to be careful.'

'Does James Carrick know?'

'Yes, I rang him as soon as I discovered what had happened this morning and he came straight over. There's been some kind of crime team in the church all day – Carrick's wondering if there's a connection with Blanche's murder.' He fell silent for a few moments and then said, 'I know you'll think I'm giving up in cowardly fashion but I don't think I can take any more of this.'

'There's no reason why you should be expected to,' was the calm reply.

His father looked a bit disconcerted. 'Oh! I was expecting you to give me a bracing rallying the troops kind of talking-to.'

'That would be downright impertinent of me.'

'Patrick, they not only killed what appears to have been some kind of bird up by the altar but smashed up part of the pulpit,' John told him in some distress.

'It's only held together by the woodworm holding hands – and a fine example of late Victorian hideousness.'

'And took what seems to have been an axe to the altar rails.'

'Ditto.'

'Most of the kneelers were piled up and had drink of some kind poured all over them.'

'That's actually a waste of good booze as most of them are full of the moth and were probably made by village ladies during the Boer War.'

After a short pause John said, 'So I've been presiding over relics, some kind of junk shop?'

'Neatly put, yes.'

'You think then that a big turnout was long overdue anyway and an appeal would be in order to raise money to replace these things?'

'Absolutely. And there's the woodcarver, Stewart Macdonald, who lives at the old smithy. You could ask him to cast his gaze over what's needed.' Patrick got up from where he had been sitting on the end of the bed and then said, 'I'm puzzled that you didn't hear this all going on. It must have made quite a racket.'

'We weren't at home. We stayed the night with our friends the Makepeaces. It was their thirtieth wedding anniversary and they had a party.'

'Who knew you wouldn't be here?'

'Any number of people as it meant I couldn't attend a committee meeting and a rehearsal for the Hinton Littlemoor Players latest production.'

'You're in a play?' I said.

'No, I do the lighting.'

Patrick smiled. 'I thought you weren't supposed to be any good with tools.'

'Not with household fixing tools I'm not,' replied John with a tilt to his chin. 'You know, hammers and saws, that kind of thing. Carpentry. Putting up shelves. Quite useless.'

'So's Patrick.' I commented.

'Have a good night's sleep, Dad, and we'll talk about it in the morning,' Patrick said. On his way out, head around the door, he added, 'I meant what I said, I'll find these people.'

'It would be unrealistic to expect James Carrick to share with you any evidence they may have turned up,' I said over breakfast, or at least during a snatched coffee and slice of toast, after too few hours' sleep.

'You're probably right,' Patrick replied. 'But I shall go off to the nick, or wherever he is, and have a go at him anyway.'

'Suppose you let me do it: he might be more forthcoming.'

Patrick gave me a look, or rather, A LOOK.

'I don't mean because he fancies me, silly, just that I'm a woman and he rather resents being pressured by other blokes,' I countered resentfully. 'You know that.'

'Sorry, but after what's happened I'm not in the mood to pander to other people's hang-ups.'

He moved to leave the room, slowly as though very tired, I was alarmed to see, without asking if I would like to go along.

'You told your father you'd have a chat with him this morning,' I reminded his rigid shoulders.

'He's still asleep. I'll talk to him later.'

'Evidence,' I muttered to thin air a few moments later, gazing through the rain-streaked window. 'Who needs evidence when you can go and find yourself some likely suspects?' Like the woman nicknamed Morticia, for example.

And, hey, nobody had said this particular consultant was off any cases.

I had, during my meeting with Michael Greenway just before Mark was born, asked him for a SOCA ID card of my own on the very good grounds that I do, sometimes, interview people when Patrick is not present. Greenway had agreed immediately, no doubt feeling it was the least he could do having stonewalled all my other concerns about Patrick being involved in the Pangborne case. Which had, I thought, savagely ramming the piece of laminated card with my photograph on it that had arrived, belatedly, through the post that morning, into my pocket, subsequently been proved more than justified.

Half an hour later Barbara Blanche, *sans* minder, peered at it dubiously. 'You've been here before, haven't you?' she said. 'With that man, Patrick somebody-or-the-other who looks as though he's never smiled in his life. He gave me the creeps.'

'It's deliberate,' I told her briskly. 'So people aren't tempted to tell him a load of old cobblers.'

'You're not a normal sort of police person either, are you?' she said accusingly.

'No, and Patrick's my husband. I've come to ask you a few questions about the break-in at the church the night before last. Understandably, the rector's very upset. And, just to set the record straight, he's my father-in-law.'

'What on earth do you think I can tell you about break-ins?' she enquired shrilly.

'May I come in?' I asked.

Slowly, she stood aside to allow me to enter.

'I'm not here to waste anyone's time,' I told her when we were both standing in the living room. 'What I need to know is whether your husband had, unwittingly or otherwise, upset anyone involved with a black magic circle.'

'Of course not!'

'I demand a thoughtful and honest answer,' I went on. 'He'd angered people with his interfering in just about every other organization in Hinton Littlemoor, frankly, in the A to Z of the whole social structure of the village. It's quite possible that people, even churchgoers, who belong to some of the more open and inclusive local clubs and groups are involved with a secret and possibly closed one that we know exists. Please think.'

She was shaking her head even before I had stopped speaking.

'All right, then,' I said. 'You.'

'Me!'

'*You're* the one who freaked out when asked about meetings

at houses on the estate in the bottom end of the village. *You're*
the one who everyone refers to as Morticia because you reckon
you can predict when people are going to die. What's that all
about then? Crystal balls, tea leaves, tarot cards?'

The woman stared at me like a rabbit caught in car
headlights.

'It's . . . it's just a feeling I get,' she finally stammered. 'A
bit of fun really.'

'Fun!'

'Well, I mean . . . whoever it is might be really old . . . and
ill, sort of thing and I say, well . . . they're next.'

'Where? At Mothers' Union meetings?' I asked sarcastically.

'No, no. At . . . er . . . the get-togethers we have at Marge's
house down at . . .'

'Down at a house at the bottom of the village,' I finished
for her when she stopped speaking.

'It's only fortune-telling and palm reading and lots of chat,'
Barbara Blanche continued almost eagerly. 'And a glass of
wine. I'm afraid we love our wine. Melvyn wouldn't have
approved. He was rather a straight-laced man. So I never told
him. I just said I was going off to another keep-fit session.'

'I simply can't believe that you and your friends didn't
discuss what went on at the piece of open ground close by.'

She sat in an arm chair and I followed suit.

'It's best not to talk about it,' she said in a whisper. 'People
who do are warned off.'

'Who's involved in it though, who? You must have some
idea.'

Staring miserably at the floor she said, 'I daren't say a
word. I told Melvyn what I'd heard, although I thought it was
no more than spiteful gossip at the time, and look what
happened. Then the rector was knocked about and now this
break-in. No. Please go away.'

'It may well have been gossip without a word of truth in
it and the rest is pure coincidence,' I pointed out.

'Oh, no. Since then I've found out that . . .'

'What?' I prompted.

'No, I can't say. I can't really believe it myself.'

'I could ask Patrick to talk to you.'

She looked up. 'Is that it? The big threat?'

'I'm not threatening you. It just that he's good at—'

'Terrorizing people,' she butted in with. 'I'm sure he is! No, go away! The damage might have been done already. They might be watching me. Go! Now!'

I had actually been about to say that Patrick was good at putting people's minds at rest, as demonstrated the previous night with his father. As it was I had no choice but to leave.

ELEVEN

What had she found out? And how?

This was going through my mind as I walked up the drive of the house next door, wondering if Ann Trelawney was at home. There was also the possibility that the widow's jangled nerves together with an incorrectly overheard conversation had caused two and two to be put together to make fifty. The problem was that I did not know whether to feel sorry for her or not and put this down to being unsure whether she was the one who had wielded the bottle of Jeyes and the vacuum cleaner nozzle.

The Land Rover, rear door open, bags of shopping visible within, was parked close to the house, sounds of activity – that is, thumping around – coming from indoors. Then Ann Trelawney appeared – and I did not imagine this – looked distinctly displeased to see me.

'More questions?' she called brightly as she marched up to where I stood by the vehicle, eyes sparking with bad temper.

'You've heard about the break-in at the church the night before last, I suppose?' I said.

'No, haven't spoken to a soul since the rehearsal for the play. Really? But everything valuable's locked up when it's not being used, isn't it?'

'Yes, but that's not the point. Quite a lot of damage was done and whoever it was performed some kind of black magic rite in the chancel.'

'Kids, I expect,' she said lightly. 'D'you like my new tree? It's a "Honey Locust", *Gleditsia triacanthos*.'

I glanced in the direction in which she was pointing and saw a pot with a twiggy little thing in it, the main stem having sharp spines.

'Can you remember exactly who was at your rehearsal?' I asked.

The woman shrugged in exaggerated fashion. 'Well, you know . . . the usual crowd.'

'Perhaps you'd be good enough to make a list of everyone who was present,' I requested stolidly.

'Look, I'm a bit busy right now.'

'Miss Trelawney, desecrating churches is a *crime*. It tends to have a very upsetting effect on the clergy who have responsibility for them too, especially when they've already been roughed up by thugs. You don't want to lose your lighting man, do you?' I finished by saying sarcastically.

There was an awkward silence and then she said, 'You'd better come in and I'll try to find a piece of paper and a pen.'

Not too difficult surely, I thought, for someone who wrote plays. The cottage in Devon had been littered with notebooks and the means to write down sudden ideas. It came to me that I would much rather be in my new home right now, in the warm working on my next novel than plodding around in the rain. Not that I had a writing room any more.

'What's the play about?' I asked on the way through the front door.

'It's a tongue-in-cheek thing on living in the country called *Mud and Magic*.'

'Magic mushrooms?' I hazarded.

Ann Trelawney had put on her reading glasses and now paused to look sharply at me over the rims. 'Of course not!'

I was unrepentant. 'I simply can't imagine how Melvyn Blanche was drawn to want to stage-manage a village dramatic society production. Surely he was too much of a snob for that.'

'Well, I suppose if you want to rubbish what we do—'

'I'm not rubbishing it, just trying to fit what people are telling me to the man he appears to have been.'

'I told you. He was a complete control freak. But I tell you one thing: we would have dropped the production rather than have him on the job.'

'Things were getting pretty tense then.'

By this time we were in the kitchen and she was scrabbling around on an amazingly overloaded Welsh dresser. 'Oh, yes. But again I say to you: I didn't kill him. I can't imagine any of those involved in the play doing it either. They're all such a bunch of sweeties.'

I decided to make up my own mind about that and said,

'Is Stewart Macdonald stage-managing it for you after all or did he give it a miss this year as he said he would?'

'I twisted his arm,' said Miss Trelawney with a faint smile.

A few minutes later, the list she had drawn up safely in my pocket, I walked back down the hill towards the village. It was in my mind to borrow Elspeth's car and call in at home – walking was all very well but in this weather I would get soaked by the muddy spray from passing cars in the narrow lanes – as Mark was colicky and I thought Carrie might like a break. But I had to go right past the Old Smithy to get to the rectory so a few more minutes asking questions of Stewart Macdonald would make no difference.

The scent of freshly worked wood led me to a side building of the cottage that must have once been the actual smithy. One of the double doors was open and as I approached I could see a short stocky man with a mop of untidy fairish hair planing the edge of what looked like a door. He heard my footfalls and stopped working.

'Ah, the lady detective,' he said, giving me a somewhat leery grin. 'Well, it's no good talking to me, I didn't kill the fool. I was in Scotland.' He picked up the door and leaned it against the wall. 'Damned weather. Even the bathroom door won't close because of the damp.'

'Business quiet then?' I asked.

'Like a grave. But even if I was up to my eyes in sawdust Cindy wouldn't tolerate the bathroom door not closing. She says the dog shoves it open when she's on the throne and reveals her in all her glory.' He sniggered. 'What can I do for you?'

'Any vibes and gossip in the Ring o'Bells about the break-in at the church?'

'Oh, that. A pile of old lumber got bashed around a bit. What's new?'

'The rector had already been bashed around a bit.'

'Well, perhaps he should live and let live.'

'You condone that kind of thing then?' I said, hearing the sharpness of my tone.

'No, look, I wasn't saying I did. And the man's getting on in years. But if people want to have a bit of fun dancing round bonfires and having a drink it's not up to him to stop them.'

'Children too,' I murmured. 'Watching chickens and people's pets being slaughtered. Is that part of life's rich pattern too?'

'It's up to parents to control what their kids get up to.'

'Do you have any children, Mr Macdonald?'

'A couple of teenage lads by my previous marriage. They live with their mother in Bath.'

'I understand that Melvyn Blanche wanted to take over from you as stage manager for the Hinton Littlemoor Players latest production.'

MacDonald was rummaging around in a stack of wood offcuts. 'Well, the silly old sod wanted to take over everything, didn't he? I have to say I hadn't been too keen on doing it again this year but rather than see the whole thing go to hell I told Ann I'd do it.'

'Everyone's glad this man's dead, aren't they?'

'How could it be anyhow else? He was like having a plague in your midst – you never knew where he was going to strike next.'

'D'you know where the key to the vestry's kept?'

He gave me an incredulous stare. 'Hardly. Do I sound like a churchgoer?'

'Is your partner?'

'Not a chance. She doesn't do all this God stuff either.'

'So it goes without saying that if the rector asks you to give him an estimate for replacing the damaged pulpit and altar rails you'll turn him down flat.'

'That's business,' Macdonald replied coldly. He grabbed a chunk of wood and went over to a workbench where he switched on some kind of large overhead drill thus rendering further conversation impossible.

I turned to leave and as I did so noticed a small axe propped in one corner by the doors. It was old, the blade notched, the handle shiny with use, probably for firewood, and in one of the notches was a tiny chip of wood. Purely on impulse I bent swiftly, pulled it out and hurried away fully expecting him to have seen me and shout. But nothing happened.

At home, half an hour later, I looked at the piece of wood through a magnifying glass. There was not a lot to see although it was fairly obvious that the wood was old: it looked like oak, and a hint of shine on one surface suggested polish. I resolved to give it to James Carrick even though aware that by touching it I had contaminated possible evidence. *And* might be confusing his investigation into the break-in.

The phone rang and it was Michael Greenway.

'I've tried to get hold of Patrick but his mobile appears to be switched off,' he said. 'Is he with you?'

I told him that he was not, adding that he might be at a location where mobile reception was bad, fairly common in this part of Somerset.

'Can you ask him to get in contact?' the SOCA man went on. 'I really could do with him at this end and despite what he said I've a nasty feeling that he might go off and try and grab Hulton himself if I don't keep him right under my nose.'

I made no comment, mainly because I was not at all sure what Patrick did intend to do.

'Is his father OK?' he went on to ask.

'Thank you, he'll be all right,' I told him. 'They're both out of the same pot.'

I tried Patrick's mobile but it seemed dead.

There was no choice but to return Elspeth's car as she needed it directly after lunch. Mark was recovering from his colly-wobbles so I left, promising Carrie that she could have the evening off to visit her mother. She was due at least a week's leave so I would either have to stay at home for the duration or get another nanny from an agency, which was not my first choice by any means.

I would just have to solve all the crimes then, I told myself grimly. ASAP.

In this somewhat bloody-minded mood I went back to the rectory, collected in passing a filled roll that Elspeth handed to me on my way out and prepared to walk home.

'You can have John's car if you want it,' Elspeth called after me. 'I've actually managed to persuade him to have the day off.'

This was an elderly Volvo estate. Elspeth hates driving it as it tends to be very difficult to get into reverse and is only kept as it is so useful for collecting items for jumble sales. I returned and gratefully accepted – the rain was torrential by this time – and then said, 'Have the police sealed the church or can I have a look at the damage?'

'Well, I think bits are still cordoned off but James did say we could have it back soon. It'll have to be reconsecrated, of course. D'you mind having a look on your own? I'm afraid I find it just too awful for words, especially after the murder.' She hastened to add, 'But I'll come with you if you want me to.'

I assured her that I would be fine on my own, collected the key from John's study and then drove his car round to the front of the church, thus giving myself a shorter dash through the rain than walking the length of the graveyard from the gate in the rectory garden.

First impressions are vital but I found it impossible to remain detached as this was literally an assault on those I held dear. The huge and historic lock on the door had somehow been forced. I walked slowly down the main aisle. There was silence but for the rain pounding on the roof high above. Before me, the area around the altar was draped with incident tape, most of the rails around it reduced to matchwood. To the left of this the more substantial carved pulpit had also been savagely attacked, a good third of the structure lying in pieces at the bottom of the short flight of steps up to it. Chips of wood were everywhere and I picked up a small one and pocketed it to compare with the one I had found in the axe-blade.

The marble flooring between the choir stalls that faced each other on either side of the chancel had been spray-painted in bright red with a clumsy pentacle and there were other, presumably occult signs on the walls, some partly covering memorial tablets. Feathers were everywhere and, in a corner by the altar was a sad little blooded bundle, the remains of a chicken by the look of it. And, as John had said, most of the kneelers had been piled in a heap and some kind of alcoholic drink poured over them; I could smell it. Leaning over the tape I sniffed closer; brandy, probably. Had whoever it was hoped to set fire to them and because everything was damp, as most old churches are, they had failed to ignite?

Brandy? A rather expensive firelighter surely.

This was nothing to do with so-called black magic: it was criminal damage.

'Yes, Patrick called in quite early this morning,' James Carrick said.

I had come face to face with him in the reception area, where he had been in receipt of some paperwork from the constable on duty at the desk. The DCI gave every impression of having been undertaking in-flight refuelling and about to jet off somewhere else.

'And?' I prompted.

'I had nothing useful to tell him: no clues at all really. As I expect you must realize, there are hundreds of fingerprints everywhere – it's a public building.'

He was all ready to go.

'Are you the smallest bit interested in what I have to say on the subject?' I enquired bullishly.

He glanced at his watch. 'Two minutes.'

In his office Carrick said, 'I'm really sorry to be so brusque, Ingrid but I'm up to my ears in work.'

'OK,' I said. 'A precis then. First and foremost: I don't believe the latest incident in Hinton Littlemoor church is the work of self-styled satanists. It's vandalism with a purpose. Either as a direct attack on John Gillard for some personal reason, or because someone wants the job of making good the damage. The local woodcarver, Stewart MacDonald, has an empty order book and a handy axe with a chip of seasoned wood in a nick in the blade – which, incidentally, I've handled – and is, in my view, a suspect and the fact that he has a couple of teenage sons by a previous marriage who live with their mother in Bath probably has no connection at all with the two who roughed up the rector previously.'

Here I handed over a small evidence bag, which I had labelled, containing the piece of wood together with another holding the sliver I had picked up in the church.

'But why would he get his sons to attack the rector?' Carrick asked.

'He's of the view that what people and their children do is none of a clergyman's business. He might be a member of the sect, or whatever the hell it is.'

'I rather thought that kind of thing was the whole point of a clergyman's business,' Carrick murmured. 'D'you reckon this character might be involved in the Blanche murder?'

'I understand the Wing Commander was trying to take over his job of stage-managing the local dramatic society's play.'

'Yes, the play. That was mentioned a few times by those

we questioned. Oh, and that hammer you found *was* the murder weapon, Blanche's DNA on crannies between the head and the helve. But someone must have quickly rinsed it off before chucking it in the shrubs of the rectory garden.' Carrick scribbled down a few notes on a pad and then looked up at me. 'I didn't like the look of Patrick. The man's not got over being doped.'

'He's under huge pressure. Greenway wants him in London but can't get hold of him and his phone appears to be switched off, which is odd. He's promised his father he'll find the people who damaged the church and attacked him. *And* promised Katie he'll clear his name over the London murders.'

'D'you not know where he is?'

'No. I rang home again just now and he's not there.'

'Are you worried about him?'

'I am rather.'

Carrick went to the door and yelled, 'Lynn! Are you there?'

I heard running footsteps and a somewhat flustered Lynn Outhwaite, Carrick's sergeant, appeared in the doorway.

'My apologies for shouting,' said the DCI, 'I'll buy you lunch, but will you please take my place at this wretched Crime Solutions for the Twenty-First Century presentation at HQ this afternoon? I've gone down with the pox, anything catching, just use your imagination.'

'Suspected,' I chipped in with. 'That'll explain why he's perfectly all right tomorrow.'

Lynn – petite, dark-haired, brainy – eyed her boss narrowly. 'A car and driver to take me there and bring me back?'

'That's fine, he'll be waiting outside for me now.'

'Lunch at The Moon and Sixpence?'

'OK,' agreed Carrick after the briefest of pauses.

'I thought you said you were interviewing a witness to a jewellery shop raid on the way back.'

Carrick snatched a file from his desk. 'Mrs Martha Timmings, Flat 4, Landsdown Parade. I hope you like cats.'

'Yes, I do actually,' Lynn replied and hurried away.

'She's a great girl,' Carrick said, turning to me. 'So where's this man of yours likely to be?'

'I don't want you to clear your diary just because—' I began.

'That's only the top layer. But I'm worried too now.'

'He might merely have stopped for forty winks in a lay-by somewhere. We didn't get much sleep last night after the drive down from London.'

'That doesn't explain why his phone's turned off. I suggest we cover the ground from here back to Hinton Littlemoor. Is he in the Range Rover?'

'Yes, I've borrowed John's car.'

'We'll go in that then.'

I rather thought that I would have seen our vehicle on the way in but did not argue, annoyed with myself for not having asked Patrick what he planned to do after talking to Carrick. I was fully expecting to find him comfortably ensconced in his mother's kitchen, having a late lunch.

'I'll make a few calls before we set off,' I said when we were in the car park at the rear of the Manvers Street police station. 'Otherwise I might be completely wasting your time.'

But Patrick was still not at home, at the rectory or answering his mobile, the latter being completely against our personal set of rules. I even contacted Greenway and he had not heard from him either.

Leaving suburban areas behind I drove at a steady pace while Carrick acted as lookout. It proved that there were no lay-bys until we dropped down into the dip before Dunkerton Hill. We stopped and spoke to an elderly couple eating sandwiches in their Ford and a lorry driver frowning at a Page 3 girl but neither had seen anyone answering Patrick's description.

'So d'you reckon he's gone off on his own to get hold of Hulton?' Carrick asked as we got back in the car.

I had forgotten that James knew about this. 'He did rather agree to stick by what Greenway wanted him to do,' was all I could say.

'Try the rural route,' Carrick suggested.

This entailed going back the way we had come for a short distance and then turning right. The lanes here were narrow with sharp bends, wending through unkempt woodland at the bottom of a steep-sided valley but not that much of a tight squeeze to necessitate passing places. There was hardly any traffic so it was possible to drive slowly. One needed to: there were any number of little tracks, driveways and entrances to fields, some with the gates wide open. We stopped and investigated a few of these on foot but found nothing.

Then, on a bend about a quarter of a mile from a junction of lanes where the left hand turning would take us to the village I pulled up sharply.

'What have you seen?' Carrick said.

I was looking at the tracks made by a set of wide tyres that appeared to have carried straight on at the bend and headed off into the woodland, here little more than connecting thickets. The ground was wet, the tyre tracks quite deep and saplings and bushes had been crushed into them.

We got out of the car and hurried, following the swathe bulldozed through the greenery and very quickly came to the cause of it, the Range Rover. It had come to rest against a large oak, seemingly gently with no visible damage to either. For some reason I assimilated this irrelevant latter information while yanking open the front passenger door, the driver's side being immersed in vegetation.

Patrick was slumped behind the wheel, his forehead resting on the top of it. I scrambled in – the car was tilted away from me – and undid his seat belt before leaning over to switch off the ignition. As I did so I heard something small fall into the footwell and automatically glanced down. It was his mobile phone, which he must have been holding in his right hand.

Carrick was already calling an ambulance, swore when he could get no signal and ran back to the car. Trying to find Patrick's pulse I heard the crash of gears as the vehicle was turned and then it roared away back in the direction of the main road.

Patrick groaned and with a lot of my assistance sat up, his head lolling against the rest.

'I'm here,' I whispered. 'What the hell's wrong with you?'

He tried to say something and then appeared to lapse into unconsciousness. He looked, as he had recently, terribly pale but his pulse seemed fairly normal, though fast: this was not a heart attack. Always aware that our names are still on the hit lists of several terrorist organizations I examined him as well as I could for bullet wounds but there was nothing, not even a scratch. The fact that the air bag had not inflated proved that the car had, indeed, come to a very gentle halt.

There was little I could do but hold his hand – was there

the smallest responding grip, or just my imagination? – until help came.

A paramedic was with us very quickly, the ambulance following shortly, and he agreed with my conclusion that there was no obvious cardiac problem. The patient was given oxygen and, after some violence to the blocking greenery, was unloaded from the vehicle and, quite unresponsive now, carried away leaving Carrick and me alone in the bruised glade.

'You needn't have stayed here,' Carrick said, still a little out of breath after his having dealt with the tree, the remark perhaps a veiled admonishment for my not having accompanied Patrick.

Fear for the life of the man I love gnawing like rats at my insides I nevertheless said, 'I know it sounds pompous but our personal rules of engagement state that when either partner is out of action but under professional medical care the one remaining should deal with other responsibilities *first*. There's absolutely no reason to leave you here with two vehicles, neither of which belong to you, when you desperately need to get back to work. I must tell Michael Greenway what's happened and can hardly keep it from Patrick's parents. It would be better if I told John and Elspeth personally.'

He said, 'Are you happy then with my decision that this is not a crime scene and the 4 x 4 should be moved immediately?'

'Absolutely.'

I got in the Range Rover, retrieving Patrick's phone from the floor as I did so. I switched it on: nothing. Either the battery was flat or it had failed. I thought the car might have done so too but it started first time and reversed from its prison easily – they are, after all, designed for rural adventures – and I carefully backed up to the lane. Carrick leading, we then drove the mile or so to Hinton Littlemoor. I made a point of testing the brakes and steering; nothing seemed to be amiss.

Just outside the village there is a bridge where the old Somerset and Dorset railway line goes over the road. There was some distance between John's car and mine by this time as it does not do to follow too closely in the event of the person in front meeting a bus or some other large vehicle and having to reverse to somewhere wider. Picturing, agonizingly, a still figure on an A and E examination table all I saw was a sudden movement above the parapet of the bridge ahead of me, something drop-ping and then the blaze of brake lights.

I too came to a dead stop and dashed to the car. The windscreen had been smashed by a rock that had landed partly on the bonnet, denting it, and then bizarrely, bounced off and fetched up on the front passenger seat. James Carrick was plastered in broken glass, frozen with shock. My opening his door roused him into action and he tore past me, leapt over a fence and went up the embankment on to the one-time railway line like a terrier after a rat, leaving a silvery trail of bits of glass. I saw him go across the bridge and then his foot-steps pounded off along the track bed into the distance.

Despite everything the thought tripped lightly through my mind: never really upset a Scotsman who plays winger at rugby.

He came back with his man; a portly, balding, blustering and red in the face – although the latter might have been from the exertion – individual whom he kept a firm hold of as they slithered down the embankment and hefted in one, sack of spuds style, over the fence.

'I'll have you know I'm chairman of the PCC,' shouted the man furiously, brushing himself off. 'I saw the youth who threw the stone and gave chase. How dare you imagine for one moment that I'm responsible!'

'Then why didn't you stop when I called for you to do so?' Carrick said impassively, not out of breath at all on this occasion. '*And* refuse to give me your name.'

'Go to hell!'

'His name's Frank Crosby,' I said.

Mr Crosby then found himself arrested on suspicion of attempted murder. Yes, Carrick was that mad.

TWELVE

I had expected bad news but it was still a shock to find that Patrick was in intensive care. This did not prove to be as ghastly as the information suggested for he was breathing unaided and was only, I was told, lightly sedated. There had been blood and other tests, the first results of which were expected at any time, but so far they did not have a clue what was wrong with him. I explained what had happened to him recently and an immediate move was made to send for his records. Being his next of kin I was permitted a short visit.

His colour was no better than when I had last seen him and he was lying there, eyes closed, on some kind of chemically induced cloud ten wired up to any amount of electronic hardware that beeped quietly. My arrival elicited no immediate response so, having drawn up a chair, I sat quietly for a couple of minutes. Then, opening my bag, I found the small bottle of my favourite perfume that I always carry with me and, spraying a little on a wrist, wafted it under his nose.

'Ingrid, why am I lying flat on my back in the car?' he asked, his voice slurred.

'You aren't,' I told him. 'You're in Bath's Royal United hospital.'

'Shit,' he whispered, eyes still closed. 'Did I prang it then?'

'No, you seem to have fallen asleep at the wheel and it trundled off into a wood and stopped when it got to a tree.'

'Any damage?'

'A few green smears and one small dent in a wing. You must have braked.'

'So when do I get out of here?'

'When they find out why you fell asleep at the wheel.'

'I could do with sleeping for a month.'

I leaned over and kissed him chastely on a cheek. 'Then do. I'll come back and see you later.'

'Can't I have a better kiss than that?'

'No, go to sleep.'

*   *   *

By now it was late afternoon. I rang Michael Greenway to tell him the latest news and of course he could do nothing other than express sympathy, offer his support and ask to be kept abreast of developments. I wondered if he was experiencing quiet relief that he did not have to worry for a while that a member of his team would act alone against orders.

Trying to behave in a rational manner while a whole range of medical conditions: liver failure, damaged kidneys, brain malfunction, brought on by the drugs Patrick had been administered with raged through my imagination – you suffer if you write – I returned to the rectory. Other than to make sure he was all right I had not pestered James Carrick, leaving him to question his suspect. He had reported that broken windscreen glass could get in some truly amazing places and that Frank Crosby was denying everything. He went on to request if I would ask Patrick's father if he normally drove along that road at that particular time of day.

'Well, yes,' John answered. 'If my dear wife had not nagged me into resting today I would have made my weekly afternoon visit to the hospice. I suppose I usually return at around three thirty. And you say that James was driving my car and that someone's been arrested for throwing a stone through the windscreen. How dreadful! Am I allowed to know who it is?'

I decided that I could don my SOCA hat and said, 'Have you had a real argument with anyone on the PCC lately?'

'On the PCC! Good heavens! No, at least, only concerning my strong stance against these stupid ceremonies that people have been holding. I was told by a couple of members that such things were a sign of the times, that by railing against them I was being perceived as old-fashioned and out of touch and was thus bringing the church into disrepute. Everyone's entitled to their opinion of course, but—'

Elspeth broke in with, 'But who, John? Who? That's what James wants to know.'

'The Crosbys. But they tend to disagree with me about almost everything.'

Elspeth snorted. 'Has it occurred to you that they themselves might be involved?'

'No, of course not!' the priest exclaimed. 'They're devout Christians and work very hard for the church.'

'It would *appear*,' I said, 'That it was Frank Crosby who

dropped the stone – no, it was a rock actually – when your car went underneath the bridge on the outskirts of the village.'

Understandably, John found this very hard to believe but was much more concerned right now about his son and went away, shaking his head, to phone the number I had given him to find out if he could visit Patrick. A few minutes later he put his head around the door.

'A doctor would like to speak to you, Ingrid.'

It was the one I had seen earlier.

'I think your husband's problem is best described to a layman – and I hope you don't mind being referred to like that, Mrs Gillard – as delayed toxic shock caused initially by the drugs illegally administered to him in London. I have to admit that there's a little professional disagreement between me and a colleague at the Nightingale Clinic about what's going on but it's clear that he's completely exhausted by the condition, and also I guess by overwork, and will require bed rest for at least a week together with medication followed by three months convalescence.'

'But no lasting damage though?' I enquired.

He hesitated for a few heart-stopping moments before replying. 'No, there shouldn't be. There's slight liver damage but as I'm sure you're aware the organ is capable of repairing itself and Patrick is otherwise a fit and healthy man. I see no real problems. But on no account must he drink alcohol during the three months rest, and only then after I've given him the all-clear.'

I thanked him, asked when the patient could come home and was told in two or three days' time, probably, as they still wanted to monitor him.

I went back into Elspeth and John's living room.

'Well?' they said in unison.

I said, 'How am I going to keep him in bed for a week, at home for three months and right away from whisky?'

'Easy,' said Elspeth. 'You can't move into the main house yet as the decorators still haven't finished and the place is freezing cold so bring him here and *I'll* wave the big stick. John, you'll have to give up drinking too, otherwise it wouldn't be fair.'

Leaving a little later, I was passing what I still could not regard as my own front door on my way to the car when I had a strange recollection. When Mrs Crosby had come to tell me, just before noon, that the church was still locked on the occasion of the discovery of Melvyn Blanche's body in the vestry I had been in the vicinity of the annex and heard her footsteps approaching on gravel.

I returned to the rear of the house and to the courtyard that will one day be partly given over to a conservatory. The quite short distance entailed walking on flagstones, the only gravel being on the drive itself at the front and the garden paths at the rear. She then, had not come around the side of the house at all but through the wide archway in the far side of the courtyard from the garden.

Why had she come that way? Had she, with or without her husband, just thrown away the murder weapon in the rectory garden? According to the pathologist, Blanche had been killed between ten and eleven. This did not mean, however, that the killer had necessarily disposed of the hammer straight away.

By now it was almost dark. I needed to check the state of affairs at home but was turning right at the end of the rectory drive when I suddenly remembered Barbara Blanche and what she had told me. If she had been speaking the truth and knew the identities of those involved in black magic rites I ought to have another attempt at getting her to reveal who it was, ask her outright if it was the Crosbys. With a heavy heart I drove in the opposite direction.

I parked at the end of the Blanches' drive, which was narrow, overgrown and, oddly, had nowhere to turn, left the sidelights on and went on foot. Blanche might have hated other people's trees but he certainly had borne no ill will against those on his own ground; the whole place was like a jungle, branches seemingly brushing the windows. I remembered from my daylight visit that the whole outside area looked neglected so he must have hated gardening. Perhaps that was it, I mused: jealousy of his neighbour's love of her little wood had been the reason for him trying to bully her into cutting them down. Everything that people partook in or enjoyed had to be controlled. By him.

Regretting having left the torch in the car and in receipt of one slap on the head from wet leaves already I walked slowly and carefully, eyes trying to pierce the gloom, not wishing to fall down a hole and thus become the Third Riveting Event of the Day.

Up ahead of me there was a sudden thumping noise followed

by a muffled shriek. More thumping, nearer, another shriek, farther away. I stopped to listen and half a minute or so later became aware that someone was hurrying down the drive towards me. They were still some distance away but this was closing rapidly; a woman by the sound of the light scurrying footsteps, the pace of someone no longer young enough to run.

She was almost upon me when I politely said, 'Good evening.'

'How dare you give me a fright like that!' shouted a voice I recognized.

'So it was you banging on Barbara Blanche's windows.'

'Get out of my way!' yelled Mrs Crosby, her voice shaky with the jitters.

'Do you know that your husband's under arrest for attempted murder?'

'Of course I do! More police bungling and I assure you we intend to sue. You're the woman with that imitation policeman, aren't you? The rector's daughter-in-law. Well, you don't impress me, Miss Hoity-Toity, and you can—'

I cut in with, 'I do actually have the powers to arrest you for antisocial behaviour. So, just to make sure that a mistake hasn't been made shall we go and ask Mrs Blanche if there are grounds for a case against you?'

In the dark I got the impression that she drew herself up to her modest height. I was quite expecting her to lash out at me.

'No. I called round on church business. But she's watching a film on the TV with the sound turned up and didn't hear the doorbell.'

'But the banging noises were outside. You were hitting the windows with your fists,' I pointed out.

'So I got sick of waiting!'

The woman then gave me a violent push, which I had been ready for, but I still ended up by stumbling backwards, whacking the back of my head on a low branch. By the time I had regained my balance she had gone. No matter, everyone knew where she lived.

I rang the doorbell, not expecting in the circumstances for there to be any response. There was not so I pushed open the letter box and called through it.

'Mrs Blanche, it's Ingrid Langley. Please open the door. The person who was banging on your windows has gone.'

After a pause, a light came on in the porch and the door

was opened, but on a safety chain. A pair of frightened eyes looked at me through the gap.

'She's gone,' I assured her. 'I know who it was. May we talk?'

'Oh, all right,' she said miserably.

Sagging shoulders, a white face, a woman on the verge of tears told it all. I followed her into the living room where she slumped into a chair and did, indeed, burst into tears. A cup of hot, sweet tea later Barbara Blanche seemed ready to talk about it.

'Please answer yes or no,' I requested. 'Is it the Crosbys who are behind unsavoury things going on round here?'

'Yes, but that's only what I've been told,' was the mumbled reply. 'I found a note written by Melvyn when I was sorting through the paperwork. He'd left it all tidy you know, all ready if anything happened to him. His will, the insurances, everything.'

Here her voice cracked and she cried again. Me, I was calling myself all kinds of names, like bitch, for example, for prejudging and despising her just because nearly everyone else did.

'I'm sorry I've been so unhelpful up until now,' Barbara Blanche gulped. 'Felicity can be a bit unpleasant and had rather brainwashed me into not wanting to talk to the police any more. But I didn't lie to you. I really had no idea Melvyn knew what was going on. I don't know if he spoke to anyone about it or tackled them face to face. I can imagine him doing it, he was like that.'

'What did the note actually say?' I asked.

'I'll show it to you.'

The big, bold handwriting executed in a fountain pen was right to the point:

> *Barbara, my dear, if I die in suspicious circumstances then I want you to show this note to the police. There are rotten practices in this village and I am pretty sure the Crosbys are behind them. I hope you never have to read this.*
>
> *All my love*
> *Melvyn*

'The window banging started before I found the note,'
Mrs Blanche said. 'And I was so scared by that time I didn't
dare do anything. As it is I can't stay in this house any longer,
not now I've shown that to you, nor in this wretched village.'

'May I give this to Detective Chief Inspector James
Carrick?'

'I suppose you'll have to now.'

'Is there somewhere you could stay for a few days? With
your sister, for example?'

She pulled a face. 'No, we've fallen out, but I have an old
friend who lives in Norton St Philip.'

'I'll take you there if you can arrange it.'

It was after eleven that night when I got home, having
called, guiltily, to see James Carrick at home to give him the
latest information. I had also been to the hospital to sit by
the side of a perfectly sleeping husband, quite unsedated
by this time apparently and no longer under such close observation. He had not even roused when given a much better
kiss this time.

I heated up a carton of soup for my dinner and then fell
into bed.

'Blanche wouldn't have been killed on account of just booze
money,' James Carrick had said the previous evening.
'Although if he knew about the goings-on and was about to
expose those he knew were involved that might have been an
incentive to murder. Crosby's still denying chucking that rock
through the windscreen of the car. That was not vandalism
but an attack on John Gillard which has to connect, in my
view, with the rector's stand against local black magic activities. I can't see how Crosby isn't involved in it but proving it
is going to be very difficult unless people start talking.'

'What about his wife?' I had asked.

'She's as good as admitted to you to banging on
Mrs Blanche's windows, tonight at any rate, but I can't really
pull her in on account of that alone. But it would suggest that
Blanche had spoken to *someone* of his suspicions about the
Crosbys and it had got back to them. I mean, the police have
been talking to just about everyone in the village so why pick
on her?'

'No, they must have known Blanche was on to them,'

Carrick's wife, Joanna, had offered. 'And I think, like you, James, that there's much more at stake here than reputations and a few pounds to leave people's pets alone. It has to be something like high-yielding blackmail.'

'Is she vicious enough to do anything else now?' James had mused aloud, not speaking to anyone in particular.

This was open to question but at least the victim's widow was out of immediate harm's way.

It was at six thirty the next morning as I made myself some tea, that I remembered the name Huggins. Huggins, the boy Clem in Matthew's class at school, who had bragged to him that his father was a warlock and who lived in Southdown St Peter.

'Which one do you want?' said the DCI two and a half hours later – it had seemed reasonable to give him time to hit his office. 'There's Darrel: grievous bodily harm and taking away cars without their owner's consent; Shane: attempted murder and affray; and Carlton: demanding money with menaces. They're brothers and their old man died when the getaway car he was driving through a red light at seventy in a thirty limit hit a mobile crane and reduced him to mince and tatties.'

'The last name sounds promising,' I said. 'Does that one have a son by the name of Clem?'

The distinct sound of the tapping of computer keys came over the line and then Carrick said, 'Three sons – Clem, who's the youngest, and Reilly and Ricky. The older two are already in trouble.'

I told him what Matthew had said and finished by asking, 'Can I have the address?'

'No, you damned well can't, they're a dangerous bunch. Even his common-law wife has form for assault and being drunk and disorderly. And if he's calling himself a warlock it's only because there's money in it.'

'According to Clem his father attends satanic meetings here in Hinton Littlemoor.' A little irritated by James's brusque manner – the all-powerful CID boss receiving a report from minion number four, I added, 'This is SOCA giving you a lead here, James.'

'Thank you, I'll follow it up. I could do with getting a warrant and giving the house a good going-over for stolen property as I've a lead there too. I actually came across a local bloke locked in a cupboard there once who they were holding to ransom but as he was wanted for murder his family hadn't reported him missing.'

I made a mental note to impress on Matthew that he must not, on any account, go within a mile of the place.

'John was roughed up by two youths who might have got on the local bus,' I recollected. 'He landed a couple of wallops on them with his stick so you might look out for unemployable yobbos wearing large bruises.'

I suppose I had been working to try to keep Patrick's promise to his father and it seemed there might be hope of some progress. Now, I had little choice but to leave James Carrick to handle everything and pray that Patrick would not fret, or worse, be driven to defy both medical and Greenway's instructions.

I need not have worried, not at present anyway. But I almost wished the reverse was true for when he was delivered to the rectory, in an ambulance, I was appalled to see that he was so weak he could hardly walk having, typically, refused point blank to be conveyed indoors in a wheelchair.

THIRTEEN

Greenway looked surprised to see me, to be expected really as I had not told him I was coming. But when I just sat there, like a dummy, and said nothing, not realizing at the time that I was as white as the blank page of the jotter pad before him and then, finally, burst into a storm of tears, his emotions were lost to me. I became aware of a strong arm around my shoulders and then a man-sized tissue under my nose. This was followed, when I had calmed down a little, by a large mug of coffee and a biscuit brought in by his secretary.

'He's that bad?' Greenway asked quietly as the door closed behind her, still sitting by my side on the large squashy sofa.

'Not really,' I whispered.

'I expect you know that he rang me the day before yesterday when he got home.'

'Yes.'

'He did mention some liver damage but the docs don't reckon it's likely to cause any lasting problems. I am aware that he was deliberately being upbeat – his voice was quite weak. D'you reckon he'll stick by what the medics are telling him to do?' Greenway quickly added, 'I'm enquiring from the angle of his own safety here, not any of my operational ones.'

'He will, mostly because right now he's under the strict eye of his mother. But when he starts to feel stronger . . .' I shrugged.

'When he feels stronger I shall get him on board in some way – hoping meanwhile that we'll either nab this bastard or someone'll come up with real evidence of what happened that morning when all those people were finished off.'

'That's why I'm here,' I told him. 'To be on board in some way.'

Greenway surveyed me closely and I noticed for the first time that his eyes, like mine, were green.

'Surely that'll be more likely to make Patrick move heaven and earth to be here instead of you.'

'No. I shall tell him that, from your point of view, I'm merely here to give you the benefit of my intuition and so I can relate any progress to him. If I say that I'm also acting as a mole, for *his* benefit, feeding him snippets of intelligence, not necessarily with your permission, he'll go along with it. The man knows he's as weak as water right now and can do little. He's not stupid.'

The Commander nodded slowly and thoughtfully. 'I welcome your presence on the team but—'

'I'm not to get involved with anything dangerous,' I finished for him.

'You don't have your normal minder with you,' he pointed out.

Privately, I had to concede the truth of this, even though Patrick and I tend to mind for each other. I said, 'Have you verified the report of the Met surveillance man being taken ill, having been, due to a mistake, working on his own and no one turning up to relieve him the next morning, the morning that everything happened?'

'No, I haven't.' Greenway frowned. 'Put like that it's three things going wrong in the same place in quick succession, isn't it?'

'And the neighbours.'

'Neighbours?'

'Patrick said that Friday nights were open house and neighbours wandered in and out. Who *are* the neighbours? Could any of them not have been neighbours at all and because everyone was plastered, doped, you name it, someone wasn't spotted as a member of a rival gang or an old enemy?'

Greenway shot to his feet. 'That's another good point. I'll get someone on to it now.' He headed for the door. 'God, we don't even know *how* many people were in the house.' And then, from somewhere down the corridor, 'Please answer my phone if it rings.'

It did.

'Commander Greenway's very temporary PA,' I said.

'What did he say?' enquired a well-remembered voice.

'That you're to stay in bed and do as your mother tells you.' A sigh.

'No, all right, he didn't say that. It's fine for me to be on

the team and make intelligent suggestions. He's just shot off
to get someone to check on Pangborne's neighbours and follow
up that business of the man who was watching the house but
left on his own and taken ill. I'll get straight back to you if
I sniff out anything. What are you doing?'

'Sitting up in bed doing the *Telegraph* crozzy. Mother's
arranged it so they eat their dinner in here with me. I've told
Dad it doesn't bother me if he has a tot as long as he doesn't
breathe all over me afterwards. Oh, and the two older kids
come straight over here after school – the bus stops by the
church – and have their tea in here with me. I'm worried about
the extra work for Elspeth really.'

'I'm sure she's revelling in it,' I said. 'But I can come home
at weekends if there's nothing doing here and help.'

'I'd like that. But I'm very boring, I tend to sleep most of
the time.'

Having, reluctantly, rung off – there was really nothing else
to say – I found myself staring at the screen of Greenway's
iMac. It was switched on and very quietly humming away,
the screen saver rather mesmerizing brightly coloured swirls
of light. Heart thumping, I touched the space bar to bring it
back to life and was rewarded by a mass of crime statistics.
Hoping that this meant I was viewing a restricted access Crime
Records Bureau website I tapped in the name Jethro Hulton.
Simply not daring to print the facts that followed I tried to
remember as much as possible – there were also several
mugshots of him bearded and clean-shaven – and then quickly
returned to the previous page and put the machine 'back to
sleep'. With not a moment to spare.

'Patrick's just rung,' I reported to explain my presence at
his desk.

'Is he coping?' Greenway enquired, mind obviously mostly
on work.

'Seems to be. Even if he doesn't actually stay in bed for a
week he'll only be pottering into his parents' living room for
a change of scenery.'

He gazed at me with a small frown creasing his brow.

'You don't know what to do with me, do you?' I said.

'You could come and meet the team.'

He had obviously forgotten that I already had, with Patrick.
On my own they would no doubt regard me as a passenger,

be incredibly polite but tell me nothing interesting. I said, 'I'd love to but first I'd like to have another look at the crime scene. I tend to get most of my good ideas by tacking the facts of the case on to what I can see and hear.'

If he thought this a bit off the wall he showed no sign of it. 'Of course. There's no need to get Rundle involved this time as I've managed to get hold of a set of keys to the place. And Ingrid . . .'

'Don't go knocking on the front doors of any big-time crooks?'

He gave me the keys, together with a big smile.

As Patrick had told us, Hulton had been born in 1970, was five feet nine inches in height, thickset in build, had brown eyes, a swarthy complexion, was usually heavily bearded and known to grow his hair long. In his youth he had served three years of a life sentence for murder in Mexico but had been broken out of a prison van taking him to another jail by accomplices and fled to Europe. The man was involved in all kinds of rackets but getting charges to stick was difficult due to threats to witnesses. My eyes had skipped this old news on the computer screen, together with the information that the man had been seen in a nightclub in Acton and followed to Chiswick tube station where he had been lost, which I also already knew. My good memory had then recorded that the nightclub was called The Last Gasp and there had been a subsequent sighting of him in a pub, The Cricketers, in Muswell Hill.

Muswell Hill? The scene of the murders.

So was this man a clever professional criminal who ran rings around the police or was Patrick's opinion correct and he was merely a stupid grown-up yob who had been sheltering in the organization of a clever woman? Given this new information I tended to agree with Patrick, unless of course, the man seen was someone else entirely.

I took myself off to Muswell Hill.

Nothing seemed to have changed in the place since my last visit except now there was no fire filling the sky with black smoke. Otherwise the clouds were still grey and the rain, sleety this time, bucketed down. After I had parked, luckily finding a space close by, I accessed the secure cubby box in the Range Rover – one has to enter a code number on a tiny key pad – removed the Smith and Wesson that Patrick has never quite got round to returning to MI5 that was concealed there and put it in my bag. If Hulton had been spotted nearby I was not taking any chances. Perhaps Greenway had not seen the latest intelligence update; if he had he might not have allowed me to revisit the crime scene alone.

First of all I wanted to retrace, as far as was practically possible, Patrick's journeys that morning of the killings and the previous night. So, before I went indoors I would walk to where his digs had been and then back. The exact time when he had actually set off from the house in Park Road to go home would probably never be known but obviously it would have been after dark so questioning people I met now was not likely to be rewarded with any valuable information.

I huddled deeper into my Dartmoor anorak against the wet and cold and set off, trying to imagine what it must have been like for someone who had probably had his drink spiked. He had said he had fixed himself an orange juice so could hardly have been drunk, a bad professional lapse anyway and not one he would have made.

It was a ten- to fifteen-minute walk, I was already aware; a second turning left from the house into a road that curved until it ran roughly parallel to the first and then one bore right where it split, carried on for another quarter of a mile or so and then the house with the digs was situated down a side street off to the left with a shop on the corner. It was the usual newsagents cum sweet shop and tobacconists, I saw when I went in, with a section devoted to groceries, mostly Asian. I picked up a few mammoth heads of garlic and went to pay.

'Are you open during the night?' I asked the venerable Indian man behind the counter.

'On Fridays and Saturdays only,' he informed me. 'People run out of food for their parties.'

'So you close at . . . ?'

'When I get fed up with them,' he said with a tired smile. 'Perhaps at around three.'

'Do you remember the night before all those people were killed in the house opposite the park?'

'Yes, truly. The fridge went bang and my young nephew

Rakshee hit his head on a shelf in his fright and almost knocked himself out. Indeed, he did knock himself out for a moment and I was just about to ring 999 when he woke up and begged me not to send him to hospital in case they killed him with MRSA. The boy is fine now.'

'What time was this?'

'At just after twenty minutes past midnight. All the lights went out, you see, and I remember looking at the clock just before it happened.'

'I'm trying to trace a person's movements that night who came from the house where the murders took place and walked to where he was living. Did you see anyone or did anyone come in the shop who you thought might have been drunk?'

'All the time,' he answered with a big smile.

'No, please think. It's really important.'

He gave me a quizzical look. 'Are you from the police?'

I showed him my SOCA ID card.

'Not in the shop, not before the fuses went,' the man replied after due thought. After that . . .' He shook his head. 'Until my brother fixed the electric, we could see nothing. My fear was that bad youths would run in and steal so I stood by the door with a big, heavy torch. There were a few people around but . . .' A shrug.

'What about the next morning? Did you see anyone then who was behaving strangely?'

'A man?'

'Yes, a man.'

'I saw a man . . . probably at a little before ten. He was dancing. But not happy dancing. Dancing in pain. A junkie, I thought.'

'What did he look like?'

'He was white, tall, a slim man. Not seeming to be the type of person to do that normally. I was cleaning the shop front and went to him. But he did not see me, in a different world, you understand, and upset. Then he said something but I could hardly hear him.'

'Can you recollect any of it?'

'It was something like "Hutton's raving mad". He said it over and over again. It made no sense to me. Len Hutton's dead, isn't he?'

'Could he have said Hulton?'

'Perhaps.'

'Is there anything else you can remember about him?'

'No, he went off, still dancing. But in a hurry, you understand. Two steps forward, one step back.'

'Which way?'

He indicated the way I had just come. I made a note of his name, having to ask him to spell it, thanked him and left.

Dancing in pain. Tears pricked my eyes.

There was nothing to see outside the house where Patrick had had the bedsit so I turned and made my way back trying to replicate the mindset of someone I knew so well and see as he had seen. He had been drugged, he was hallucinating, he was armed, he was focused on rescuing the child. What did he do?

The rain had eased off a little when I got back to the house. All exterior signs of what had taken place here had been removed; no seals on the front door, no incident tape. I let myself in, quietly, and then closed the door securely behind me, standing still for a moment. There was complete silence and the smell of stale blood had coarsened into that of putrefaction. It caught at my throat and I retched.

Another smell, no, a scent, a perfume, something utterly alien to this place somehow reached me, possibly borne on a faint draught coming down the hall from the rear of the house. I took the gun from my bag, placed the latter on the floor and followed my nose towards the kitchen, moving as silently as possible, finally diving to one side and through the door, the weapon two-handed just the way I had been taught.

'Good morning,' said Richard Daws, one-time head of D12, fourteenth Earl of Hartwood, tall, steel-blue eyes, faded fair hair damp from the rain, back leaning against the worktop, arms crossed, not remotely alarmed.

I lowered the gun, a bit lost for words.

'I opened the window,' he said. 'You must have heard me.'

'No, it was your Ralph Lauren aftershave,' I told him. 'Never smell of anything if you want to stay undetected. You should know that.'

We both laughed and then he said, 'Mike told me you were on your way here so I thought it a good idea to catch up on all the news.'

I was not fooled by this; the man probably knew what colour

lipstick I had on and the size of clothes I wore. I went back into the hall to retrieve my bag and returned the gun to it. Most of my bags smell of gun oil.

'So what do you think happened here?' he asked when we were both standing in the room where the murders had taken place.

'If you mean who killed these people I don't know,' I said. 'Otherwise my view is that what occurred is the same as the account that Patrick has given minus the bits he can't remember. I've just spoken to someone in a shop near here who saw a man who answers Patrick's description making his way, with difficulty, in this direction just before ten on the morning of the murders. That would tie in with the time I spoke to him in his digs when he'd just come round and was throwing up. The missing bit is the period of time from when the child was shot in his arms until he was found in the access lane at the end of the garden.'

'With his gun in his hand, the weapon having been used to kill several people.'

'Right,' I acknowledged evenly. 'The Glock had been wiped of fingerprints except for one clear set of his own. Which rather destroys any theory that he'd used it as he'd hardly wipe it clean and then pick it up again.'

'Unless he was forced to for some reason. Unless he simply didn't know what he was doing. Unless someone overpowered him at that point and then left him, unconscious, out the back.'

'But it was still Patrick's gun that was the murder weapon. He can't have been too gaga not to have known that that fact would incriminate him so why go to the bother of wiping his prints off it? And, for God's sake, if he really was away with the birds would he have been able to shoot so many people so accurately?'

'You don't think he did it? Not in your heart of hearts, ignoring all personal feelings?'

'No. He'd have easily, *easily* shot Hulton after what he told him he was going to do with Leanne. But not the others.'

'No, nor do I,' said Daws after a short silence. 'The problem is I'm not too sure why I think that, but nevertheless, I do. But I have to say that if the cleaner had whispered to him that Hulton was in the house, as Patrick insists she did, then I would have gone after the man first and saved the child afterwards.'

'Leanne came out of her room though, didn't she?'

'Yes, and we can't pretend that Patrick's judgement wasn't affected by what had happened to him. The big question is, by how much? And please bear in mind that at the moment we can't discount the version of events given to us by the cleaning woman.'

A feeling of despair and helplessness washed over me.

'I'm prepared to give Patrick every support,' Daws went on. 'But there has to be answers to several very important questions before we can move on from this – and, it goes without saying, the real killer must be found.' He took a card from the top pocket of his suit jacket and held it out for me to take. 'I have a new contact number. For emergencies only, you understand. Now, can I give you a lift anywhere or do you have your own transport?'

I wondered why he had come here for, obviously, Greenway had told him I was on my way. To see if I had any amazing theories or just to offer his physical protection?

This consultant had no theories whatsoever.

I got back in the car, observing Daws being whisked by in a dark-green Jaguar, his own, I knew, and I recognized Jordan, the driver, who also acts as his bodyguard and part-time butler. For some reason seeing him started a chain of thoughts. A chauffeur-driven car, the privileged, royalty, the Queen.

Almost running, I went back to the corner shop.

'Is there a lady round here who takes several corgies for walks?' I asked the surprised to see me again proprietor.

'Oh, yes, that's Ma,' he told me happily. 'We all call her Ma but don't ask me her name. She's always trotting about with her little dogs.' He mimed a woman trotting, holding leads.

'Where does she live?'

He spread his arms expansively. 'Somewhere not too far away. People complain to me that the dogs never stop yapping so perhaps it would be good to follow your ears.' He went on stacking shelves, chuckling to himself.

I then had an amazing piece of luck, spotting a postman coming out of the entrance to a block of flats.

'Ma?' he echoed. 'Yes, I know her. Mrs Goldstein, Flat 4, Albert Villas, Lilac Grove.' He pointed. 'It's down that road off to the right there, third street on the left. Watch out for the dogs, they're killers.'

He was turning away when I registered that he was nearing retirement age and had a large and filthy sticking plaster on one hand. Only just preventing myself from grabbing him by the front of his jacket, I said, 'You were the one who was thrown into a bush by a man on the morning of the murders!'

'I did give a full statement to the police,' he said stiffly, moving to carry on with his round.

'You can tell me about it too,' I declared, shoving my ID under his nose.

'I've a job to do.'

'Either here and now or down at the nearest nick,' I said, not at all sure if I had the authority. Hey, yes, I did.

'It's still not properly healed,' said the postman, going into aggrieved mode and showing me his hand. 'I'd sue him if I knew who he was.'

'It might do if you keep it clean,' I countered. 'And I happen to know that you were shifted out of the way to prevent you from stopping a bullet in the event of a shoot-out. Tell me exactly what happened.'

He slammed the bag of mail he was carrying down on the pavement. 'All right, lady, all right. I was walking along that road, Park Road, when—'

'Time?' I snapped.

'Dunno, exactly. After ten some time. Anyway, I saw that the front door of that particular house was open. Someone was smashing glass. I thought it might be a break-in and people were trashing the place.'

'Did the sound of breaking glass seem to be coming from inside the house or out the back somewhere?'

'It was hard to tell but possibly outside if there was a back door open. So when this man happened along and looked as though he was going in I—'

Again, I interrupted. 'Surely though, what you heard wouldn't have been that suspicious. A door open, the sound of glass breaking. That might merely have been someone having a disaster with some bottles they had been just off to the recycling place with.'

'No, not bottles being *dropped,* smashed one at a time.'

'People do have bad mornings.'

'Well, anyway—'

'No, sorry. There must have been something else. Did you have any post for the house?'

'Yes, I'd gone in and—'

'You went in?'

'Folk don't like their post left in full view on the doormat where people can pinch it.'

'You could have still pushed them through the letter box and they would have been out of sight behind the door. So you went in?'

'And put them on the hall table.'

'What did you see?'

'Nothing. I just came straight out again.'

'Tell me the *truth*!'

The man bit his lip. 'Look . . .'

'This is a murder inquiry!' I bellowed at him.

He gazed around nervously. 'Look, if this gets about . . .'

'It'll get about that I've arrested you if you don't tell me what happened.'

After a protracted silence during which he carried on biting his lip nervously, he said, 'I shall lose my job and I've only got a few months to go so my pension'll probably go out of the window too.'

'I don't think I can help but if it's possible I will,' I told him. 'What happened?'

After another long pause he said, 'I spotted a full bottle of whisky on the floor just inside the room nearest me. I know I shouldn't but I can't afford it any more so I . . .'

'You took it?' I asked when he stopped speaking.

He nodded miserably. 'I picked it up and then saw that there was a load of folk in the room all sprawled about stoned out of their minds. Some of them were even on the floor.'

'Are you sure they were alive?'

'Yes, some of them had their mouths open, snoring. I saw one guy twitch.'

'But couldn't they have been just asleep?'

'No, they were all of a heap, as though they'd just collapsed where they were.'

'How many of them were there?'

'It was difficult to see. There was a woman there too. Six or seven perhaps. I didn't want to stay, just beat it.'

'With the whisky.'

'Yes,' he muttered, shamefaced.

'Then what?'

'I ran straight into this bloke at the front gate. He didn't look too good either.'

'And?'

The postman breathed out gustily. 'Well, I'd been caught red-handed, hadn't I? He wasn't the sort you argue with so when I saw his gaze on the bottle I gave it to him and said I'd just picked it up off the path. He didn't believe me and chucked me in a bush.'

'No, he said you were persistent.'

'All *right*, I told him about the smashing of bottles to distract him from what I'd done.'

'Did you tell him about the people in the front room?'

'No, because I reckoned he was part of the same bash and had popped out to his car or something.'

'What did he do then?'

'Heaved me into the bush.'

'Didn't he *say* anything?'

'Get out of the bloody way . . . no, keep out of the bloody way.'

'There's a big difference in meaning between the two, isn't there?'

'Yes, I suppose there is.'

'And then?'

'Well, I'd badly cut my hand as I'd landed under the bush and when I'd sorted myself out and tried to stop the bleeding with my handkerchief he'd gone.'

'D'you think he went in through the front door?'

'No, I just saw him turning a corner into a side lane when I went back out into the street.'

'He took the bottle of whisky with him then.'

'No, he . . .'

Silence.

'What?' I demanded to know.

'He . . . he'd . . . chucked it into another bush. I'd heard the thump as it hit the ground. So I . . .'

'You took it anyway?'

'Er . . . yes.'

'Was the seal broken?'

'Yes, but only a little drop had been drunk.'

'Have you drunk any of it?'

'No . . . I . . . er . . . couldn't, not after I heard about the . . .'

'Thank God for that! Where do you live?'

'A couple of miles from here.'

'We're going there right now and you'll give it to me. Later, when you've finished work, you're to report to your nearest police station and make a full, revised statement. Is that understood? They'll be expecting you and you'll receive a visit from the police if you don't. All I can do for you is say that you volunteered the information after I'd asked you if you knew where the lady with the dogs lives.'

Half an hour later, having spoken to Greenway, I contacted DCI Rundle and then took the evidence to Wood Green police station.

FOURTEEN

Mrs Goldstein was at home but, seemingly, just about to go 'trotting' with her dogs. Keen canine ears had heard my approach up the stairs and by the time I rang the doorbell the barking had reached such a level that I was surprised she heard it.

'Shuddup!' the short, matronly, silver-haired lady roared at the animals bounding around at her feet. Her bright, dark eyes peered up at me appraisingly. 'You like dogs?'

'They're fine when they're doing something useful,' I said.

'You hear that, Misha?' she said to one of the dogs. And then to me, 'She's never done anything useful in her life except try to eat the postman.' She wheezed with laughter. 'What can I do for you?'

I explained and, again, produced my ID card.

'You'd better come in.'

Thankfully, the Corgis – there were five of them – were sent off to a bed in one corner of the living room and stayed there.

'You want me to remember a man who might have seen me on the morning of the murders? Is he the killer?' Mrs Goldstein said when we had seated ourselves and I had explained the purpose of my visit.

I was a bit disgusted with myself the way it came out so pat. 'We're just trying to eliminate him from our enquiries.' I went on to describe Patrick.

'Yes, I saw him. He was staggering all over the place. I asked him if he was all right – silly of me, as he obviously wasn't, but what the hell else do you say? – and he just smiled at me, rather a lovely smile actually, and said he was a policeman. All I could do was tell him he was doing a splendid job and off he went. He looked as though he knew where he was going so I didn't worry too much about it. Very odd though.'

'Did you go anywhere near Park Road that morning?'

'Oh, I go everywhere, dearie.'

'Please try to remember.'

She stared into space for a few moments, then said, 'No, I think we went round to the shops on the parade for a few bits and bobs. Yes, and to make an appointment at the dentist's – I'd lost a filling and couldn't get through on the phone to them for love nor money – always engaged.'

'Where is your dentist?'

'Over the Halifax Building Society next to the betting shop. He has the whole of the first floor.'

I knew where the parade of shops was – nowhere near the crime scene. I thanked Mrs Goldstein and left. At least another piece of Patrick's account of what had happened had been fitted into the puzzle.

Daws' presence in the house had utterly distracted me from my original errand. I went back and again stood in the hallway, the smell of putrefaction in my nostrils, the silence of this place of death seeming to press on me. I walked the few feet to the entrance to the living room and saw all over again the blood- and brain-streaked walls, the vomit stains, the over-turned furniture. I stood there for quite a long time.

It was clear now from what the postman had said that the people in this room had been drugged in some way, probably from drinking doctored whisky, possibly the reason that someone was out the back smashing the bottles, hoping to destroy any evidence.

The first question I asked myself was had Patrick walked in and shot them all in the head and then smeared the resultant mess on the walls to make it look as though they had been shot while standing up?

No, he had not. For several very good reasons it made no sense.

Had a lunatic bent on revenge for some past grievance or keen to de-clutter his life of people who had become a nuisance murdered the lot and then indulged in a little wall-painting to declare his triumph and show what a clever boy he was?

Yes, he had.

I went closer to the wall and stared at it through half-closed eyes and then backed off a little, carefully avoiding the gaps where the floorboards had been removed, until I was standing in the space in front of the bay window. Even with the use

of a little imagination I could make out nothing that looked
like letters or a word. I put my head on one side to the left
and shut my eyes even more, wondering if whoever it was
had written something and was right-handed, inclining the
writing. Nothing. And then I tilted my head to the right.

HILIK. Sort of.

Concluding that I had given Rundle enough evidence to be
going on with for one day and not even sure that this little
idea might even be classified as such I went back to SOCA's
HQ. Greenway was out and I was shown into the large room,
generally referred to as The Hole, where his team worked.
They were, I knew, drawn from all the organizations that
comprise the agency: the National Crime Squad, the National
Intelligence Service and the investigations divisions of HM
Customs and the Immigration Service.

'Miss Langley,' said a dark-haired man with an acne-scarred
face I knew to be Greenway's second-in-command by the
name of Andrew Bayley. 'How nice to see you.'

I was encouraged to be seated and asked if I would like
coffee. It was actually well after my lunchtime by now so I
refused with a smile.

He didn't know what to do with me either. I helped him
along by giving him the report about my encounter with the
postman and Mrs Goldstein I had hastily produced on a
borrowed computer in an outer office. He read it and then
said, 'This is Mike's operation really but it's interesting and
I'm glad we're beginning to build up a picture of your
husband's movements that morning.'

'And you might,' I said. 'Ask Google about Hilik.'

I spelled it out, adding that I had no idea how it was
pronounced and not adding that it might merely be the product
of a writer's overenthusiastic imagination.

He hit buttons.

'Town in Serbia, population two thousand, three hundred
and forty-nine. There's even a website. Why do you want to
know?'

'Anything crime-wise happened there during the past, say,
twenty-five years?'

He became much more interested.

'There's nothing about *that* on the website,' he reported after
a couple of minutes. 'But as they appear to want to promote

the place as a tourist attraction – it's up in the mountains – that would figure. But I can find out. May I ask what prompted the enquiry?'

I explained and showed him the photographs I had taken of the wall with my mobile. He squinted at the tiny screen and then asked if he could download them on to his computer. To my total embarrassment the memory content included several pictures of a happy but red in the face mother with baby Mark, shortly after he was born, the battery of Patrick's phone having been flat.

'So where's the sprog now?' he queried as though I had left the pram somewhere on the Embankment.

'At home with the nanny, our four other children and closely monitored by his father, not to mention grandparents,' I replied.

Bayley went fetchingly pink and busied himself with the keyboard.

'It's not exactly clear,' I admitted when the pictures of the wall came up on the screen.

'Umm . . . no.' He glanced at me. 'I'll dig into this, especially as we now know for sure that some of those killed originated from the Balkans and had got into this country illegally.'

'Any more news on Hulton?'

He shook his head. 'No.'

'I find it staggering that he was spotted in a pub in Muswell Hill,' I remarked, throwing out a baited line.

I was subjected to a searching stare. 'I wasn't aware that you knew that.'

'It's counterproductive to keep your adviser's consultant in the dark about *anything*,' I said, staring back.

'I'll tell Mike you called in,' Bayley muttered, dropping his gaze.

'I think I'll get myself a bite to eat,' I told him, rising.

'If you're going to the canteen the salmon's good.'

'Thank you.'

I wasn't.

The Cricketers pub was situated at one end of the open ground on the western side of Park Road. Modern in appearance I could nevertheless imagine a time when a tavern had stood on the site and local teams played cricket on the adjacent village green. I went in and there were indeed pictures of such matches on the walls of the bars, faded photographs and a couple of watercolours, together with signed bats, caps and, in a showcase, some tarnished trophies.

That was how the place could be summed up: tarnished. It was also drab, the table I sat at sticky and the man serving behind the bar looked as though a heavy soap and water tax had been imposed upon him. But the place was practically full, they served real ales and everything on the menu was advertised as home-made. It was man-food; the usual assortment of steaks, pies and sausages, not a salad or anything south of Dover in sight.

It was cold and I was famished as it was getting on for two o'clock so I ordered steak and ale pie. I had just done so when, unaccountably, loneliness and misery swept over me. If Patrick were here now he would have that to eat too. We would talk over the case, exchange ideas, plan the next move, in it together. I actually took my phone from my bag to ring him and then put it away again. No, it was selfish to spread unhappiness.

Then it rang.

I stared at it for a moment and then answered it.

'Hi, I have a new mobile. The other one had died. Matthew went into Bath with Dad and bought it for me. Same number. Hope you're in the warm, there's snow forecast.'

'I am, and just about to have a late lunch.' Truly, the man must be telepathic.

'Good. Mother's feeding me up so it's been soup and dumplings. Oh, and the doc popped in to take a routine blood test and said that whatever the specialist says she thinks I ought to get up a few times a day this week and move around gently or I'll stiffen right up. I didn't tell her I already have been.'

I did not remonstrate, asking him instead how he was feeling.

'Still worn out – as though I've just run a marathon. I just seem to sleep all the time.'

I went on to tell him about my morning's work. He seemed impressed.

'You could ask Greenway if they really were Met people doing the surveillance at Park Road. I'm wondering if anything like that is ever farmed out to private firms when it's just a question of watching a house and taking photographs of who goes in and out.'

'I'll do that straight after lunch,' I promised.

'We mentioned weekends earlier. It's Friday tomorrow. Are you coming home?'

'It depends on what turns up.'

'You are working with Greenway's team, aren't you?'

'Of course.'

'I don't want you going off and acting independently.'

'I understand that.'

'You will keep in touch, won't you?' he finished by saying wistfully.

'Of course I will.'

No lies told there then.

While eating my meal I covertly glanced around. Although not for one moment expecting to trip over Jethro Hulton it seemed logical that his having been seen on these premises, or at least someone who closely resembled him had, that there would be an undercover police presence. I amused myself wondering who it might be – the builder's labourer, his clothes white with plaster or cement, the city type reading *The Times,* a man and woman with several bags of shopping? – and if whoever it was would report *my* presence.

As I left I made a play of searching for the ladies' toilet, going into the other bar and having a good look round. The place was far larger than the outside appearance suggested and I had an idea that several tiny rooms at the back where a man was shifting beer kegs, the area otherwise used as a general dumping ground, were actually the original building. As it was the loos were situated half below ground in a grim cellar; damp stone walls, tiny barred windows, like a dank dungeon.

I did ask Rundle Patrick's question when he phoned me a little later with news that the whisky definitely contained barbiturates. This was only a preliminary finding and I gathered that he had given the lab hell until they had made the job a priority. More tests would follow as would those on blood samples taken from the murder victims and, for the present, until he had it in writing, the DCI would not update the case notes.

'No,' the DCI said, in response to my enquiry. 'We don't use private help for that kind of thing. Some of the personnel are retired police officers who want to keep their hand in for various reasons, mostly financial these days, but otherwise it's all strictly in-house.'

'Is the man who was taken ill better now?'

'Yes, fully recovered, thank you'

'Does he know what made him ill?'

'God knows. I haven't asked him. They live on takeaways you know, and apparently the empty house they were in was filthy.'

'Chief Inspector, has it crossed your mind that he might have been deliberately poisoned?'

'Frankly, no.'

'And then there was a mix-up with the rota and all this co-incided with multiple murders at the house he and others were supposed to be watching where it would now appear that the victims were first drugged with doctored whisky.'

'I'm fully confident that it was a dreadful coincidence and that my staff are above reproach,' Rundle said stiffy. He then said that he was very busy and rang off.

Well, I hadn't actually been accusing anyone of anything.

Greenway had on his desk the report I had earlier given to Andrew Bayley. 'It's coming together,' he said, giving it a tap with a chunky forefinger.

I told him about Rundle's call.

'I'm amazed he's telling you things like this. Great news! It means that it's certain now that when Patrick entered the house all those people were unconscious.'

'But we're no nearer to finding out who pulled the trigger,' I pointed out. 'How do I get to talk to the cop who was left on his own and went down with food poisoning? I don't think Rundle's generosity stretches that far.'

'You still think there's a grey area there, don't you?'

'I don't like thundering great coincidences, that's all.'

'No, nor do I. I'll find out who he was.'

'Any news on Hilik?'

'Not yet, but although Andy's got a lot on he's sent emails off to various outfits in Serbia.'

'It's a very long shot.'

'They're something I do like. It's amazing how often they

make a hit.' Greenway stretched his arms above his head. 'Going home for the weekend?'

'You wouldn't say that if it was Patrick sitting here,' I remarked tersely.

'No, but—'

'Incidentally, there's a man who works in the cellar in the Cricketers pub. He's swarthy, thickset and has a beard. It might pay to find out who he really is.'

At which point I felt I had done enough for one day.

The Serbian Embassy is in Belgrave Square. The next morning I spent around an hour in the building assisted by a very helpful young clerk and came away with several pages of paperwork that he had kindly printed off for me. On my way to the tube – parking difficulties and the congestion charge meant that I had left the car in the hotel car park – I kept a good hold on my bag with its precious contents. This time I had left the gun behind as well.

Hilik was notorious, or rather had been. There were even local jokes that something in the water was the cause of it being a bandit factory. My helper, who spoke perfect English, knew quite a bit about the place but was at pains to point out that, these days, things were different. Crunchtime had come around twenty years previously when rival gangs, in effect Mafia-style whole families, had engaged in one last shoot-out. Over thirty people had been killed and the police had arrested most of the survivors. The source of this information even provided a list of the dead.

As this was the Balkans, I reasoned, old feuds would still be simmering below the surface. Like volcanos. Whatever the truth it did appear that I might have a motive for the Park Road murders and duly went to present my findings to Greenway. He was at a meeting so I placed it carefully on top of the stuff in his in tray.

Again, I felt drawn to the crime scene for answers, this time to examine the area to the rear, something I had put off, frankly, because of the teeming rain. This had stopped but the morning was bitterly cold, a strong north wind whipping across the wide open grassed space that fronted the road and finding its way down the access lane at the rear of the gardens with a ferocity that was Arctic.

There would be nothing to see after all this time, I told myself, and it was silly to think that the luck I had had with the postman could continue. I found myself wondering why the Met had not tracked the man down and asked questions. The answer had to be that, as far as Patrick's account of what had happened was concerned, they had hardly believed a word of it.

'So,' I said to myself, standing in the back lane facing up the garden. 'Theory one: someone carried an unconscious Patrick from the first floor of the house and out here where they dumped him down, wiped the murder weapon and placed it in his hand. Why?'

Why indeed? Patrick is six feet two inches tall and weighs around twelve and a half stone. Carrying him with his long legs down the staircase, which was not particularly wide, would not have been easy so if anyone had done that they would have had to be very strong. Hulton was no doubt strong, but why bother?

I walked up the garden path. The whole area was neglected; long grass and assorted rubbish, and any rear boundary hedge or fence had been removed to enable vehicles to pull in on to a makeshift and uneven brick and concrete block parking space. If the murderer intended to blame Patrick for the killings he would hardly have brought him out here with a view to loading him into a car and taking him somewhere.

This was ghastly: I kept coming back to what appeared to be the only answer, that Patrick had shot everyone in a drug-dazed living nightmare, staggered out here and collapsed, having, in his confusion, wiped the weapon before picking it up again.

But what of the person who Patrick had said shot Leanne on the upstairs landing? Another dream? He had, after all, thought he had seen his parents out for a bike ride. But, surely, as with Mrs Goldstein being the Queen, he had merely spotted two ordinary cyclists. OK then, the man on the landing must have existed. This person shot Leanne, having possibly rendered Patrick semi-conscious first, and then went downstairs to kill everyone else.

It occurred to me that my husband may have been trying to escape through the back door after hearing the shots as the others were murdered and having somehow come down the stairs under his own steam. He no longer had his gun, he was in no fit state to do anything, not even to use his knife, the weapon these days strictly for last-ditch self-defence purposes.

'Knife!' I practically shouted. 'Where was it? Where is it now?'

I grabbed my phone.

'Where's your knife?' I blared when a sleepy-sounding voice answered.

'What? Oh, sorry, must have dozed off. What did you say?'

'Your knife,' I repeated. 'The Italian-made silver-hafted throwing knife from which you're never willingly separated. Where *is* it?'

There was a shocked silence and then he started to swear at himself for forgetting about it. 'I don't know,' he finally admitted. 'It had completely gone from my mind.'

'Suppose you factor that in to what you've remembered already and have a think.'

'As I said earlier, it's Friday. Suppose you come home for the weekend and we can talk about it then.'

'Look, I'm standing in the back garden of the house in Park Road. Could you please have a little think now?'

'OK, I'll phone you back in a minute.'

Approximately thirty seconds later my phone rang again.

'I might have thrown it,' Patrick said.

'Thrown it!' I exclaimed.

'It might only be one of the hallucinations. I threw my knife somewhere out in the open. I was being chased by a monster of some kind, an invisible one.'

Hulton, I thought, a monster who had just killed his own daughter.

'Well, I found the Queen,' I told him. 'I'll have a hunt around and then come home. Oh, and by the way, there's a man who works at the Cricketers pub in Muswell Hill who answers Hulton's description.'

'For God's sake stay away from the place then.'

'Yes, all right.'

I knew how far he could throw his knife and how accurate he usually was. There were no trees in the garden but it was surrounded by overgrown hedges that could easily conceal several cannon and a small howitzer, never mind a knife.

Working on the theory that even in extremis he would still not miss any target by a lot I began a search of the whole of the rear of the house, up to a height of about eight feet plus the ground directly beneath. I found nothing, nor were there any fresh chunks out of wooden window or door frames. I spread my search to the vegetation nearby and still failed to find it.

Moving the search area farther down the garden I examined every inch of what had once been a lawn, kicking through the rough grass and praying that I would encounter metal. I found nothing. The tangled borders were virtually impossible to hunt through but I reasoned that if someone had been chasing Patrick down the garden then anything thrown, which presumably missed, would be found somewhere within a few feet of the path, which was slightly to one side of the centre of the garden.

Nothing.

I had been looking for over an hour now and was very cold. Disconsolately going back towards the house I suddenly noticed that a small pane of frosted glass in the window of what looked like a downstairs toilet had a hole in it where one corner had been broken. There were no slivers of that kind of glass beneath it although there were what could have been smashed whisky bottles. I let myself back into the house through the front – I did not have a back door key. Truly, I told myself as I quick-marched to the rear, I shall have nightmares for life if I have to enter this literally bloody place again.

What might have once been a ground floor bathroom was now a dingy utility room: washing machine, tumble-dryer, central heating boiler, and shelving on the wall opposite the window that was crammed with old newspapers, pairs of boots and shoes and sundry other items.

Patrick's knife was buried up to the hilt a couple of inches above the heel of a Wellington boot. I photographed it in situ with my phone and then took it, boot and all, back to SOCA's HQ.

This was still not proof that he was innocent of murder.

FIFTEEN

It was three days later when I descended a flight of steep and slippery with half melted snow steps to the entrance of The Last Gasp nightclub. It had been difficult to locate but I had finally found it in a dimly lit alleyway just off the main shopping street in Acton. At the bottom of the steps I pushed my way through a very stiff to open door that slammed behind me like the jaws of a gin trap. The third obstacle turned out to be an extremely large gentleman with a mouth also like a gin trap who required to see my membership card.

'I'm here to see Terry,' I told him, or rather yelled to make myself heard over the din.

He grimaced and jerked a thumb in the direction of a nearby curtained archway.

It was dim within but for a diminutive spotlit stage upon which, to the deafening racket that some might describe as music, a mostly naked woman writhed her way around a large fluffy red toy snake. My eyes just about succeeded in piercing the gloom and I congratulated myself that I had got it right as far as the rest of the females present were concerned. I can do tart very nicely, something that greatly amuses Patrick. It's mostly a matter of make-up, hair and deportment but a bosom that threatens to escape from confinement helps.

I was here with Greenway's blessing, in a way, and my reply to the doorman-cum-bouncer, an undercover policeman, had been a prearranged password. The stipulation had been that I would provide my own minder, something he had probably thought I would be unlikely to achieve. There were SOCA personnel already watching without, and within, the club, and although the Commander had not actually said that none of them could be spared to watch over a female loose cannon that was just about the truth of it.

I did not really mind: I would merely turn up with one of the best.

Terry Meadows had been Patrick's assistant in our MI5 D12 days and could be relied upon to drop everything, in practice his security consultancy business, and help out the person he still jokingly refers to as 'the governor'. I spotted him almost immediately for he was one of the few men sitting on their own.

'No thanks,' he said as I seated myself, a move that co-incided with someone slaying the hi-fi system, the damsel getting her way with the snake, or whatever, both disappearing to desultory applause. He then did a wonderful double take. 'Ingrid! I didn't recognize you with –' his gaze strayed downwards from my face – 'with . . .'

I helped him out. 'Big boobs? It's temporary and just about the only advantage of getting pregnant. But you know that, you've two children of your own now. How are they?'

His good-natured features split into a big grin. 'Fine, but exhausting.'

'And Dawn?'

'As gorgeous as ever. What can I get you to drink?'

'I'd better have orange juice too,' I replied, eyeing the tumbler that was in front of him. 'Thank you.' I put a hand on his arm. 'It's really good of you to come.'

He asked the question when he returned with my drink. 'So what are we doing here?'

I gave him a short history of events so far, and, professional that he is, he only refrained from closely surveying those assembled once during my account and that was when I told him that Patrick had to convalesce for three months.

'Not a chance!' he said turning to stare at me in surprise. 'He'll be off out as soon as he feels better.'

'He's a little older and wiser now,' I countered.

Terry just smiled. He is younger than Patrick by just over ten years, of strong build and has conker-brown hair. Once upon a time I had almost fancied him and he me – we almost succumbed but not *quite,* ending up by having a very cold shower together instead.

'Jethro Hulton,' Terry mused. 'D'you have any mugshots on you?'

I did, having wrung them out of Greenway.

'He's got the boring kind of face that asks to be played around with, so he does,' Terry concluded, frowning at the three photographs. 'Sometimes a beard, sometimes long hair, sometimes a moustache. Disguise apart, he probably has an ego problem because he's so nondescript.'

'But hairy everywhere else,' I said, realizing that Terry was probably right.

'Hairy?'

'Yes, on his body. Andrea Pangborne liked hairy men.'

'Right, so I'm looking for a woolly mammoth with clothes on.'

'No, I haven't asked you along to find anyone for me. You're just here to ride shotgun for me because Patrick's not around. SOCA rules and regs.'

'That's a real shame. I can feel a nostalgic, old times sort of mood coming on.' Unconsciously, perhaps he rubbed the knuckles of one hand against the palm of the other.

'There are probably more police in here than genuine customers,' I breathed, a little alarmed. This was definitely something he had caught from Patrick; the love of occasional and well-orchestrated mayhem.

I had driven straight to Devon after delivering the boot with the knife in it for forensic examination. Worried and pleased in roughly equal measures upon finding Patrick up and dressed and planning to move into the main part of the house, the decorating having almost been completed, I had said nothing about that until we were temporarily on our own.

'You'll have to negotiate the stairs.'

'No, I'm going to sleep on the sofa. The heating's on in there now so I can keep an eye on things. Besides, I'm under Mum and Dad's feet staying here and I know they feel that having their favourite TV and radio programmes on is intrusive.'

He had not been able to conceal from me that he was still very weak and walking with the aid of one of his father's sticks to steady himself as he was suffering from occasional dizzy spells. His complexion remained unhealthily pallid despite the fact that he was still taking a lot of medication.

'I found your knife,' I had told him, going on to say where it had been.

'Pity I missed the bastard,' was all Patrick had muttered when I had elaborated on my theory.

'Have you remembered any more about it?'

'No.'

It had not been a happy couple of days. Even the two elder

children had been subdued – all we could tell them was that
Patrick was suffering from a virus, an untruth that made me
feel very uncomfortable. But what else could we have said?
I am afraid I had spent a lot of time with Justin, Vicky and
Mark, convincing myself that it was about time their mother
showed up and played with them.

'You're really worried about Patrick, aren't you?' Terry said,
breaking into my thoughts.

'Yes, I am. All I have to go on is that he said his hand
aches for a while after he's fired a handgun and it didn't. Like
a few other people I can't see how he'd have noticed that
when he'd been doped to the eyebrows and possibly knocked
out for a while as well.'

'The man's always skated on very thin ice.'

I looked him right in the eye. 'Do *you* think he did it?'

'No,' Terry immediately replied. 'To use your words: integrity
tends to inhabit the subconscious as well.'

I found that I was smiling reflectively. 'It was actually
Patrick who said that, to Joanna before she and James Carrick
were married and he'd been accused of drink-driving when
his car went through a hedge. It turned out he'd been set
on because he'd witnessed a fight during which a man was
killed and they'd tried to do away with him as well and make
it look like an accident.'

'We three have certainly worked on some weird cases
together,' Terry commented. 'D'you remember when we were
out in Canada staying with a diplomat's family and trying
to prevent some Brit engineers from getting topped and
Patrick and I swapped undercover roles? He was the scummy
gardener and I swanned it indoors as the man from MI5.
Richard Daws blew his top when he found out.'

'Yes, definitely not cricket,' I said, laughing. 'He did all
their winter pruning for them too.'

Other memories crowded into my mind: of Terry's correct
diagnosis of Justin's screams one night when he was a very
tiny baby of being boiling hot in a woollen vest that an over-
anxious new mother had dressed him in; of his calm bravery
in very tight corners but fainting every time medics went near
him with needles. Of his unquestioning loyalty to Patrick and
me, even when the former had given him a bad-tempered
and unwarranted reprimand.

More and more people were arriving, a group that Terry described as a 'sawn-off' jazz band set up shop on the stage, alcohol flowed as though it was being given away. By now it was just after midnight.

'So why were the Bill watching this club in the first place?' Terry said, gazing around disparagingly at the tatty interior that someone had had a go at disguising with a coat of crimson emulsion paint and lighting effects.

'Because, according to Greenway, according to the Drugs Squad, it's a favourite rathole for dealers and those who ought to be detained at Her Majesty's pleasure, but aren't.'

'I'm surprised. They usually soon rumble that the eye of the law's on them and move on.'

Another hour went by and I was on my third orange juice. I began to wonder what the hell we were doing here on the grounds of one doubtful sighting. The jazz band had a rest, the lights dimmed and the female with the snake returned for Round Two, only with rather less on, the girl, that is. I stifled a yawn, wondering if this was the time when customers did their business deals, in the comparative darkness.

The snake was appearing to be getting the upper hand when there was a shout, then the crash of overturned chairs followed by utter pandemonium. Nearly everyone made a dive for the exits, emergency and otherwise, almost falling over one another in their panic. This was compounded when all the remaining lights went out leaving utter darkness but for one or two tiny red gleams that I guessed were the indicator lamps on electrical equipment.

Terry and I got to our feet just as there was an inrush of people carrying powerful flash lamps.

'Police!' someone yelled. 'Stand still! No one move!'

'God help us,' Terry drawled into the ensuing silence. 'It's the good officers of the law.' He dropped back into his seat again adding, 'Who have screwed up yet again.'

Torches were shone right in our faces.

'SOCA,' I said. 'Mr Meadows here is my protection officer.'

'ID?' a deep voice grated.

'You don't imagine that I carry it with me when I'm working undercover, do you?'

Someone put the lights back on to reveal half a dozen police wearing some kind of riot gear *sans* shields plus four or five other people who, like us, had stayed put and were now looking less than enchanted. A man not in uniform strode through his dark-blue clad troupe to the front giving every impression of being in charge.

Speaking quite loudly, but not to him or his underlings, Terry said, 'Questions. Was there a lookout who made sure everyone dodgy, including the staff, got away before this lot had even squeezed themselves through the front door? Yes. Is Jethro Hulton likely ever to show his stupid face in here again? No. Has he ever actually done so or did one of the plods' oppos confuse him with an Estonian delivery driver who had called in to ask the way? Quite possibly. Do we go and chuck these Noddy cops, together with Big Ears here, in the nearest sewage works? Yes.'

And, to a man, those who had been in the club all night moved forward.

The one in charge, who did indeed possess rather large ears, went a little pale, jerked his head in the direction of the exit and the police contingent clomped out.

'I need a beer,' someone said. 'I've been hanging out in this effin' dump for a week. All for bloody nothing now.'

Terry flexed his arms in businesslike fashion and headed over to the bar. 'Then I reckon they owe us a pint or six. Your orders, gentlemen.'

I left them all to it, drowning their frustration, and found a very late taxi.

Michael Greenway was a big man, broad-shouldered, around six foot four, and usually as placid as Virginia Water. On the morning after this fiasco though and when I had given him a fairly detailed verbal report I got the impression that he was coming up to a slow simmer.

'Rundle,' he brooded darkly. 'We will find this Rundle and ask him about the individual who didn't arrive to do his turn on watch in Park Road that night due to what was referred to as a mix-up. I emailed him about it and got no reply. The guy with guts-ache should have been relieved at six the next morning but wasn't so perhaps we ought to find out who that should have been as well.'

'So there's two on at night and one during the day?' I queried.

'It depends on staffing levels. But yes, usually. Hoodlums

are busier during the night, like rats, and it's safer to have two on as they can watch one another's backs. And this was a particularly dangerous crowd, of course. It's not unknown for surveillance teams to be found out.'

The Commander had been sort of overspilling from one of the smaller upright chairs in his office but now stood up and said, 'Coming?'

'What, now?' I asked.

'Now. I'm in the mood to cause a few knees to knock together and I've a spare couple of hours.'

Apparently Rundle was at home, on a day's leave, so it was just as well that Greenway had checked before we left. This meant driving out to Enfield. I wondered why the Commander hadn't merely contacted whoever had been left in charge of the case or called Rundle on his mobile but it appeared that it was the DCI's knees that were required to knock.

We were leaving the building when my phone rang and I paused to answer it. It was James Carrick.

'Sorry to be so tardy in getting back to you,' he said 'But I had to release Crosby and he went off to see his solicitor to sue the police for wrongful arrest. I hope whoever that is has the sense to tell him to get his head down below the parapet and keep it there. He's insisting that he saw a youth drop the stone and then slide down the embankment on the far side into a concealed track. I've been back there and there's no concealed track nor signs of someone having slid down anywhere. But I've no real evidence against Crosby either. On top of that, Hinton Littlemoor seems to have gone into a state of suspended animation, hardly a leaf moves, they're *all* keeping their heads down.'

'You need to make something happen,' I remarked.

'Yes, I'm sure that would be your next move. But this is the Somerset and Avon Police, not Gillard and Co. How is he, by the way?'

I told him.

'I'll call in tonight and see him.'

'That's good of you. Ring the bell of the front door of the rectory itself, he's moved in there so he's not under John and Elspeth's feet all day.'

'Roger.'

There was no one in at the Rundle household. Greenway

got back in the car, took a deep breath and found his mobile. It soon transpired that the DCI was in B&Q with his wife before taking her to a doctor's appointment. After that they were both due at the dentist's.

'I don't *think* this man doesn't want to see me,' Greenway muttered, glancing at his watch. 'I'm really sorry, Ingrid, but I shall have to leave it here. Are you coming back with me or do you want the authority to speak to him when he finally turns up? You can charge a taxi fare to expenses.'

Which was why, moments later, I found myself standing alone on the pavement outside a very boring semi-detached house in a stultifyingly boring suburb of north London. I worked out that Rundle would not show up for at least two hours and walked back to a row of shops that I had spotted on the way where I found a little bistro and had coffee.

It was quite wrong to assume that Patrick was at the top of Greenway's list of priorities but the longer all this went on, the more we found ourselves on barren ground; no leads, no real fresh evidence to add to what we already knew, then it was obvious that the patience of everyone in authority would become exhausted. Patrick would be asked, quietly, to resign, the multiple killings would remain on file and he would live the rest of his life with a shadowy charge of murder hanging over him. Worse, he would not be able to keep his promise to Katie.

By lunchtime, the Rundles had still not come home and I was beginning to despair. I wondered if Greenway, trying to be helpful, had phoned the DCI back to tell him that I was waiting to talk to him and he had, for whatever reason, decided that he did not want to talk to me either. Perhaps there had been a major failure with surveillance matters generally that he did not wish to come to light.

Perhaps I should follow my own advice to Carrick and make something happen.

After waiting another hour to no avail strolling around, buying a sandwich and eating it in a tiny square nearby, I abandoned Enfield and took a taxi to Muswell Hill – a long way but I was not in the mood for a journey achieved using, no doubt, nine changes of buses or five different railway routes. I had not thought to ask Greenway for the address of the house used for the surveillance in Park Road and knew only that it was an empty upper floor flat a little way down the street on the opposite side. As it happened finding it was easy as a FOR SALE sign was displayed on the top floor of the first house on the end of the terrace next to the recreation ground.

Patrick's 'burglar's' keys came in very handy to open the outer door which had an old-fashioned lock and a more modern one, the latter off the catch, perhaps only locked at night. I went up the stairs, which were carpeted, though worn, ascending to the top floor through a lovely aroma of cooking: garlic, herbs and frying meat. I supposed I could have gone to the estate agent, shown them my ID and asked for the keys to the flat but patience has never been a trait of mine. This lock – the door was at the top of a narrow flight of twisting stairs – was slightly more sophisticated but I must have been a good pupil for it only took me a couple of minutes to open it.

The door opened directly into a typical studio flat: a large room with a huge window. There was only one bedroom which was at the front, from where the police must have kept watch. I was surprised to see that a single mattress was on the bare boards of the floor with a couple of blankets folded up on it. In one corner was a suitcase and an old chair that had a motley collection of items on it: clothing, a pair of trainers, a towel . . .

The towel was damp as though it had been used recently.

I went quickly into the tiny kitchen, little more than a curtained-off recess, and saw a carton of milk, fresh, an opened loaf of bread and other things that pointed to someone actually living here. A nasty cold, tingling sensation travelled down my spine. A matter of feet away was an equally cramped bathroom, or at least, a room with a toilet, shower and minuscule basin. Shaving gear was dumped on a shelf, together with a somewhat disgusting toothbrush in a plastic mug.

'And who the hell might you be?' said a man's voice behind me.

I spun round. He had approached with the silence of a cat.

'You should have checked to see if the door to the roof terrace was locked before you had your snoop round, shouldn't you?' he said smugly, coming a little closer. 'It wasn't and that's where I went when I heard you trying to get in. I asked you a question, who are you?'

'SOCA,' I told him. 'And I know who you are. Jethro Hulton – you've just shaved off your beard – the whiskers are all over the basin. I saw you in the pub.'

He shook his head. 'No, you didn't.'

'It was you, you were working in the cellar. As I've just said, I saw you. You're pigeon-toed too and there's a tattoo of a bird in flight on your right hand, just like the man I saw.' The police description had not mentioned those details or the rotten teeth, yellowish eyes, the general demeanour of a mangy and deranged hyena.

He walked right up to me in his strange hunched-over, hulking way, oddly seeming to be fascinated by my presence rather than angry. 'Before I kill you tell me how you knew I was here.'

I was desperately wondering how I could defend myself and stop him doing just that. Fool, fool, why hadn't I said straight away that I was from the estate agent's? Why had I left the gun in the Range Rover? 'I didn't,' I said. 'I've just come to have a look at the flat the police were using to watch Pangborne's house.'

The man swore and then laughed. 'So SOCA's as useless as the Met! They weren't here! That was the place next door but one!'

'What are you doing here?'

'If you want to hide from the law, stick around. It's worked before for me and it worked this time – until you came along.'

'You're under arrest,' I said, drawing myself up to my full height.

'You and who else is going to take me in?' he jeered.

'For murder,' I went on as though he had not spoken, determined to keep talking and wring responses from him while I worked out what I was going to do in order to stay alive.

'You mean that lot over there?' Hulton replied, wide-eyed and waving an arm vaguely in the direction of the window. 'Not a chance!'

'You shot them all,' I countered. 'The cleaning woman was terrified because you were in the house.'

'I called in. They were all sleeping off their excesses. I left again.'

'No, you shot them. Even your own daughter.'

'I did *not*, Mrs SOCA,' he retorted. 'I did *not*. Some other bastard, or bastards, did that. They murdered my little girl. That's another of the reasons I'm sticking around, just in case he comes back.'

'Cheap that, coming from someone who was going to sell her to the sex trade.'

'Oh, no. I would never do that. Who said that?'

'You drugged a man and then told him that's exactly what you were going to do – after you'd fetched Pangborne to finish him off.'

'I drugged no one.'

'I'm sure you wanted them dead though.'

'Of course. They were messing up my life with their stupid ways of going about things. That woman, she thought she was some kind of god. She had told me to get out or she'd kill me. And now someone has been arrested, a man from SOCA. How could this be?'

'You tell me. You were in the gang so you know him.'

'There was only one clever one, the man who said he'd been a soldier. I believed him. Perhaps he went off his head. I knew he'd killed before, there was something about him – dangerous.'

'He'll kill you, slowly, if you hurt me,' was the only thing I could think of saying.

The horrible eyes widened. 'You're his woman?'

'I'm his wife.'

He must have moved as quickly as a cat then and hit me, for darkness swallowed me up.

SIXTEEN

My phone was ringing. It stopped when the messaging service must have cut in and then, some time later – a minute, an hour, a week? – rang again. I opened my eyes and was presented with a woodworm's eye view of dirty floorboards. But only just, it was practically dark. The side of my face hurt, the side ground into the dust and roughness of the floor, and I seemed to be lying in a heap.

The phone . . . had stopped again.

What was the point of a phone you couldn't answer? I thought dully. It was useless – would have to go.

I struggled to sit up, head spinning, felt sick, had a little rest and finally, retching, got myself into a sitting position, my back to a wall. The phone was in my coat pocket and I took it out after getting very cross and swearing at everything for not cooperating and glared at it, or tried to, my eyes refusing to focus.

Then it rang again, making me start violently.

Somehow, I must have pressed the right button. 'What?' I bawled, making my head swim nauseatingly.

'I've been trying to call you,' said Patrick's voice.

'You don't have to tell me that!' I raved at him. 'It's been ringing for bloody ages!'

'Ingrid, what's wrong?' he asked sharply.

'I'm just furious because the damn thing keeps ringing and I haven't been able to answer it,' I told him. What the hell else did he think was wrong?

'Where are you?'

Where was I? Oh, yes, there.

'I'm in a studio flat at an end of terrace next to the playing fields, or whatever. Where the police were keeping watch, only they weren't.'

'Is this at Muswell Hill?'

'Where else do you know about that has playing fields recently?' I yelled, beginning to get extremely upset about everything now.

'Please tell me why you weren't able to answer it.'

'Because he hit me and it's left me feeling a bit weird, that's why. You keep asking the most *stupid* questions.'

'Who hit you?'

'HULTON!'

And I hurled the phone right into the large living room where it hit something and skittered along the floor out of sight.

'Look, I'm sorry but all I was trying to do was take a look at where the surveillance was carried out,' I said to Michael Greenway. 'That flat seemed the obvious venue as it was empty, or at least looked empty, and was up for sale. Only it was the wrong place.'

He seemed to have aged ten years.

'And you bumped into Hulton,' he said wearily. 'I really don't know why you're still alive. And if Patrick hadn't phoned you and then contacted me you'd probably still be in that bedsit walking round in small circles.'

I had left out the bit about telling Hulton Patrick would kill him if he harmed me. Mostly because it was true. I said, 'I did tell you about the man in the pub. It was him. If he'd been checked out, right under your noses all the time—' I broke off, there was no point in getting angry, again.

It was a little after two the following afternoon and we were in the room furnished with easy chairs next to Greenway's office which he used on the rare occasions when he was able to relax for a while. I had been examined by a paramedic, deemed not to need hospital treatment and someone had taken me back to the hotel. From there, in bed, I had tried to ring Patrick to thank him for alerting people to my plight and tell him that I was all right but for some reason he had not answered, probably in the shower, so had left him a message. Then I had phoned Elspeth just to be sure someone was aware of the state of affairs, making light of events by saying I had tripped and hit my head – which actually seemed to have occurred as I had a lump on the side of it as well as a bruised jaw – but was now perfectly all right. Surprisingly, my phone was fine too. It probably didn't ache all over though.

I had already related to Greenway what had happened during

my encounter with Hulton, and written out a report, so there
was not a lot more to say.

Greenway said, 'I don't have to tell you that half the Met's
out there now, looking for him, under their own noses as well
as everywhere else.'

'I should have remembered to carry Patrick's gun,' I said.

'Then you could well have been dead right now. If he'd thought
you were armed . . .' Greenway left the rest unsaid and rose to
pace the room restlessly, like something caged.

'I'm really sorry I couldn't arrest him,' I said.

The Commander, who momentarily had had his back to me
over by the window, turned quickly. 'Ingrid, for pity's sake
don't apologize! Judging by his past record we'll need a bunch
of Royal Marines to bring the man in. I can only assume he
thought you were some unimportant clerk, or somebody like
that, and there was no kudos to be had in killing you.'

I was alive so had to be grateful. Unless I was now in some
kind of parallel universe and everyone was now grieving for
me in another one.

'You're sure you're OK today?' Greenway said worriedly.

I gave him a big smile. 'Fine.' Perhaps I had had a glassy
look in my eyes.

'We're still no further with this,' Greenway said to himself.

'What about the knife?' I enquired.

'Oh, Patrick's fingerprints are all over it. No blood, nothing
else. As you said he must have thrown it and missed.'

'Thrown it at who though? At someone who was pursuing
him down the garden, the person who caught up with him,
he having possibly passed out, and dumped him in the lane?
The murderer?'

'We might never know.'

I was sensing his reluctance to go any further with the investigation. It was taking up too much of his time, using scarce
resources and costing too much money and he was working
out how he was going to break it to me gently. A dead sort of
feeling settled in the pit of my stomach.

'I don't know what to suggest we do next,' Greenway
observed slowly. 'And until Hulton's caught – and believe me,
he will be . . .'

'What about Rundle?' I asked.

'*I'll* talk to Rundle. I see no reason why you should hang

around in the cold waiting for a dozy DCI to turn up. Meanwhile . . .'

'You'd rather I went home.'

He shrugged helplessly. 'Until Patrick's better and I've heard from Complaints – not a word yet, I'm afraid – then I don't see . . .' Again, he stopped speaking.

'OK,' I said, getting to my feet.

'But I don't want you to go away thinking that you've achieved nothing,' he said hastily. 'On the contrary—'

I interrupted him. 'Will you contact me when there are any developments?'

'Of course.'

I left.

The word 'failed' seemed to hammer into my brain at each step I took down the stairs from the first to the ground floor. Failed, failed, failed, failed . . .

Just outside, in thin winter sunshine that was having no effect on the freezing temperature, Elspeth called me.

'Sorry to ring you during your working day,' she began.

'Is something the matter?'

'No, at least, I hope not. It's just that Patrick seems to have taken himself off somewhere. We've been out all morning and have only just got in. I'm not *particularly* worried, it's just that . . .' Her voice trailed away.

'But . . . but I have the car,' I stammered.

'Yes, I know and he hasn't borrowed mine or John's, not that he would without—'

'Was he well enough?' I butted in.

'Well, look, I don't want to worry you any more than necessary but he might have stopped taking his medication.'

'*What?*'

'Early yesterday he said that he was suspicious that what-ever some of the tablets were they were the cause of his feeling dizzy and still weak. I said he could hardly stop taking everything just because something wasn't quite right for him. He didn't answer – you know how Patrick does that when he can't agree with what you've just said.'

Did I ever.

'And he hasn't even left you a note?'

'Oh, I didn't think of looking. I'll ring you back.'

I went straight into a café nearby, for the warmth, and rang James Carrick.

'Is there something you ought to tell me?' I said, in the mood for scorched earth policies.

'I was asked to contact you about now,' he countered after a short pause while he had obviously left whichever room he was in and was now, judging by the slight echo when he spoke, in a corridor.

'Oh, fantastic,' I said sarcastically.

'Ingrid, I do *not* argue with that husband of yours when he's got it into his head to do something and starts issuing orders. I called in last night as I said I would and he was ready for off and about to ring for a taxi. He didn't say much, only that he'd had a call from you that had worried him and he'd had to phone Mike Greenway. Are you all right, by the way?'

'Absolutely fine,' I said.

'Good. I pointed out that his parents would be worried even more if he just upped and went and he told me he'd already left them a note.'

'So you drove him to Bath station?'

'Yes, that's where he wanted to go.'

'Elspeth says she thinks he's stopped taking his medication.'

'He might not have done. He went off somewhere and came back with some boxes of pills and chucked them in his bag. He seemed slow-moving and a little low key but otherwise OK, if that's any consolation.'

Well, it was something.

'Did he say where he was going?'

'No.'

I thanked him, adding an apology for snarling.

'Please keep me posted. If things get desperate you know where to find me.'

I fetched myself coffee and a croissant. I had planned to check out of the hotel and go home. What now? Was it necessary to inform Greenway of this latest development?

'No,' I said to myself. 'Greenway has just about washed his hands of it.' Very regretfully, the Commander was going to cast off his man from MI5 who, at best, would be sent out into the world with a slur on his character, at worst, and despite anything Complaints might or might not say, arrested and charged with murder.

Elspeth rang me back.

'The note was in the bathroom,' she said. 'It doesn't say much, just that there's something he wants to do and not to worry as he's feeling much better. I also discovered that he's been sleeping upstairs after all. I have to say I half expected him not to stick to doctor's orders – mothers just have to lump it, don't they?'

'Please tell John to carry on being careful, won't you?' I urged, furious with Patrick for causing her this anguish after all her efforts in looking after him. 'There are still people messing around with black magic and a murderer at large.'

She promised she would.

I almost stuck to my original plan to return to Hinton Littlemoor. But I did not. I went back to the scene of the crime in Park Road and, having given back the keys, used Patrick's.

The cleaning woman's phone number – at least, I hoped it was her, Rosa Jerez – was in a tattered notebook I discovered jammed at the back of a drawer containing a jumble of things in a table in the hall. I wondered why the police had not found and removed it and remedied the omission myself, handling it with gloves and putting it in a plastic evidence bag in my pocket. The Smith and Wesson was in the other pocket and I took it out now and went into every room of this increasingly stinking property in case Hulton had decided to continue thumbing his nose at the Met. I was in the mood to wing him meaningfully and painfully and *then* complete his arrest.

It had seemed too much to hope for that anyone would answer when I rang the cleaner's number and no one did. But, back at the hotel, I became intrigued with other information I had already noticed scribbled down on the crumpled pages. Donning gloves I went through them carefully. There were phone numbers, mostly of what appeared to be the ordinary information a large percentage of the population has to hand: local garages, a window cleaner, a pizza delivery service, the local Chinese takeaway. There were other numbers with just initials alongside. People? Places like shops or stores? Dodgy solicitors? There were also addresses, all of people with foreign-sounding names, and whole paragraphs in German and what I thought was Serbo Croat. There were even diagrams, rough plans of various floors in buildings. I took the notebook down to the ground floor and copied all the more interesting-looking information in the hotel's Internet room.

Obviously, the notebook would have to go to Rundle. But my purpose here, in London, was not in order to hand bits of evidence on a plate to the Met. I was busying myself doing just that while not having the first clue where I was going to go from here. Why had I believed what Hulton had said? Because even the most vicious criminals tend not to murder their own daughters.

I suppose I sat there, in introspective misery, for twenty minutes or so. I had tried ringing Patrick's mobile but there had been no reply. I rang Rundle, damned if I was going to go trotting over to Wood Green again: he could send someone to collect it. He was not in so I left a message, asking whoever it was to get him to phone me back. I had a call almost immediately, a DI Latimer wondering if I could take the notebook to West End Central police station, just off Oxford Street.

Well, yes, I could. And then, perhaps, a cup of tea and something to eat – I did not feel like having a proper lunch even though it was getting on for two thirty – followed by a quick look around some shops. Anything to try to take my mind off the hell that I was living in and postpone making decisions.

The room phone rang and it was a call from reception.

'Miss Langley, there's a gentleman here who says he's your husband and would like to speak to you.'

'Please put him on,' I said.

'Hi,' said Patrick's voice. 'I've a good tip for tomorrow's two thirty at Ludlow, Cuckoo Spit.'

'I don't bet on horses,' I said.

'Plus a dead cert for the three fifteen, Snuggems.'

'Room 207,' I told him.

I must be really twitchy, I mused, asking for two proofs of identity. No, actually, I was still furious with him.

I let him in and he gazed at me searchingly, angry. 'How the hell did you manage to run into Hulton?'

'Calm down and I'll tell you.'

This I did and when I had finished Patrick said, 'I don't know why you're still alive.'

'That's exactly what Greenway said. Hulton seemed more interested in how I'd stumbled across him.'

There was a short silence before Patrick said, 'This is me having one last stab at trying to sort everything out. I simply have to push to the back of my mind what's going on in Hinton Littlemoor and give this priority. Otherwise I'm finished.'

'You're not well enough to be doing anything,' I countered stonily. 'I'm surprised you were even strong enough to get on a train.'

He shrugged, not about to respond to points of view with which he did not agree. 'Sorry if you've been trying to get hold of me – I hadn't charged up my phone properly.'

The man put his weekend bag on the bed, unzipped it and rummaged, presumably for the charger. He glanced at me, then held my gaze, a question in those wonderful grey eyes.

'Oh, come here,' I said, holding out both arms. After a long, long, silent hug I whispered, 'Please tell me why you're going against medical advice.'

'The docs couldn't agree in the first place. The consultant you spoke to on the phone probably only won the argument because he had possession of the patient. I've just been back to the Nightingale Clinic to see the specialist I saw first as he impressed me rather and the pills I'd been given in Bath were making me feel like death and affecting my coordination. One lot of pills, that is. I've been taken off them. He agreed that most of the trouble must have been total exhaustion but still didn't go along with the drugs prescription. I've just about had my week's rest and he wanted me to go back home and carry on taking things easy but I'm damned if I'm going to.' Wrongly putting my silence down to disbelief, he added, 'That's the truth.'

'You've never lied to me,' I whispered. 'But the liver damage?'

'I had more blood tests and apparently it's not as bad as the other bloke thought and improving already. I'm still strictly on the wagon though and on tablets for that. That's the bad news.'

'Welcome aboard,' I said, kissing him.

He gently stroked my face where it was bruised. 'I really hate it when somebody hurts you.'

*   *   *

I slept for three hours, having intended to put my feet up for a few minutes while Patrick had a shower, and when I was woken by my mobile ringing I saw when I had switched on the bedside lamp that he had been asleep by my side.

'Do you know where Patrick is?' Greenway's voice said, sounding tense.

I could never explain afterwards why I lied. 'Sorry, no. He should be at home.'

'No, he's not at Hinton Littlemoor and neither James Carrick nor the rector and his wife knows where he is. Or say they don't, anyway.'

'Why do you want him?' I asked, ignoring the slur on their characters.

Greenway breathed out hard down the phone. 'Jethro Hulton has been found hanged. In that flat where you ran into him and I really, really want to talk to Patrick before the Met get hold of him.'

'Hanged from what?' I gasped. I could not remember anything in the place that would support the weight of a body.

'Apparently there's a pipe in the bathroom that emerges from the ceiling and then goes through the wall into the kitchen. He'd been strung up by a length of broken sash cord from one of the windows.'

I could do nothing else but express my shock and tell him I would keep in touch.

Patrick was looking at me, wide awake now.

'Hulton's body's been found strung up at the flat where I ran into him and Greenway wants to talk to you before you're arrested by the Met.'

'Er, no, he'll want to be seen doing the right thing by handing me over.'

'That's really cynical!'

'The man has no other choice and I wouldn't expect him to do anything else. So, it's crunch time then: do I go quietly and hope that the whole thing's sorted out satisfactorily, in other words, that I'm found to be innocent of the shootings, or do I go on the run and sort it out myself, D12 style?'

'As far as the latter goes are you that confident of the outcome?'

'No, for the simple reason that I still can't remember what

happened. All I have to go on is gut feelings. These tell me that I'm not guilty of their murder.'

I had opened my mouth to speak when there was a thunderous knocking on the door.

'Open up! Police!'

Without exchanging a word we both got off the bed, I grabbed the gun and car keys from my bag, shoved them in the pocket of my slacks and went over to the door. After pretending to fumble with the lock to give Patrick a few more seconds I opened it, looking suitably apprehensive.

'What on earth's this all about?' I said to several large coppers.

'We're looking for Patrick Gillard,' replied the one at the front.

'But there must be a mistake – we're both with SOCA,' I whinnied.

'Sorry, but that's my orders.'

I pulled the door wide and they all trouped in. I tripped and then shoved the last one, who had probably positioned himself at the rear on account of being the smallest, and this created a most satisfying domino effect, the man at the front not quite recovering his balance and clouting his head on a chest of drawers on the way down. It only took a few seconds for me to scoop up my jacket and Patrick to commandeer their radios as they floundered around on the floor and then the two of us had run out, slamming the door.

Old MI5 habits had ensured that I had checked the inner workings of the hotel's emergency exits and now led the way to a staircase that, while it might not be an official fire escape route did lead, eventually, to the underground car park. All one had to do was go through a door marked PRIVATE on the ground floor, descend to the basement by means of a staircase with a STAFF ONLY notice on it and then go through double doors that I had an idea were alarmed. For obvious reasons I had not tested the system, having merely glanced though the small window in one of them into the gloomy interior of the car park before retracing my footsteps.

They were exceedingly alarmed, a deafening bell commencing to ring as I burst through them. I am also someone who makes a point of remembering, exactly, where she has left her car and headed for it now, at the run, hoping that Patrick was not far behind. In the driving seat, the engine running, I unlocked the passenger door just as he appeared, tossing the radios into a rubbish bin of some kind in a dark recess as he went by.

'I did glimpse a police car blocking the exit,' he panted.

The much despised stainless steel bull bars on the front of our vehicle are not expressly for maximizing the injuries to any pedestrians one was unfortunate enough to hit, as detractors sneeringly suggest, or for show, but were fitted because they might just come in useful one day. They enabled me to gently shunt the squad car out of the way, the mouths of those witnessing this assuming the shape of large round 'Os', and then we were away.

'Where to?' I demanded to know.

'A safe house I know of in—'

'I've a better idea,' I interrupted.

'What?' he snapped.

'A house I know of in Enfield.'

SEVENTEEN

t was dark by now, nine forty-five, and the roads were unusually quiet. Expecting to come upon a police road block
at any moment I stayed well within the speed limits, taking
short cuts through side roads where I was familiar with
the terrain, driving the big car quietly so as not to draw
attention. Patrick let me get on with it, probably thinking,
rightly, that I needed to concentrate. To his credit he did not
question my choice of destination either. At least, not until
we arrived.

'Rundle!' he exclaimed, having spotted the car parked in
the drive.

'Rundle,' I agreed, yanking on the handbrake and turning
off the engine. 'I have a theory – tentative, I admit – that he
has one or two rotten apples in his surveillance squad.'

'He will try to arrest me.'

'So we'll talk him out of it.'

'Do you have anything to go on at all?' Patrick enquired
lightly.

'I've made a little progress, including a list of people killed
in a Serbian shoot-out around twenty years ago at a place
called Hilik. That had been scrawled in all that mess on the
wall at Park Road.'

'It never occurred to me that anything had been written
there.'

'I also found a notebook today at the back of a drawer in
that table in the hall there which I've promised to drop off at
West End Central. But we can give it to Rundle now if he's
at home.'

'Anything interesting in it?'

'Too early to say. I've copied the more fruitful-looking
pages.'

'May I have a look at the list of the dead?'

I switched on the vehicle's interior light and gave it to him.
He studied it for a few minutes and then murmured, 'I've
heard some of these surnames before – and not from D12

days. But they might not have been the real names of the
people involved.'

'Who were they?'

'Criminals,' he replied simply, giving back the list. 'Thank
you, it's changed everything.'

'How's that?'

'You'll find out in a minute, when we're inside.'

'Apparently Hilik produces crooks like some towns make
black pudding and meat pies.'

In the somewhat dim light he gazed at me worriedly. 'It's
just occurred to me that you probably shouldn't be driving.'

'I'm *sure* you shouldn't be.'

We both sighed heavily and got out of the car.

There was a light on in the ground floor front room of the
house and another upstairs. I hung back, leaving it up to Patrick
exactly how we made the approach. Not particularly surprisingly, he rang the bell. After half a minute or so a bored-looking
teenage girl opened the door.

'Yeah?' she asked, slouching against the door frame.

'We'd like to speak to DCI Rundle,' Patrick said in his best
Sandhurst manner.

'Who wants him?'

'It's business,' she was informed quietly.

The girl prised herself upright and drifted off inside. We
followed.

'Dad, there's a bloke to see you,' she called. 'He says it's
business.'

'Oh, right,' said Rundle's voice from somewhere to the rear
of the house. 'Show him in to the living room.'

But before she could do so the DCI came up the hall and
entered the room before us, moving quickly to cross the quite
appalling purple and brown carpet to stand by the only other
occupant, a woman who was presumably his wife and who
had just jumped to her feet.

'We are both perfectly safe and so are you,' Patrick said
serenely, seating himself in one of the armchairs. I followed
suit.

'And why should I believe that, Gillard?' Rundle grated
sarcastically.

'Ingrid's just shown me a list of names of those killed in
a shoot-out between criminal families in a town called Hilik

in Serbia about twenty years ago. One of those names is Draskovic, another is Horovic. Horovic, or Larovic, are the names Andrea Pangborne appears to have used in her native Serbia. The chef she ran off with was a man by the name of Zoran Drascovic. She killed him when she got fed up with him, having found a much more productive friend, Hulton. A little research might be necessary and there might not be any connection at all between these people but I'm wondering if those particular families were from the same enclave and on the same side in whatever feud triggered this all off, if you'll forgive the pun, or she wouldn't have gone off with him. Another name on the list is that of Mladan Beckovic. This man is obviously dead but I happen to know he has a son who uses his father's name and at home was described as a serious criminal. It's now thought that he's over here, in the UK, but has gone off the map. Mladan junior could well have sworn revenge if Zoran was a friend of his or had a connection with his family.'

Rundle was distractedly endeavouring to shepherd his wife from the room but the lady clearly did not want to go and irritably ducked under his guiding arms to reseat herself in her chair. She appeared to be finding Patrick too interesting to miss.

'So you're not suggesting that the gun-battle in Serbia had anything to do with the murders in Muswell Hill,' Rundle said, giving up.

'No, not *necessarily*. But why go to all the trouble of writing the name of the place on the wall?'

'It's a terribly far-fetched story full of "ifs" and "mights". And I have to tell you that—'

'I'm under arrest?' Patrick said. 'Wouldn't that be the action of a man just carrying on grabbing the first suspect who comes along? We've brought you the list, together with a notebook full of phone numbers and things like that that Ingrid found at the house in Park Road earlier today – that your people had missed. I think you know about that.'

'Oh,' said Rundle. 'Yes, I do.'

'And we want to know who should have relieved the man watching the house on the morning of the killings and didn't, plus the name of the man who should have been on duty with him overnight and didn't turn up. This is probably the fourth time you've been asked for this information. Photographs of the pair would be helpful as well.'

'I've already emailed this information to Commander Greenway – not that I think it has any relevance.' Rundle opened his mouth to continue but his wife spoke first.

'Gillard?' she said. 'Patrick Gillard?'

Patrick gave her a really lovely smile.

'Not the army major who'd been drafted in from MI5 and saved the life of Prince Andrew from a mad knifeman several years ago?'

He cherishes the solid gold cufflinks with horses designed by Stubbs that were a discreet thank you gift after that particular episode.

'Only doing my job,' Patrick said in time-honoured fashion.

'I thought I recognized you. I saw it on the TV news.'

I could almost hear Rundle thinking.

'By the way, we resisted arrest at the hotel,' Patrick went on to say. 'Their radios are in a bin in the underground car park.'

I had an idea that Mrs Rundle badly wanted to laugh. But if she did she managed to refrain, saying instead, 'Surely there's no harm in giving them the information, Harry.'

'Do you have any kind of alibi with regard to Hulton's murder?' Rundle asked Patrick, ignoring her suggestion.

'You haven't told me the approximate time of death.'

'Answer the question.'

'Well, I left home at about six thirty last night with Detective Chief Inspector James Carrick of Bath CID – who's a friend of mine – who took me to Bath railway station. I caught the seven forty-two train to London and stayed the night at an officers' club of which I'm still a member. At eight fifteen this morning I asked a member of staff to call a taxi for me and went to the Nightingale Clinic as, the day before, I'd made an emergency appointment to see a specialist, Gordon Lefevre, who originally treated me when I was found unconscious at Park Road. That was at nine. I stayed there for the whole morning, seeing him, waiting around and having tests, returned to the club for lunch as there was someone I wanted to see, and then went to the hotel where I knew Ingrid was staying, arriving there at two thirtyish. There, I had a shower and then a nap and we were both woken by a phone call from Michael Greenway who wanted to know where I was as Hulton had been found hanged and he'd been told I wasn't at home.'

'Who saw you yesterday after you'd spoken to Ingrid when she told you she'd come upon Hulton and he'd knocked her about?' Here, the DCI's gaze fixed on me for a moment.

'No one but Carrick. Just before that I'd been with my parents and our two eldest adopted children, Katie and Matthew. We all had tea together. They come over after school.'

'I'm surprised you didn't drop everything and head here, seeing as your wife had been assaulted.'

'As soon as I'd spoken to Ingrid I contacted Greenway who organized medical assistance and an area car. He rang me back shortly afterwards to say that Ingrid wasn't badly hurt and had been taken back to her hotel. It was then that I decided to come to London to see the doc and bring Ingrid home, if that's what she wanted. And obviously, I'm still trying to clear my name.'

'So, if she'd felt up to it, you'd have done a bit more sleuthing, even though I understand you've been forbidden to do so.'

I found myself wondering how closely he had been liaising with Greenway.

'That's right,' Patrick agreed. 'Mainly because nobody else bloody well is.'

'Who did you see at the club who would verify your story, the person you had lunch with?'

'I met up with Richard Daws, my old boss in MI5. He's now one of those in charge of SOCA.'

'Hoping he'll protect you from prosecution?'

'No, not at all.'

'Are you carrying a weapon?' Rundle asked, seeming to come to a decision.

Patrick looked surprised. 'Hardly. You should be more than aware that my Glock 18 and my knife are helping you with your enquiries.'

'I haven't changed my mind. I still think you killed those people, whether you were aware of doing so or not or even intended to commit murder. You also killed Hulton. You knew where he was, he'd hurt your wife and—'

'But Hulton would hardly have stayed there or gone back

later and hung around waiting to be arrested' I butted in furiously. 'No, someone with whom he was in close contact killed him. Someone who knew where he'd gone to ground. Besides which, Hulton was a heavily-built man. How on earth do you think Patrick could have overpowered him to hang him up in his present state of—'

Rundle impatiently waved me to silence and then I was again forestalled from finishing what I was going to say, by Patrick this time.

To me, he said, 'We were rudely interrupted back at the hotel when I asked you how you thought we ought to handle this. What do you think?'

'We did make the decision,' I pointed out.

'Regrettably . . .' Patrick said to Rundle just before we headed quickly for the door. In the hall he grabbed the back of my jacket as I headed for the front door.

'Back way,' he hissed.

'There might not be one,' I observed, no louder, seconds later when we were in the kitchen.

Usefully, or not, a pair of security lights came on as we exited through the back door, illuminating a small garden. There appeared to be no way out of it to the rear and, as we had already seen, the garage was at the side of the house. Then we heard Rundle's voice, shouting somewhere out the front.

'They're in the garden! Come in through here!'

Rundle had seen us arrive and called for assistance. I heard Patrick swearing under his breath.

There was a plastic compost bin with a lid in an almost screened off corner at the bottom of the left-hand side of the garden and, behind it, the boundary was represented by an untidy conifer hedge. Patrick went straight over to it, climbed on to the bin and then disappeared from sight into the greenery.

'I'll catch you,' he said from somewhere out of sight on the other side when I was teetering on the top of the bin.

I launched myself through the top of the hedge and was caught, just.

'You didn't have to go into orbit,' Patrick muttered.

We discovered that we were in a much larger, overgrown garden and swiftly made our way from the sounds of activity behind us. If they had a dog with them we were finished.

Moving as silently as possible between shrubs in the near darkness, we bore left, walking through long, sodden grass. Soon, we came to a broken-down wooden fence and squeezed through a small gap in it into what appeared to be a yard to the rear of either shops or a small industrial unit. The area soon proved to be semi-derelict and, thankfully, there were no working security lights here.

Making our way carefully around what appeared to be piles of fly-tipped rubbish, trying to see where we were going in the weak glow from street lights some fifty yards ahead of us, we eventually peered around the corner of the building into what seemed to be a cul-de-sac. Nothing moved but it was crazy to think that they had not fanned out to look for us.

'What did Daws have to say?' I whispered as we paused there for a few more moments.

'He wondered when I was going to be able to avoid controversy.'

I supposed the man had a point. I said, 'But this has hardly been your fault.'

After a short silence Patrick said, 'Have you still got the Smith and Wesson?'

'Yes, but—'

'Keep it with you at all times.'

'Why? What are you going to do?'

He turned to me. 'I'm going to give myself up.'

'But – but you can't! You said—'

'Think. Soon there'll be dogs, choppers with thermal-imaging cameras and God knows what else hunting me down. I asked Daws to meet me to clarify matters and it's what he told me to do. They're not interested in you. So go. All I ask is that you stay out of danger for the children's sake. It would make me really happy if you went home. I'll do everything I can to get the car back for you – I haven't been using it here in London, after all.'

I flung my arms around him and held him tight.

'Please go,' he murmured, a break in his voice. 'Go to the hotel and rest. You don't look very well.'

'But I'm in this with you,' I protested.

He misunderstood, or might have chosen to do so. 'No, they're not interested in prosecuting you for helping me resist arrest. Greenway'll pull strings. Daws promised that you'd be protected too.'

Still I held him, appalled that it was all my fault for bringing him here.

'Please go,' Patrick said again. 'What you've found out has probably cleared me of everything already.'

I let him go and he kissed me quickly and then went off down that ghastly, blighted dead end back towards the main road, walking tall but limping just a little as he does when he's very tired.

What stopped me from running headlong round to Rundle's house and putting a bullet into his thick, stupid skull?

I still don't know.

EIGHTEEN

I was not permitted to have the car, which was requisitioned as 'evidence', and succeeded in finding a taxi to take me back to the hotel. As I half expected to find a reception committee in the shape of one of the large coppers I had upended earlier waiting to charge me with 'perverting the course of justice' or 'assisting an offender' or some other such codswallop, it went towards lifting my black mood just an iota to encounter nothing of the sort.

The cruel pictures were there, in my imagination: you suffer when you write. They would have made him lie face down in the road before searching him for weapons. They would have handcuffed him where he lay before hauling him to his feet and, because of his service history, he would then have been taken to an extra secure police station, Paddington perhaps, where terrorist suspects are held.

It was all utterly, utterly unbearable.

My phone rang.

'Yes?' I sort of gasped, realizing that tears were running down my cheeks.

'The grapevine's in overdrive,' said James Carrick's soft Scottish voice.

'They've got him,' I sobbed. 'This fine courageous man who's served his country for most of his life has been carted off like some filthy, murdering yob and . . .' I couldn't speak any more.

James talked to me. I can't really remember what he said, only that the words washed over me like a warm, comforting blanket.

'But the man's used to this kind of thing,' I do recollect he finished up by saying. 'All that training for Special Ops; being dragged through the mud and chucked in rivers. D'you want me to come up?'

'How can you?' I asked, staggered.

'Easy. I'll throw a sickie again.'

'Patrick would prefer me to go home.'

'Well he would. But it's up to you.'

Carrick did not ring me when he arrived at the hotel as it was the early hours of the morning by then as he had driven up. But he did the next morning and we met for breakfast where he bullied me into eating something.

'As far as I can tell there's been nothing in the media,' he said after dealing briskly with a full English. 'They're keeping it strictly in-house. So what d'you plan to do? Storm the nick where he's being held?'

This I knew was to make me smile and he succeeded.

'I just want to wring the neck of whoever committed these murders until he confesses,' I replied. I had brought him up to date with events and showed him the information I had obtained from the Serbian Embassy as he ate, including what Patrick had said to Rundle at the DCI's home.

'Does Patrick reckon this has anything to do with that shoot-out years ago?'

I shook my head. 'No, he doesn't think so – but it might.'

'We still don't know the names of these surveillance people.'

'I forgot to mention that bit to you. Rundle said he'd emailed them to Greenway.'

'Then let's go and talk to Greenway.'

'I think you'll find that he's no longer involved. It's Met business now.'

Carrick brooded. I wondered if he was thinking of the time Patrick had found him when he had been shut up inside an old boiler at a derelict factory and left to die. Patrick had had to fight his way through three of the gang responsible in order to rescue him. And the cases they had worked on together when we had been with MI5, including when Patrick's brother, Larry, had been killed.

'When you had a snoop round that flat thinking it was where a watch was being kept on the Pangborne place, only it wasn't, and came upon Hulton . . .' he began thoughtfully.

'The right flat was next door but one,' I said, guessing what his next question would be.

'Let's go and have a look round that.'

'Unofficially?'

'Oh, aye. I'm in bed with the flu. Anyway, bugger the Met.'
And, reverting to type, 'Are ye armed, hen?'

'Too right.'

'We haven't discussed that.'

Police vehicles were still parked outside the house where
Hulton's body had been found, a wide area cordoned-off with
incident tape causing Carrick to leave his car some distance
away. A constable standing by the front door was stamping
his feet, trying to keep warm.

Next door but one there were curtains at the top window
that faced the street, which would have made it easier to
observe a property farther along on the other side without
being spotted. The front door to this particular house in the
terrace was open and we went straight in and up the stairs.
An elderly woman was mopping the floor at the top of the
first flight.

'Oo are you?' she demanded to know, straightening her
back with a wince.

'Police,' said Carrick, producing his warrant card but
not giving her time to read it. 'Is anyone living in the top
flat now?'

'Nah, but a bloke's been dossin' there. Gorn now though.
Could 'e be the one what done in that bloke in the end house?
This place has never seen nuffink like it.'

'Who was he, do you know?'

'A rough type. I kept right away from 'im, I tell yer. 'E broke
in. Smashed the lock. Someone's supposed to be fixing it.
Next Christmas I 'spect.'

'This was after the police used the flat for surveillance
work?'

'So that's oo they woz! Ho yus. After that. Just for a coupla
days it was.'

We thanked her and went on up, my companion perceptibly
fizzing with enthusiasm.

'Gloves,' Carrick muttered when we were standing outside
the damaged door. 'We don't know who this man was. Do
you have any with you?'

'That's what handbags are for,' I told him, finding just one
pair. 'You have them, you're the professional detective. I won't
touch anything.'

Warily, we went in. The place stank but, after all, someone
had been rather ill in here. I expected the layout to be the
same or similar to that of the other flat but this was a
series of small rooms including a proper bathroom and
kitchen, the former definitely a no-go area as far as I was
concerned. The room at the front, the largest, was about
twelve feet square, and like the others it was empty of furniture. The only item in the place was a supermarket bag full
of rubbish in the kitchen. Very carefully, Carrick began to
go through it.

'So was it Hulton?' I wondered aloud. 'He knew the police
had been here.'

'But why the hell was he hanging around?' Carrick said,
dubiously unwrapping what turned out to be the mouldy
remains of a takeaway. 'You saw him at the pub, he was next
door but one and he might, *might* have been here too. Was
he hanging around hoping to catch up with the man who killed
his daughter?'

'That theory has a lot going for it,' I said. 'But why would
whoever it was come back here?'

Carrick looked up at me with a glint in his eyes. 'Because
it was his job to do so?'

'Oh, brother,' I whispered. 'Did Hulton think it might have
been one of the cops on watch?'

'One of the cops who'd changed his name from his Serbian
one?'

'Mlandan Beckovic!' I exclaimed, suddenly remembering
the name.

'It's happened, you know. Not all that long ago a Super in
the Met was interviewing new entrants when he recognized
someone he'd arrested for murder nine years previously. The
bloke had assumed a new identity.'

'I can't believe that if it was Beckovic he joined the Met
with a view to settling old scores.'

'No, but crooks *do* try to join the police, as in the case I've
just mentioned. It gives them a huge advantage. And now that
identity theft's on the increase . . .' He broke off and whistled
softly.

I had been looking around the rest of the kitchen. 'What
have you got?'

Carrick delved into the bottom of the bag. 'There's an empty bottle in here. The sort that drugs are kept in in pharmacies and hospitals.'

I went over and we looked at the label.

'Amytal Sodium,' he read out loud. 'It's a barbiturate. It looks as though we might have found the stuff that was put in the whisky. God, if this was full and whoever it was tipped it all into three or four bottles of Scotch then I'm surprised they lived long enough to be shot.'

'There might be fingerprints on it.'

'Quite. You wouldn't have a specimen bag on you, I suppose? – although I might have some in the car.'

I handed one over.

Carrick said, 'If the guy on duty the night before the shootings was nobbled, poisoned, in some way there's still plenty of evidence in the bathroom. Did anyone investigate that, do you know?'

'They didn't,' I told him. 'But please don't ask me to take samples.'

'Och, I'll do it. I might even have some wee plastic sample phials in the car too . . .'

He did and more potential evidence was gathered.

'I reckon something went a bit wrong with their plan,' Carrick said, removing the gloves. 'I mean, if the man here on his own was dosed with something to make him ill during the night it would have had to be done somewhere else, before he arrived, as time would have been needed for it to take effect. I'm sure they would have wanted to take out the people over the road under cover of darkness, as they say in corny detective stories. Only for some reason their plans went a bit wrong. Therefore, and still I'm guessing, the murderer was the one who should have been here on duty with him, not the man who was to have taken over from him next morning and who must have received some official-sounding message telling him he wasn't needed.'

'Unless they were both in it together.'

'That might be stretching it a bit. Whatever the truth we must find out everything about these surveillance people.'

'Where are you going to take the evidence?'

'You're the one who works for SOCA.'

'Yes, but as I said earlier, it is Rundle's case.'

'I don't like the sound of him at all. Is Greenway interested in getting Patrick off the hook?'

'He is, but I don't think he can justify throwing much in the way of resources at it.'

'Does *he* like Rundle?'

'No.'

James grinned.

I rang Greenway and, without explaining further, asked if I could see him. He sounded surprised but immediately said I should come to SOCA HQ.

There were to be more surprises; first another for Greenway on seeing Carrick and then a further one when James and I caught sight of Patrick sitting in the Commander's office, drinking coffee. I got the impression that he had not been there long.

'I threw my weight around,' Greenway said, having been patient during the handshakes and hugs and provided extra coffee. 'I don't do it very often but –' he seemed for a moment to be in danger of losing his temper again but mastered it and, his voice thick with anger, continued – 'Rundle crowed. That shitty little DCI crowed to me that he'd made one of mine lay in the gutter to be arrested. More importantly as far as the law goes, he has no evidence to connect Patrick with Hulton's death, none at all, and that was what he had arrested him for. We've checked and just about his every movement yesterday can be accounted for. The morning at the clinic, taxi rides when, just to be on the safe side he took the numbers of the vehicles, then lunch with Richard Daws – God above, is there a better alibi in the whole universe than that? – and then another taxi to the hotel where the receptionist remembers he arrived just before she went off duty at two thirty. By that time Hulton had been dead for just under five hours. We know that because his watch was smashed and had stopped at nine sixteen, after Patrick had booked himself in to the clinic.'

'Who found the body, sir?' Carrick enquired.

'I take it you're here in the capacity of Ingrid's minder in the assumed, at the time, absence of her husband and taking into consideration the hazardousness of the investigation.'

'That's right.'

'Admirable. There was a tip-off.'

'Oh?'

'Yes. Stinks, doesn't it?'

'What about these surveillance men whose details Rundle said he'd sent you?' I said impatiently, having thought that it was perfectly possible for Hulton's killer to have altered the time on the watch before smashing it.

'Their names are Kenneth Hills and Daniel Rushton-Smith. Hills is a one-time traffic cop and due for retirement. He hails from Manchester. Rushton-Smith is thirty-nine years old and has been in the force only eighteen months. According to his CV he has mid-European antecedents. Take a look, I've printed off his photograph.'

'I've already seen it,' Patrick told us quietly. 'He bears a remarkable resemblance to the mugshot of Mladan Beckovic we actually have in this building.'

The colour photo came into my hands and I stared at the dark, somewhat sullen features. 'Is this the man who was upstairs at Pangborne's house?' I asked Patrick.

'I still don't remember seeing his face.'

Greenway said, 'So now I'm not tiptoeing around this any more for fear of offending our colleagues in central London I intend to have him picked up. He's on his second day off this week, apparently.'

'I can't understand him being stupid enough to leave that barbiturate bottle in the kitchen of the flat,' Carrick commented. 'If it was him, of course.'

'He's probably a lousy policeman,' I said.

'The four of us will go with back-up,' Greenway decided. 'Unusual, I know, but a lot is at stake here. I want to see this man's reaction when he and Patrick come face to face.'

'In that case I'd like to put in an official request to carry a firearm strictly for self-defence purposes,' Patrick said. Then added with the trace of a smile, 'Sir.'

'Request denied. But doesn't Ingrid have your one-time MI5 short-barrelled Smith and Wesson?' He shot to his feet. 'Well? Are you coming?'

We gulped down the remains of our coffee and followed him out.

Rushton-Smith, according to Met records, lived in Hammersmith. Only he did not, the house empty, the windows boarded up. Greenway, determined seemingly to be right at the forefront of events, pounded on the front door of the semi-detached house next to it and there was a short conversation with a woman. Patrick, Carrick and I, plus the driver, remained in the Commander's car, another with reinforcements parked right behind us, watching and waiting.

'She doesn't know where the owners or tenants of the place are,' Greenway reported on his return. 'It's been empty like that for several months and she's never seen anyone living there who looked like the man in the mugshot I showed her. So it's either a phoney address or he hasn't bothered to update his details.' Back in the car he turned to flash a big smile at the three of us in the rear seat. 'I'm getting quite excited about this.'

'Where to now, sir?' asked the driver.

'Wood Green nick. We'll talk to Kenneth Hills. No, hang on, I'll find out exactly where he is first.' He grabbed his mobile.

Rundle gave the information immediately. Hills was on duty with the colleague who had suffered food poisoning and they were at an address in the centre of Wood Green keeping watch on a Chinese restaurant thought to be employing illegal immigrants. There was, the DCI added, a car parking area to the rear of the shops. I thought the advice pointless as Greenway was in the mood to block the road and bring the place to a standstill. But as it happened the pair were watching the rear of the premises in question across the car park from a storeroom-cum-office they had commandeered over a charity shop that fronted on to another road.

'The four of us will go but do try not to look like cops on the way over,' Greenway announced. 'I don't want to bust the cover of these blokes and I'm not for one moment suspecting them of anything dodgy. However, a little exposure to firepower never did anyone any harm.' Unlike Richard Daws he did not pronounce it 'far-par'.

No wonder Rundle had been so helpful, I mused, he was still recovering from his own singeing. I also wondered what had made Greenway change his mind about interfering, not just because Rundle had become a bit cocky, surely.

We wandered over to the charity shop, Patrick and I first, the others following half a minute or so later, and discovered that the rear entrance was locked. We found our way round to the front and went in, Greenway waving his warrant card at the two

Oxfam ladies on the way through and giving them one of his big smiles.

'Morning!' said the Commander loudly at the top of a flight of narrow stairs.

'Morning, sir,' said one of the two men with cameras and other surveillance equipment in the gloomy and cramped room we found ourselves in – the grubby curtains were almost closed – which instantly became very crowded indeed.

Rundle had warned them then.

'Which one of you is Kenneth Hills?' said Greenway after quickly introducing the rest of those to whom they were talking.

'I am,' said the man who had first spoken; of medium height, slim, with a thin moustache.

'Tell me, in no more than twenty words, why you didn't report for duty on the morning of the murders at Park Road, Muswell Hill.'

'I got a phone call from Dan saying that he would stay on and do the first shift as well.'

'That is Daniel Rushton-Smith?'

'Yes, sir.'

'Did you question that at all?'

'No. He gets a bit funny if you argue with him. He said he'd had a row with his girlfriend and wanted to stay out of it for a bit longer.'

Greenway turned to the other man, 'And you? Sorry, I don't know your name.'

'Keeting, sir. Philip.'

'Are you prone to stomach upsets?'

'No, not at all.'

'But you were really ill.'

'Yes. I thought I was going to die. The docs said I must have eaten something horribly off.'

'Had you had anything in the hours previously that could be regarded as suspicious?'

'No, I couldn't think of anything. No seafood or stuff like that.'

'Had anyone fixed you something to eat – other than in the nick canteen?'

'Dan had fetched several of us coffee earlier that day. But he only had to go out to the machine in the main corridor, not go to a greasy spoon place.'

'Do you know if anyone else was taken ill?'

'If they were I didn't hear about it.'

'OK. Where does this Dan live? His records are out of date.'

Both men looked at one another in surprise.

'Dunno,' said Keeting.

'No idea, sir,' said Hills. 'He's a private sort of bloke.'

'No idea at all?' Greenway asked in amazement.

They both shook their heads.

'Think,' Patrick said, stepping forward from where he had been standing in a corner. 'He must have given you some clues.'

They frowned in perplexity.

'Come on!' barked the parade-ground voice, making everyone jump. 'You're bloody *cops*!'

'Well – well, he doesn't drive in,' Keeting stuttered. 'Moans about the trains.'

'Tube trains?'

'Er – no, surface ones. He got stuck at Hornsey not so long ago. I don't think that's on the tube.'

'It's only the next station to Wood Green down the line,' Greenway commented. 'So that doesn't help much.'

'Either of you got his mobile number?' Patrick asked.

'Yes,' said Keeting. 'I have.'

'Be so good as to write it down for us.'

This was done.

'Do you happen to know if he's back with his girlfriend?'

'Er – no,' Keeting answered. 'Do you, Ken?'

'No,' said the other. 'And I haven't liked to ask.'

'It sounds to me that he's none too pleasant,' Carrick said.

'He's OK as long as you stick to chat about the job and nothing personal,' Hills said. 'But you get the impression, at least, I do, there's loads there, deep down, that he won't talk about.'

All we had then, was the mobile number.

'I find it quite mind-blowing that we have no other way of contacting a British cop!' Greenway burst out with when we were back in the car.

'Shall I phone him?' Patrick offered.

'And say what, for God's sake?' the Commander blared, swivelling round in his seat.

Patrick tactfully bore with the momentary lull in his boss's constructive thinking. 'If he is using an assumed identity someone must know; friends, family, whoever. There might be people in the UK with whom he's in regular contact and who have his mobile number. If we're wrong about this man, we're wrong and no harm done, but suppose I phone him and pretend to be a friend of Zoran's, the chef who Pangborne got bored with and killed, the reason this bloodbath might have happened in the first place?'

'And?'

Patrick just smiled like a great white shark.

'God, I get really uneasy when you do that,' Greenway muttered. 'OK, do it and see what happens. The worst that can go wrong is that we have to put a watch on railway stations and airports for him.'

Having kept quiet for a long time in the company of so many people who really knew what they were talking about I felt that the oracle ought to utter a word of caution. 'No,' I said, 'Far worse things can happen than that. Patrick touched on it earlier: this man may well be in possession of weapons.'

Greenway nodded. 'Yes, point taken.' And then, to Patrick, passing over the slip of paper with the number written on it, 'Do you know what you're going to say?'

'Yes, but you'll have to be patient. You won't get him until tonight. And I shall ring him from a payphone somewhere, not my mobile or SOCA HQ.'

'Good thinking,' said Greenway, turning to the driver. 'Right then, somewhere warm that has a phone and more coffee – well away from this dump.'

NINETEEN

'So what happened?' Greenway asked urgently when we were in a café, Patrick having just returned from making the call.

Patrick sat down and stirred his coffee with deliberation. Then, in a thick mid-European accent and miming huddling around a phone he said softly, 'You don't know me but I knew Zoran in the old days. I got your number through an acquaintance who is someone you keep in regular contact with.' He paused. 'No, don't ask, my friend, it is never best to know these things. Through my own grapevine I understand congratulations are in order and to thank you myself and to bless the memory of Zoran I want to buy you a drink, several drinks. We get drunk together, eh? Shall we meet soon?' Another pause. 'Where?' A longer pause. 'I shall find it.'

'The Last Gasp nightclub,' Patrick said, emerging from his re-enactment. 'Tonight, ten thirty.'

'Did he question your story?' Greenway wanted to know.

'No, but I got the impression that he was pretty suspicious. And who knows, if he's on the line he might be merely satisfying his curiosity and wondering if I'm worth arresting. He must know that the nightclub is quite often stiff with his undercover colleagues in the Met.'

'I notice you didn't call him by the name we're assuming is his real one.'

'No, too risky.'

Greenway stared into space, thinking, and for a little while no one spoke. Then, after a gusty sigh, he said, 'OK, so be it.'

We returned to SOCA's HQ where, over a working sandwich lunch, the plan was made, Patrick drawing on his military experience to advise where necessary. It was decided – and Greenway had had no choice but to liaise with Rundle over this – that the Met would provide support, some armed but not initially within the club premises, SOCA, in the shape of Greenway and a couple of others, as 'bodyguards' for Patrick. Timing was vital, the details complicated and to be honest I did not take a lot of notice.

This was mostly because the oracle was deemed superfluous to requirements, on the grounds of her health and safety, which put Carrick out of the running as well. I made no protest, not sure afterwards if Greenway had wondered about this given my past record, but he did not comment. Also, I had soaked up a smiling remark from the man in my life to the effect that, 'We need no cuckoo-class back-up, only those who know what they're doing.' Greenway had replied, sniffily, that he was sure the Met did not employ cuckoo-class anything. Patrick had quickly added, looking worried, that he had only been joking.

'I'd better return home and undergo a quick recovery,' Carrick said when the meeting had broken up and we were walking along a corridor, leaving the building. Patrick was free until the agreed time to go to the club.

Patrick paused to look around before replying. Seeing there were others within earshot he just said, 'Can we give you a lift back to the hotel then?'

The offer was possible because Greenway's tantrum had further manifested itself in the return of the Range Rover, which we had been told was in the car park at the rear. Carrick's eyes widened slightly when Patrick went over the vehicle with a mobile phone-sized electronic device that he has not had for very long which detects the presence of things that should not be there. The gizmo having not got excited about anything we then got in.

'I'm meeting him at nine thirty,' Patrick said.

'*Nine* thirty!' Carrick exclaimed. 'But—'

'I have a very nasty feeling about all this,' Patrick said. 'The last thing we want is another bloodbath. I think that if all our hunches are right this character's likely to fancy an action replay. If he deeply suspects what I've told him and the arranged meeting he might just be feeling that he's been rumbled and walk into a trap. I don't want to be responsible for more killings. I shall take him – if he even turns up. But at least we can rest easy in the knowledge that if the 'ifs' are wrong then no one will have been killed.'

'And you'll be back to square one with your career and whole future,' James said.

'Please don't remind me.'

'What do you want me to do?'

Patrick gave him a smile of thanks. 'Will you get into trouble over this?'

'It depends on how badly you want me to behave,' was the instant reply.

We all laughed: I could not remember the last time I had done so.

I already knew that Carrick had previously worked undercover, first with the Vice Squad when he was with the Met and, more recently in Scotland, when he had become involved with a case Patrick was working on for MI5, one of the few of which I had not been a part. For that, he had successfully taken on the role of a criminal, replacing the genuine article being smuggled into the UK. This had culminated in a gang of would-be crook and terrorist importers being arrested near Paisley, a town in the west of Scotland, the only redeeming features of which are the magnificent Gothic Abbey and its railway station, where you get off the train for Glasgow airport and thus have the opportunity of leaving the place behind altogether.

Even knowing his history I was unprepared for the unsavoury-looking individual who emerged from shadows beneath a narrow railway bridge not far from Acton Town station. For a moment I did not recognize him. I actually felt Patrick, by my side, tense. Then he chuckled.

'But you can't have had those clothes with you!' I said to James.

'No, I did as you always do and went to a charity shop.'

The overall effect was that of a slightly down-at-heel mobster; a shirt the collar of which was several sizes too big for him, plus unkempt hair, a slouching gait and, as we had first spotted him, with a good line in sullen scowls. The two men made a good pair, Patrick having had merely to don black shirt and jeans, and his leather jacket, also black. The belt, plastic, with the brass skull buckle sporting red glass eyes which I have never been able to separate him from was there as well; he insists it brings him luck. The rest of the 'disguise' lay, like Carrick, in deportment, having his normally wavy hair smarmed flat with gel and a superior leer that made even his wife want to give him a good smack.

For authenticity's sake the female addition to the trio was attired in her 'tart's rig' similar to that which I had worn for my first visit: micro skirt, tight top and sundry bits of bling all topped with a fake fur jacket resembling a yak with mange that I had bought in a jumble sale at Hinton Littlemoor. These and other garments take it in turns to reside in a bag kept in the car.

'So James is your sort of minder?' I enquired of Patrick as we strolled, with a few minutes to spare, in the direction of the club to which I was acting as official guide. I was aware that he had gone along to Carrick's room for some kind of council of war while I was in the shower.

'No, not at all,' Patrick answered. 'We're going to disturb the peace. Aren't we, my Jockanese friend?'

'Aye, we are that,' said Carrick with relish.

A short distance farther on I halted and said, 'There, on the other side of the road. It's down that alleyway between the building society and the burger bar.'

'How far down?' Patrick asked.

'Thirty yards or so.'

'Off you go then,' Patrick said quietly to Carrick and the Scotsman went, hunched into his jacket – it was almost as cold as last time – and, pausing to wait for a gap in the traffic, crossed the road. Patrick and I loitered, pretending to look in shop windows.

'What else is down the alley?' he suddenly said.

'Not a lot – the side entrances to various premises, the sort that are locked at night, a couple of bars. That's only in the bit on the way to the club, I didn't go all the way down.'

'Why not? It's always a good idea to know exactly what's what.'

'Sorry!' I raved at him, getting well into character. 'It was bloody freezing and I was on my own not wishing to have to fight off being forcibly picked up by various drunk, pig-brained men who were hanging around the doorways and thus draw attention to myself!'

Patrick staggered off for a few paces as though I had hit him and then returned to put an arm around my shoulders, giving me a fierce grin. 'To The Last Gasp,' he announced. 'My last gasp.'

'What do you want me to do?'

'What you always do, watch my back.'

'You don't have your knife.'

'I have the spare.'

Which I knew was not anywhere near as good.

'But what are *you* going to do? Wasn't the original plan to sneak you in to the club so you could come face to face with this man?'

'Yes, but I'm going in making as much noise as possible.'

'And?'

'It'll be the last thing he's expecting. Then play it by ear. If he's brought reinforcements then it'll immediately become apparent.'

'But *how*?'

'Human nature. Trust the old warrior, eh?'

I took his arm and felt the slight shiver, saw the fear of failure in his eyes, the horror of having to go home and confess to Katie that he was a murderer after all.

Was he strong or well enough to do this?

It was exactly nine thirty. There were the usual hangers-arounders in the alley, seemingly mostly those who had emerged from the club or bars for a smoke. Patrick and I sauntered along, his arm proprietorially around my shoulders, and I noted the wary looks the other men were giving him. I have never been able to fathom exactly how he emanates this aura of menace, how he thus becomes a different person to the one of five minutes previously.

In the next second I found myself confronted by James Carrick, who had appeared from nowhere, and all three of us came to a sudden stop. Carrick gave me a wonderful smarmy smile, boozed-up lechery writ large. Another second later and the front of his far too shiny jacket was bunched in Patrick's fists. The hands were knocked down and they stood still, glaring at one another.

During working on a film not all that long ago when Patrick was asked to be stand-in for the main lead he did a lot of work with a fight director. Watching what followed I began to realize exactly what he had learnt and also, how much he had managed to impart to James in the time available. But pretend scrapping on a filmset and falling on to out-of-shot mats is not the same as trying not to injure your chum in a gloomy London alleyway. There would be a few bruises.

They fought like tomcats, deliberately, I think, amateurishly, all the while 'drunkenly' shouting abuse at one another. Word of it spread and half of Acton turned up to watch. The bit of totty did her bit, screaming encouragement on the sidelines to her man, which helped no end to attract an audience. This had been going on for a short while when someone must have fetched the club's bouncer, a different monolith than last time, just as Carrick headed, mostly in reverse and at some speed, in that direction. Rather than try to put a stop to the proceedings the bouncer fielded him and tossed the hapless man back towards his opponent thus lining him up for a clip to the jaw that I was sure connected. Carrick staggered but it was a feint and then darted at Patrick, head-butting him in the chest. Both overbalanced and fell backwards.

The bouncer closed in, grabbed the pair of them, hauled them to their feet, crashed them together like cymbals, got them by their collars and, before anyone, watching or otherwise, could draw breath he then shoved them in front of him down the steps and kicked open the door of the club. It slammed shut like the gates of Hell after them.

This, obviously, was not part of the plan. I did as people might expect: ran down to the basement entrance and battered on the door with both fists, not imagining for one second to be let in. I carried on banging on the door and when it suddenly opened, almost fell in. A blare of jazz met me.

'Get out of my way!' said a man right behind me, not waiting for me to move and violently shoulder-charging me from his path. He hurried in, together with a few others and I heard him snarl, 'I'm a member and these are my guests, fool! Shift your ugly carcass!' presumably to the bouncer.

I picked myself up from where I had ricocheted off a wall, ricked my ankle and landed on the floor. The bouncer appeared, ignored me completely, slammed the door again and locked it before striding out of my sight. Over the music I heard him say to someone quite close by, 'In a moment. First I'm calling the cops to take away those two who were fighting outside. You don't want to lose your licence, do you?'

'Make it quick. Beckovic isn't happy when he doesn't get the red-carpet treatment,' another voice said.

'Well, you go and lick his arse then.'

'Don't speak to me like that! I only agreed to let you have the job for one night as a favour.'

I rounded a corner and saw, tucked away in the opposite direction to the entrance into the main area, a tiny office. The bouncer almost filled the doorway, blocking my view of the person to whom he was speaking.

'What do *you* want?' said the bouncer, noticing me.

'You've got my man,' I snivelled.

'They're in the gents. Sod off.'

Patrick and James were indeed in the gents, the former wincing as he rubbed his shoulder, the latter seemingly endeavouring to untwist something wrong with his back.

'What?' I hissed, 'Is going on?'

'He's not pleased,' Patrick whispered grimly.

'Well, you've been well and truly rumbled. What now?'

'We wait.'

'Beckovic has just arrived. He shoved me out of the way.'

'He's here!' Patrick exclaimed, only quietly.

'Yes, I heard a man who must be the owner of the club say so.'

'Was he alone?'

'No, at least, he came in with several men but that doesn't mean they were actually together.'

A few minutes went by during which time I had to retreat into the corridor as men entered. Then came a thundering on the outer door.

'Well, of course I locked it,' I heard the bouncer call over the jazz band. 'You didn't want them doing a runner, did you?'

The two then did just that, dashing past me into the club, and, hard on their heels, I saw that it was packed. Patrick has always said that war is organized chaos and this is precisely what happened: war. Tables were overturned, the jazz band routed, chairs were thrown over the bar, glasses and bottles smashed.

I had not seen the face of the individual who had knocked me aside in the doorway but I saw him now as he jumped to his feet, recognized him even though his hair was styled differently to that in the photograph. A surprisingly slight figure given his strength of shoulder, he was with two cronies. I fought my way towards them through the clubbers stampeding for the exit. Then I saw that one of the men was grabbing into an inside pocket of his jacket. In the mêlée Patrick must have seen the movement too for when I next glimpsed him he was right upon him, only coming from behind. Moments later the man had disappeared, presumably felled and on the floor.

Patrick and Beckovic stood face to face, the surviving henchman apparently having been turned to stone.

'You!' the man bawled above the turmoil of people falling over furniture as they scrambled to leave. 'You're in custody for murder!'

I arrived in a clear space near a wall – people seemed to be finding their way out through an emergency exit – and stayed there, able to hear what was being said and aware that James Carrick was not far away either.

'As you can see,' Patrick said with one of his stock-in-trade nasty smiles. 'Not so.' He commenced to sway slightly from side to side, staring fixedly at the man he was talking to and although I could not see from where I was standing I knew his eyes were like crazy, living pebbles. It makes the recipient, frankly, shit-scared.

'You phoned me and pretended to be a friend of Zoran! You lied!' For all the shouting and bluster he was a weedy sort of man, his lips specked with spittle as he yelled.

'I do sometimes if it catches murderers,' Patrick said in a bored voice.

A forefinger was pointed accusingly. 'What's that supposed to mean? You're some kind of hit man for God's sake! You were working for *her*! Just the sort to go off your head and blast the lot of them to hell!'

'Yes, and I'm a cop,' Patrick said. 'Just like you.'

I edged a bit closer. Even in the poor lighting I saw the colour drain from the other's face.

'No!' he yelled, his hands shaking. 'You can't be! That's what you said when I doped you, but you're lying! You killed those people! I saw you, you were staggering all over the place!'

'How did you see me?'

'I was on watch farther down the street.'

'No, you weren't. Keeting was on his own. You saw me because you were in Pangborne's house.'

'No! It's your word against mine. No court would ever believe you after you'd had a gutful of that whisky.'

'I had no whisky. What whisky?'

'You did. Someone poured some in your drink – what looked like orange juice. The Scotch was doctored to make them all unconscious.'

'How do you know about that? Nothing's been said about that by your mob because Rundle's still waiting for the full written report on that and blood samples from the murder victims.'

The henchman suddenly came to life and decided to leave, walking backwards, the second person that evening to do so and find himself cannoning into the bouncer, who had silently approached. This time the big man, without shifting his concentration away from what was being said, contented himself with chopping the invader of his space neatly across the neck and heaving the untidy result to one side.

'You're under arrest,' Patrick said to Beckovic.

Beckovic panicked, completely, and before I had had a chance to move lunged forward and grabbed me by one wrist in a vicious heave that almost dislocated my shoulder. Then a knife was held across my throat, I actually felt the edge of the blade slit my skin. Out of the corner of my eye I saw that Carrick, who had the Smith and Wesson, had drawn it.

'You killed that child,' Patrick said through his teeth and might have said a lot more if the bouncer, actually Michael Greenway, had not shouted first.

'Release the woman!'

'She dies, just like that Serbian bitch deserved to die if you try to stop me!' Beckovic frantically shouted almost right in my ear. 'Move aside and let me through!'

Whereupon this woman decided she did not want to die right now and I threw myself backwards, stamping heavily on his feet with my heels as I did so. He yelled in pain and we both crashed to the floor. I was cast aside and, when I had stopped rolling over and over, I saw him start to bolt from the room. Then, he turned and flung the knife, straight at me.

Instinctively, I curled, with my hands over my head, but was far too slow. All I heard was a single, sharp metallic clang, a bit like a small clock striking one, and then a clatter. No agonizing stab of pain. Perhaps you don't feel anything when a knife first buries itself in you, the thought went through my mind. I looked up.

Two knives were on the floor, still shivering from their collision.

'Bloody hell,' Greenway whispered. And then to Patrick. 'You're wasted in SOCA. You should get a job in a circus.'

Mladan Beckovic had run into a wall of cops in the entrance hall.

It would be a long day for Patrick and me tomorrow; statements, interviews, but for now, at one thirty in the morning, we rested. I think Patrick and James had just about forgiven Greenway for the battering together he had subjected them to, authenticity or no, but Patrick, I knew, was ready to drop and functioning on will-power alone. At least we were taking it easy in a very pleasant VIP lounge at HQ while we waited for the Commander to tie up a few loose ends before we could all go our various ways for a few hours' sleep.

'It was a complete fluke,' Patrick said, discovering that my gaze was upon him and not for the first time in a few minutes. I think I was in a state of mild shock: I could have so easily been in hospital with a horrible injury.

The knife was ruined, a nick in the blade, and had taken its place in the investigation, no doubt as Exhibit Z.

No, it wasn't a fluke.

Greenway breezed in, still wearing the horribly tight suit – the only suitable attire he had been able to lay his hands on in the time available – he had suffered in all night with the green shirt and pink tie. Muttering something he wrenched himself out of the jacket and hurled it overarm into a corner. The tie followed.

I said, 'If you really want to get comfortable I can . . .'

He gave me a big grin. 'No, I can survive for a few more minutes, thank you, Ingrid.' He surveyed us all gleefully. 'Well, he's singing his heart out already. It was all Hulton's fault, who was in it with him. That's a lie. Someone threatened to kill him if he didn't top the lot of them. That's a lie. He'd contacted the Pangborne woman before she came to this country, asked for a job so he could infiltrate her mob and she turned him down flat after a short meeting on the grounds that he was a wimp. That might not be a lie. It was all for

Zoran, who was his best chum. That's probably partly true
too. Personally, I think the man's raving mad.'

The Commander had already told us that he had made a
few more plans after we had left, not entirely trusting his
'adviser' to stick to what had been decided. He himself had
thought it wise to turn up an hour before the agreed time and
make sure he had back-up, just in case. He had told no one
that he intended to be right in the middle of things and had
had a quiet word with the usual doorman, one of Rundle's
undercover people, to phone in saying he was ill but recom-
mending a 'friend'.

I had not actually been present when Greenway had
conducted a debriefing with Patrick and Carrick and had rather
received the impression when the Commander had lured me
into this room with coffee and a plate loaded with chunks of
iced fruit cake that if I attended then it would cramp his style,
in other words, he would be forced to moderate his language.
The three had joined me after twenty minutes or so, the one
nearest to my heart ashen, but giving me a rueful smile. I had
refuelled them with coffee and cake.

'So this was all purely for revenge?' I said.

Greenway nodded briskly, with a mouthful. Then, 'We don't
know yet what connection there was with that shoot-out in
Hilik all those years ago but there must have been one or why
write the name of the place on the wall? Nor do we know if
there was monetary gain to be had in it for him. The shrinks
will talk to him and I'm no expert but it might be something
to do with knowing that he *is* a bit of a wimp, not at all like
his father who Patrick informs me was physically a big man
who carried a lot of clout locally. So if the son could lead a
double life, fool the Metropolitan Police and use the data that
was available to him in order to track down the killer of his
friend that might have boosted the little rat's ego.'

'But why kill Hulton?' I said.

'We don't know that yet either.'

To Patrick I said, 'So it was Beckovic and the men he was
with who broke into your flat and doped you.'

'And as it would appear that I'd been slipped some of that
whisky after all it would explain why I didn't know who the
hell it was.'

Greenway turned to Carrick. 'Whatever I said just now,

James, I want you to know I very much appreciate your help. I know you understand that nothing can appear in official records about your off-piste presence on this case but want you to know that if there's anything I can do to help you in the future then just give me a call.'

'Thank you, sir,' Carrick said quietly. 'I'll have a couple of hours' sleep then I must go home and find myself a murderer in Hinton Littlemoor.'

'Well, you'll just have to apply the three Oracles of Murder: motive, means and opportunity,' Greenway said jokingly.

'Yes, but everyone hated the victim's guts. I have around a hundred suspects.'

'Then who stands to gain?'

TWENTY

I t was established, but much later, at his trial, that Beckovic
himself had been the 'insider' who had leaked the story to
the media of someone working for SOCA being involved
in the shootings as a ploy to draw any possible suspicion away
from himself. The coincidence he had created of there being
only one police officer watching the house, to be taken
seriously ill – he had introduced a few drops of juice from
putrid raw prawns into Philip Keeting's morning coffee – had
worried him.

Beckovic finally admitted having planned to gun down
Pangborne, plus anyone who got in his way, breaking into the
house while everyone slept. Watching and biding his time
nearby that night, waiting for it all to go quiet, he had seen
Patrick leave the house at around four thirty in the morning
and, wondering why he was still on his feet, decided to follow
him, calling upon two friends, the pair with him in The Last
Gasp, who were also hanging around in the area in case they
were needed. They had burst into the bedsit, taking Patrick
by surprise mainly on account of his having consumed a small
amount of the whisky, and jabbed him with truth drug. It was
never established why he had told Patrick that he planned to
sell Leanne to a paedophile ring, or even that he had pretended
to be Hulton. They had left him semi-conscious and returned
to Park Road where they had discovered everyone unconscious.
Beckovic had sent his henchman away and, quite forgetting
that he had doctored the whisky earlier – to do this he had
entered through the back door, kept right out of Pangborne's
way and told those he met he was a neighbour – had taken a
couple of mouthfuls from one of the whisky bottles. He had
woken in a bedroom just after ten the following morning not
knowing how he had got there.

The drug seems to have had a disastrous effect on him, either
that or he panicked when he left that room and saw Patrick
talking to Leanne. Overpowering him for the second time that
day, he had taken Patrick's gun, shot the child – because she

was screaming – and then cold-bloodedly shot all the others. It had probably taken only a couple of minutes. He had then realized that someone was banging around in the cupboard on the upstairs landing and found the cleaner, Rosa Jerez, who had indeed seen Hulton earlier. She had begged him not to kill her and for some reason – had he been sickened by what he had done already and terrified the sound of the shots would quickly bring people to investigate? – he had released her after making her swear to tell the police that Patrick had committed the murders. He had then snapped her wrist as a reminder of what would happen to her if she broke her word. Making his escape he had again come upon Patrick, outside, and dumped him at the end of the garden when he had collapsed after throwing the knife at him.

Of course, hardly any of this had been established when our part in the case was over. Except, that is, the new account of what had happened from Rosa Jerez after Beckovic had been arrested, to the effect that she had been forced to lie. He had told her he would find and kill her, wherever she tried to escape to, if she implicated him. The irony of all this is that if Beckovic had left her in the cupboard and gone away instead of letting her out, his hands still apparently having been covered in blood from smearing it on the walls, she would have been none the wiser as to the identity of the killer. To be quite sure on this matter Patrick had been suddenly introduced into the room where Miss Jerez was making this statement. She had practically fallen on his neck, weeping, thanking him for hiding her away and thus, and despite her coming face to face with Beckovic, probably saved her life as he might have otherwise, in a frenzy, killed her with the rest.

We had stayed a further two days in London, endeavouring to play our part in unravelling what had been a complicated case and were now on our way home with the golden knowledge of Patrick's innocence. He actually had a copy of the statement in his jacket pocket in the event of any more visits from Complaints, which organization remained as silent as a grave. Officially, he was still on sick leave.

'Hilik though?' I said, breaking what had been a long silence on the drive home, Hinton Littlemoor a matter of minutes away.

'Better than Hilik,' Patrick murmured, imitating Beckovic's

voice, making me shudder. 'Mladan's a big man now. Mladan can gun people down with the best of them.'

'You really think that's what it was?'

'Yes, after he'd killed Pangborne, his original target, he thought he'd prove himself. And, don't forget, he'd been hoist by his own petard, the whisky which had to have affected any judgement he had left by then.'

By this time it was around four thirty in the afternoon and we had already decided to go to the rectory first. I had told Patrick he owed his mother a very large bouquet of flowers and these were residing fragrantly on the rear seat of the car together with a gift for John that my husband had promised me faithfully he would not, if offered, even taste.

It was teatime in the annex kitchen, Matthew and Katie with their grandparents just about to sit down to cold chicken and salad sandwiches and home made cakes – no pot noodles ever here. They were not expecting us.

'Oh! Oh!' Elspeth cried when presented with a walking flower bower. 'Oh, thank you. How wonderful!' she said when her son was revealed. 'You look happy. Is it all all right now?'

'It's all right,' Patrick assured her.

'You're not still under suspicion?'

'No. We caught him.'

There was then a mass hug, Patrick unashamedly in tears, Katie clutched to his chest, one hand resting on her bright chestnut hair.

We moved into the rectory, in more snow, and for a few days – no, I must be honest here, the best part of the fortnight – we strove, with Elspeth and Carrie's help, to gain some kind of domestic order. Patrick was still not back to full health and had to go to bed early but his blood readings were improving. Then, on day fifteen after the move, James Carrick rang to ask if he could call in for a chat and Patrick immediately invited him, and Joanna, to dinner that night.

The cook battered off in the 4 x 4 through the still snowy lanes to the shops.

James, we discovered, had had the flu and was still suffering from a racking cough. There had been the ghost of an idea in my mind that he might be in need of help in connection with the local murder investigation, which was soon proved to be the case.

'I'm under a hell of a lot of pressure to get a result with the Blanche case,' he said not long after being in receipt of a pre-dinner glass of wine.

Joanna sighed. 'Can't you forget work just for a couple of hours?'

Patrick gave her a sympathetic smile and then said to James, 'Commander Greenway's offer of help does extend to his troops, you know.'

'I don't want you actually to *do* anything as you're still recovering,' the DCI hastened to say. 'But a few ideas . . .'

'The weather seems to have put a stop to any black magic antics although they've probably been driven indoors. Did you have any luck with forensics as far as the samples of wood that Ingrid took from the church and the axe in our local woodcarver, Stewart Macdonald's, workshop were concerned?'

'Not enough to hang a charge on anyone. They were both oak of some age and *probably* from the same source.'

'Pity.'

'Does your father intend to ask him to quote for repairs or replacements?'

'No, not now. Macdonald called in to see him a few days ago and virtually asked for the job. He's not a churchgoer and probably expected to find a doddery old pushover. He didn't get one. Dad took an immediate dislike to him and told him that the church couldn't afford to employ a craftsman to make things from scratch and he would suggest to the PCC that second-hand replacements would be cheaper. The idea had just popped into his head. Since then someone went on the Internet and arrangements have been made to buy stuff from a chapel that's being demolished in Bristol. A couple of members of the congregation are sufficiently skilled in woodwork to adapt it for our use.'

'What was Macdonald's reaction to your Dad's reply?'

'He was very rude and slammed out.'

'So, perhaps then, even if there's no prosecution to be had there – and I have no intention of abandoning that crime – we can rule out that particular episode as relevant to the murder case.'

'I think that would be fairly safe.'

Carrick just smiled wryly and took a sip of wine.

'It's fairly certain that Frank Crosby dropped the rock on the car surely?' Patrick went on to say.

'Yes, but again I can't prove it.'

'And his wife was banging on Barbara Blanche's windows.'

'She was, and as you probably know, Ingrid was a witness to that. Was this in an effort to drive the woman from the village do you think?'

'No idea. But all in all, they're a pretty poisonous pair and they might have murdered Blanche because he'd found out something about them. Ingrid reckons the woman had come through the churchyard and into the garden and not up the drive when she came round that morning, ostensibly about the flowers. She could have thrown the murder weapon, the hammer, into the rectory garden then.'

'But the pathologist reckoned that Blanche had been killed a while before that.'

'Yes, but they might have worried, if they'd just left it lying around, that some evidence that could connect them with the murder might be on it. People know all about DNA testing these days. The woman might have gone back for it with the view to chucking it away somewhere.'

'Hardly very far away though if it was in your garden,' Joanna commented, obviously having kept abreast of the case.

'People panic,' Patrick said. 'She would have been terrified someone would see her, any number of people: the postman, the newspaper boy, anyone. The Crosbys are your best bet.'

Carrick said, 'I shall have to prove exactly what it is they're up to. But I can't really see them being involved with satanic practices.'

'Blackmail?'

'You mean they might be running something anonymously and blackmailing those who are drawn into dancing around naked and sacrificing animals or whatever other nonsense? That's a bit of a long-shot.'

'Possibly, but like Blanche, they might be hooked on the power it gives them over people.'

'One would have thought that someone in the village would have come forward by now – if not to the police then to your father.'

I said, 'We already have a name, although not from the village, the father of Clem Huggins who's in Matthew's class at school. He's supposed to mess around with black magic.'

'Carlton Huggins,' Carrick recollected. 'I went out to their particular rats' nest and no one was at home. That family is really bad news – not the sort the Crosbys would normally associate with. It just doesn't add up.'

'There has to be a common denominator,' Patrick muttered.

It was over coffee after dinner that the discussion continued.

'OK then,' James said. 'How long has this black magic caper been going on for?'

'Only for a couple of months as far as anyone can tell,' Patrick answered.

'How many people do you think are involved?'

Patrick shrugged. 'No one really knows but it can't be many. Perhaps no more than a dozen.'

'Let's change tack and work on the presumption that the black magic bit's a front. Leaving blackmail on one side for a moment but bearing in mind that if a Huggins is involved there's money in it where does that get us? Following a phone call, your father, Patrick, went down to where dodgy goings on appear to take place at the bottom of the village on some spare ground. He was roughed up. Rightly, he's been preaching against this sort of thing in church. Is it a distraction and other members of the Huggins clan are otherwise gainfully and illegally employed nearby somewhere?'

'That could be it,' I said. 'Winter months, long, cold, dark nights. Law-abiding folk kept mostly indoors, especially the elderly, except for visits to the pub, or events and meetings in the village hall. Otherwise they get in their cars and go farther afield, to Bath perhaps, for a meal out. What finer further incentive to keep people firmly at home than the prospect of rough characters getting drunk and killing things down on the site of the old station? People would have asked themselves who these people are. Would they bump into them and possibly be attacked if they went for a walk after dark, as John was? He might have been lured down there for no other reason than for the resultant publicity.'

'Go on,' Carrick encouraged.

To Patrick, I said, 'You know this area really well. What kind of target for criminals might there be round here? Any big and

remote country houses that would be worth breaking into where
the owners are away? Old buildings in the middle of nowhere
whose roof lead might be worth stripping off that aren't checked
very often, if at all?'

'There are quite a few properties but people don't tend to
leave them unattended these days. The best thing to do would
be to dig out the OS map. James, do you have any recent
burglary cases involving country houses?'

'One, but it was a good twenty miles from here. As far as
this immediate area's concerned there's Priston Manor. The
Lord Lieutenant of Somerset lives there, and I happen to know
they're not away. I also know that the place bristles with security devices and there are live-in staff.'

'What was Frank Crosby's job before he retired?' Joanna
asked.

Patrick did not know and went through to see if his father
did. When he returned there was an enigmatic smile on his
face. 'He had an antiques business in Midsomer Norton.'

'Wow!' Joanna exclaimed.

'*Now* can you see why I fell in love with my sergeant?'
James said.

She threw a cushion at him.

'If this theory is anywhere near the mark we're talking
about a lot of money being involved,' Patrick said. 'If they're
going to the bother of arranging so-called satanic meetings,
where I should imagine the real draw is booze, probably free
booze, then that costs money. They must regard whatever their
own returns are for this scam as worth it.'

I said, 'Matthew told us that Clem invited him to wherever he lives – I take it the whole lot don't live under one
roof—'

Carrick interrupted me. 'Sorry to butt in, but they do. In a
corner-site one-time council house with tatty extensions
erected without planning permission surrounded by several
caravans parked in what used to be a large garden. Their fore-
bears were either tinkers or what used to be referred to as
gallows-fodder. You say Matthew was *invited* there?'

'Clem wanted to show him his Dad's magic stuff. Apparently
Clem goes to some of these meetings but isn't allowed to
attend others. I'm wondering if this man really is involved
with devil worship.'

'Which mostly involves booze, drugs and sex,' Patrick said dismissively. 'I'll go and ask Dad about other possible targets where parishioners are away.'

When he came back he reported, 'Old man Huggins once stripped lead off this church roof, probably the nearest he'd ever got to the place so there's a bit of family history of that. He made the mistake of leaving something behind that had his name on it.' He added, 'Before your time though, James. Then there's the old mill at Wellow which is apparently empty and up for sale. But it's in a pretty bad state with not much worth taking, Dad doesn't think. And the Harley-Brownswords, who live at a house by the name of Fir Copse, are on holiday in the West Indies – although his brother is house and dog sitting.

'I mentioned the Huggins lot,' Patrick continued, 'And other than comments along the lines of their names always seeming to be in the local papers after being arrested for something or other there was nothing useful there. *But,* for some reason Mum suddenly remembered that the Crosbys had some rather rough-looking men painting their house not so long ago.'

'Did they have a van with a firm's name written on it?' Carrick wanted to know.

'No, just a battered plain white one.'

'Who lives in the Grange, next door, now?' I enquired.

'The Rollasons,' Patrick answered. 'I'd forgotten about them. They always go to their house in South Africa during the worst of the winter months. They're probably still away.'

'But surely your parents would have noticed anything going on there,' James said.

'No, by no means. There's a high wall all the way round and a lot of trees,' Patrick said. 'I actually know the lie of the land round there quite well because Ken Rollason asked me about security measures when they bought the place.'

'Did he mention anything he owns that he had particular concerns about?'

'No.'

'It doesn't sound as though the house would be at risk from the likes of the Huggins tribe then.'

'It depends on what anyone's been getting up to,' Patrick replied dryly. He stood up. 'I'll phone to see if they're there.'

This he did and there was only the answering machine.

'A little sortie?' Patrick suggested.

'What now?' Joanna said. 'It's freezing and really snowy out there.'

'All the better to see any footprints that shouldn't be there. Not *all* of us,' Patrick remonstrated gently when everyone had jumped to their feet. 'Too noisy and creating too many footprints of our own.'

He won the argument on the grounds that specialized knowledge was required and he and I ended up by putting on our boots and anoraks. James insisted that he would hang around in case anything important came to light.

There is a gate in the boundary wall between the two properties that dates back to the days when the squire and his lady took a short cut through the rectory garden to attend church in order to save themselves the mire of the lane and having to rub shoulders with the villagers. We made our way towards it now, everywhere starkly bright with the moonlight on the snow. I wondered if the Rollasons were aware that Patrick had a key to the gate, a relic from recent times when close friends of the rector and his wife lived in the house and it was useful for the ladies when popping in for coffee or a short cut to track down the family Labrador that always seemed to turn up at the rectory at mealtimes.

'There's snow piled up against it,' I whispered as we approached.

'It opens the other way,' Patrick hissed back in a manner that told me to stop talking.

I could not see that anything might be going on over there right now but did as I was told. The old key made hardly a sound as the gate was unlocked, proof that everything was kept well oiled. Patrick's stone-cold professionalism at such times always has exactly the opposite effect on me, making me want to giggle. The hinges did not squeak either but no one had trimmed the ivy on the wall on the far side which unloaded a pile of snow on our heads as we went beneath. Patrick turned to give me a look as a huge bottled-up chortle emerged as a faint squeak.

The garden, here a large lawned area dotted with small trees, the shadows of those above our heads, much taller, thrown across it, stretched with virginal perfection before us; no footprints, except those of birds and what might have been a fox. Across the lawn was the western side of the house: as one would have expected, all the windows were in darkness. Leaving the gate open – a pile of snow had fallen into the gap – Patrick turned right and set off along by the wall. I followed, giving him room.

Continuing along by the wall we soon arrived at another pristine area of grass, the wall bare now but for a few climbing roses growing in the border. From here we could see the drive, lined with mature trees, and the front of the house. Patrick carried on, still walking along by the boundary wall until we reached where it turned at ninety degrees at the southern limit of the property where there was a lane that gave access. Carrying on, we came to the inside of the large entrance gates, which were closed. There were plenty of footprints in the snow covering the drive itself and vehicle tracks where the postman had made deliveries. Patrick signalled to me that we should walk up the drive and from here it was possible to see that the front of the house was also in darkness.

'There doesn't seem to be anyone around,' Patrick said under his breath when we were side by side. 'Round the other side is a building that used to be a coach house and stables. Ken didn't say if he stored anything there but hinted they might turn it eventually into some kind of office or living accommodation. I think we should take a look at that first.'

'What does he do for a living?'

'Dunno. Something in the city probably.'

'What did you make of him?'

'Bit of a smart-arse.'

There were footprints around the side of the house too, where the drive continued, only narrower. Patrick stopped and shone his 'burglar's' torch down at them.

'These are recent, possibly this morning or last night. Three people coming and going. As you can see there's just a little fresh snow in the prints – it snowed again a bit last night – and they've thawed slightly and then frozen again as it chilled off tonight.'

We came in sight of the carriage house and stable block, a rather fine stone building that matched the house. There was an archway that carriages would have once been driven through into an inner courtyard. We followed the footprints; they led straight under the arch. But we did not go that way,

Patrick's natural caution causing him to turn aside to follow
the outside wall. There were several windows, quite high up,
with bars and no other openings until we reached the rear
where there was a smaller archway. Inside the arch, which
did not directly face the larger one opposite, were a couple
of doors, one on each side. Patrick tried the handle of the
first we came to. It was locked. As was the other.

We made our way under the arch, keeping out of the moonlight as much as possible, and emerged into what would have
been the carriage yard. It was quite small, enough room to
manoeuvre a modest carriage drawn by two horses, and there
were stable doors facing inwards where the animals would
have been housed. The carriage house itself was immediately
around to our right.

There was no choice now but to emerge into bright moonlight. For some reason I half expected to be shot at, especially
when we discovered that the same footprints led right up to
the large double doors and the padlock fastening them had
been cut off. Patrick kicked a little bump in the snow nearby
and found it, pushing it into a corner by a drain pipe with his
toe so as to be able to find it again.

Warily, we pulled open one of the doors wide enough to
enable us to enter. Once inside Patrick shone the beam of his
tiny torch around. In its limited illumination there seemed to
be nothing within but lumber, together with what must have
been a couple of tons of logs and an old Transit van. Patrick
went over to the van, which was parked close to the left hand
wall, and peered around behind it.

'Give me a hand,' he whispered.

The handbrake had either failed or had not been applied
and we were easily able to roll the vehicle forward. Behind
it was an old bedspread acting as a curtain. Behind that was
another door. It was of solid construction and the two bolts
on it plus a padlock had been either jemmied or cut off.

TWENTY-ONE

'This would have been the harness room, surely,' Patrick murmured, thinking aloud as he hitched back the curtain. 'And we mustn't contaminate any evidence here.'

Taking down one of several lengths of old rope hanging from a nearby rusting nail in the wall, he made a loop with it and used it to pull down the handle of the door, which opened inwards. All was completely dark within. We went in and the torch beam picked out stacks and stacks of boxes, some cardboard, most of wooden construction.

'Better not put the lights on,' Patrick said in an undertone as the little pencil of light flicked over a couple of wall switches.

Shining the torch in other directions revealed that the damp room was about twenty feet square and that some of the boxes had been opened. Packing – tissue paper, bubble wrap and wood shavings – was scattered on the floor. We went over to one of the opened boxes that appeared to have been discarded on one side. Half buried in some hastily rammed back bubble wrap was a large silver coffee pot with a monogrammed escutcheon on it. Careful probing on Patrick's part exposed another, smaller one, a jug and, right at the bottom, a gallery tray, all solid silver.

We investigated other opened boxes, finding china packed in several, probably a whole dinner service, that was heavily decorated with gold, hand-painted country scenes and a coat of arms. We discovered Chinese pots, glass claret jugs, gold-plated and silver cutlery and Royal Worcester vases. There were cleaner areas on the dusty floor that gave every impression that some boxes had been removed altogether.

'So is Ken a dealer or a fence?' I whispered.

'Impossible to tell at this stage. But it looks as though someone's pinching it who has to be a fence. You notice that most of the obviously traceable stuff has been rejected. No, come to think of it, Kenny boy isn't likely to be a dealer otherwise this lot would be kept somewhere much warmer and drier.'

'Consulting with you on a friendly basis about security was all a bit of a front then.'

Patrick chuckled humourlessly. 'Perhaps he thought I carried local clout and was an open door to drinks parties with the upper classes and so forth. But Paddy boy doesn't like being used by crooks.'

'My money's on the Crosbys,' I said.

Patrick's mobile rang and he muttered a few expletives for having forgotten to switch it off. I stood close when he answered it so I could listen in. It was Carrick.

'I hope I haven't ratted anything up for you but this is important. Your father's just received a call from someone he described as a nervous lady parishioner who said there's people down on the old railway site making a real row dancing round a bonfire. She lives nearby apparently and wants to know if she ought to call the police. Naturally, he came straight through to me.'

'For God's sake tell him to stay right away from the place!' Patrick said, not keeping his voice down.

'Don't worry, he's not even thinking of going down there. I was wondering if it means something else is happening tonight.'

'You might like to come over to where we are,' Patrick told him. 'Because something just might.'

When James found us, having followed Patrick's detailed instructions, and presumably our footprints we closed the outside door, draped the curtain where it had been, shifted back the van and shut the inner door. Carrick had brought a bigger torch with him and by its light we moved a few of the boxes to give us room to conceal ourselves between them and the wall. But we could not disturb them much, not enough to be really noticeable. Our hiding places were exceedingly cramped and when the torches were switched off it became very, very dark.

About three million years went by.

I was endeavouring to rub a bout of cramp from my right calf when I heard muffled noises: feet being stamped with cold or to remove snow perhaps. Moments later the outer door was opened and people entered the coach house. I tried to guess how many of them there were; they were not trying to be particularly quiet. Three or four perhaps.

Huffing and puffing noisily they then moved the van and, after a longish pause, came through the door. Seconds later the lights were switched on. I already knew that Patrick was close to me, but Carrick was somewhere round a corner out of sight.

'They're coming home in two days' time,' a thin reedy voice I recognized said. 'So, as I told you earlier, this is the last run. Rip open as many boxes as you can this time and I'll take a look inside and decide what we take. Just the really good stuff.'

'How d'you know when they comin' back?' someone asked.

'I have my sources,' the first voice, Frank Crosby's, I was convinced, said pompously. 'Just get on with it and stop talking or you won't get your cut.'

Patrick had already said to James that this was his, Carrick's, war so he would follow the DCI's lead. I guessed that he would wait until they had some of the booty actually in their hands before making a move and this is exactly what happened some three or so muscle-racking minutes later.

'Police!' Carrick suddenly shouted. 'Stay right where you are! You're all under arrest!'

Patrick and I jumped out of hiding. The first thing that became apparent was that it was two to one: there were six of them. The second was that they had no intention of being arrested. Third, five were well-built oafs.

'Don't move!' Patrick bellowed, enough to shake dust from the rafters.

They all moved. Two threw full boxes at James and Patrick. I did not see the outcome of this having gone for Crosby. He kicked out at me, missed and ran out of attack ideas after I'd got him by his jacket lapels and slammed him into a wall a few times. I then tipped him backwards over some boxes and parked him mostly upside down in a corner where he was forced to stay.

Patrick was fighting off three of them. One came hurtling towards me after a flailing fist had caught him on the jaw so I let his momentum carry him onwards, guiding him over the boxes as well so that he thundered down in a cloud of dust on top of Crosby in the corner. Another left his original target alone when I got him by the hair and lined him up for a haymaker from Carrick who was making like the wild Scot part of him that he calls up in emergencies.

Out of the corner of my eye I saw someone fleeing through the door. I tore after him, jumped on his back, one arm around his throat, tightly, the other over his eyes. Off balance, he ran straight into the back of the van with me still on board, hitting one of the rear doors hard enough with his forehead not only to dent it, we discovered afterwards, but send it rolling across the coach house to crash into the opposite wall. My mount collapsed sideways and I hit the floor hard. I found my feet, grabbed another piece of rope and tied his ankles tightly together.

Back in the inner room the war was over; Carrick breathing deeply, rubbing his knuckles, Patrick leaning on some boxes as though absolutely done in. He was.

But very happy.

'And, not only is your neighbour at the Grange a fence,' Carrick told us joyfully the following afternoon, 'It would follow that he's involved with a gang that specializes in stealing antiques, possibly the boss man. Crosby's probably nothing to do with the gang – he's still not talking – but my guess is that he went round to the Grange wearing his good citizen hat doing a charity collection and was told of the impending departure for South Africa. Only time will prove me right or not.'

'What are the Huggins mob saying about all this?' Patrick wanted to know, the haul having comprised three brothers, one cousin and a son of Carlton, busy with his magic down in the village.

'They're all singing like canaries. According to them – although, as you might imagine, there are varying accounts, mostly completely exonerating the person actually speaking, of course – Crosby was the brains behind it. Whether the man was invited in next door and saw a few rather nice pieces of furniture, and so forth, and decided to have a snoop around when the place was unoccupied we don't yet know but the Huggins' accounts all tally on one point, Crosby already knew the stuff was there. It's worth a fortune. The Arts and Antiques Squad have hardly started looking at what's stored in the coach house but we know already that there are even items stolen from National Trust properties.'

'And our new neighbours?' Patrick asked him with a wry smile.

'They'll be arrested as soon as their feet touch the ground at Heathrow.'

'Blanche must have found out,' I commented. 'But how?'

Carrick said, 'He may well have only found out about the people behind the black magic sessions. His note to Barbara only spoke of "rotten practices" if you remember, which is bad enough but doesn't suggest stealing antiques. If he said something like "I know what you're up to" to either of the Crosbys they could have thought he knew everything.'

'And lured him to the church that morning on some pretext and killed him,' Patrick mused. 'Have you arrested the wife?'

'Too right. I can't believe she didn't know what was going on, at the very least. The business of going round to ask Ingrid for the key so she could check the flowers, in effect that Blanche's body would be found, was merely to divert any suspicion. Oh, and the eldest son of Carlton Huggins, Riley – the one you tackled, Ingrid – has admitted that he and his younger brother, Ricky, were the two who roughed up the rector. Riley seemed to think we were going to make him pull his pants down to show where he still had the bruises where John walloped him if he didn't own up.'

'And of course you wouldn't have suggested he did anything so demeaning,' Patrick said with a laugh.

'Of course not,' Carrick replied, looking shocked.

There had been a very strange end to the 'party' by the bonfire that had put an abrupt stop to it, hopefully for always. Suddenly – those taking part well drunk, including a few younger ones definitely under age including Matthew's classmate Clem, his father Carlton Huggins in all his finery invoking the Devil – there had been a flash and a loud bang. Then another, centred on the bonfire. Then when they were all running, a much bigger explosion that had rattled local windows and blown the fire to pieces, sending blazing bits of wood raining down on the fleeing 'worshippers' and setting light to Huggins' robe. He had last been seen jumping into the nearby river.

'Thunder flashes are one thing but a *hand grenade*,' I reproached. 'Please don't tell me you're keeping things like that at home.'

Patrick gave me a Mona Lisa smile. 'Never. Rest assured any emergency items like that are kept in a very, very secure place.'

I did not enquire further. No one has yet been convicted of killing Jethro Hulton and I haven't asked Patrick about that either.